The Spark of Wrath

BOOK 2 - THE MASON JAR SERIES

A NOVEL BY ELI POPE

© US COPYRIGHT 2020 – Steven G Bassett
All rights reserved.

No portion of this book may be reproduced, stored in a retrieval system, or transmitted in any form or means including electronic, mechanical, photocopied, recorded, scanned, or other, with the exception of brief quotations in reviews or articles, without prior written permission of author or publisher.

Scripture quotations are taken from the Holy Bible, NIV®, MSG®, KJV®

This novel is a work of fiction. All names, characters, places, and incidents are either from the imagination of the author or used fictitiously. All characters are fictional, and any similarity to people living or dead is coincidental.

Cover Design – Steven G Bassett
Interior Formatting – Sharon Kizziah-Holmes
Audiobook Narration – Paul McSorely
Audiobook Music Creation – Nikki McSorely – nmcmusiccreative.com

Published by 3dogsBarking Media LLC

Also available on Audible.com

ISBN: 978-1-7358159-2-3

DEDICATION

This story is dedicated to all the lost souls of this world who for one reason or another feel like they've fallen away, believing that giving up is their only answer.

With one's eyes closed, the world seems swallowed by the darkness forever. Prayers someone can teach you how to open them once more and allow the light to brighten up your path.

ACKNOWLEDGMENTS

There are far too many to thank for me not to accidently leave someone out but I will attempt to name the ones who have been irreplaceable.

My editor Julie Luetschwager has not only fixed my many mistakes and pointed out changes that make me appear to be a smarter author than I truly am, I say thank you, thank you, and thank you. You've helped keep me inspired to move forward.

Sharon Kizziah-Holmes @ PaperBack Press for her formatting. She makes the look!

All the beta readers that stay loyal to my writing, I appreciate you all very much.

My Springfield Writers Guild fellow author friends who share ideas, critiques, knowledge, and occasional beers. Thank you!

And my wife who puts up with the hours my head is buried in my other world. I love you and couldn't do it without you.

It truly takes a village to make it all work!

1

The salty breeze blew placidly across the bay like every other day in the small Gulf coast community. The heat not only brought a sultry sweat, making teens have that "nasty boy odor", but it also invited tension. Anxiety had been especially thick through the season this year.

It would soon be the first day of Darrell's senior year. Class of 1981.

Summer had started horribly, and although he no longer addressed him as such, his poppa recently moved back into town as if nothing ever happened. Life was instantly changed in Darrell's world, again. It was horrible. It was also the driving force in his "growing up quick." He'd been treated like a small child ever since the "incident." Darrell thought that was such a bullshit word to describe what had happened just outside the home he and his momma had lived in, since Poppa ran.

To Darrell, the word "incident" was an insult, and he boiled every time it was used on the television or when he would overhear it in the grocery store. Anywhere people would talk.

Each day still contained daily struggles for him, as one could expect. But he'd finally managed to convince his momma and the Watkins, to give him the breathing room he needed.

"Mom, I'm f'ing eighteen now! Geeze." Darrell stormed out through the front door and it slammed forcefully against the jam. It was the last Friday on the last week of summer. School would begin Monday.

"I'm a damned adult now. I don't need to be babysat—and I don't need to answer to anyone." He blew off his steam to Chubbs, who was now his best friend. They sat on the pier talking—close to where they'd first officially met.

Simple fact was, Chubbs was Darrell's only friend up to this point. When you have a background as the Caders do—life wasn't exactly a normal one.

Darrell could still remember the day he met Chubbs. He'd been fishing from the pier and wasn't having any luck, not even a nibble. He walked out farther to the end where this really chunky, curly-headed boy was standing with his line in the water. Darrell asked the boy if he'd mind him fishing just to the other side of where he stood.

Chubbs turned to face the voice and immediately recognized who Darrell was. The "incident" had just taken place only weeks back, and was now being broadcast constantly on the tv and radio. Every local conversation was rehashing what happened three years ago; the murder of Billy James by the boy's father, Billy Jay Cader. Now the latest event was Billy Jay Cader being shot by his younger son, Darrell Lee, when he showed back up in town unannounced. This was the boy who now stood beside Chubbs.

Everyone seemed to finally let the first story sink into the past. But summer began and along with it exploded this newest chapter of the Cader family troubles. Full bore public.

It seems the old bastard, Billy Jay, had come back into town and Darrell tried to kill him, claiming he was protecting his momma, after seeing his poppa attack her.

Anyway, Chubbs' first thought was to drop his rod and run; worried that crazy kid, would for some reason, try and kill him. Once Chubbs looked Darrell in the eye—that fear left him and instead they talked. By the end of the afternoon, Chubbs had befriended him, and for that, Darrell was grateful. He now had his first real friend—ever, since his brother Billy had died.

Chubbs was riffraff, or white trash. But Darrell respected him for not turning away because of his circumstances, and besides, he was by no means any socially higher on the scale. The murder of his brother, the three-year fugitive status of his 'poppa' who committed the crime, and, of course the fact that he tried to blow his poppa's brains out with his pastor's shotgun—when one thinks of it like that Darrell was just white trash too.

Darrell explained what his summer had brought to this new friend of Chubbs' he'd just met, "You know, uh, Kyle, is it?" He hesitated, not remembering the long-haired kid's name for sure.

Chubbs nodded, acknowledging that Kyle was indeed his friend's name. "Kyle Jones, from Arcadian Shores, upper East Coast."

"So, like I was saying, Kyle, when you've lived a life like mine, here in Apalachicola—I'm not exactly your typical run-of-the-mill teenager. Sheriff Burks seems to watch my ass closer than a dog's tongue is when he licks his own butt. That son-of-a-bitch just has it in for me. Well, me and—you know, the murderer I was telling you 'bout. I don't acknowledge him as my dad or poppa no more. Fact is, he ain't shit to me. It's 'cause of that son-of-a-bitch my only brother is dead. He likes to think he's working his way back in," Darrell guffawed, "but he sure as hell ain't."

Kyle stared at Darrell in disbelief. "You gotta be making this crap up. Come on, here in small-ville-pecker-town America? There ain't no exciting murderers or shit going on here. I think you're talking bullshit!"

Darrell glared over at Chubbs. "You better get your boy up to date. I don't wanna hurt nobody just before school starts—but shit's gonna go down if your friend don't apologize—really damn quick!"

Chubbs leaned over, saying something in Kyle's ear. Kyle's eyes widened.

"Okay, I'm sorry. Maybe you're not full of it. Chubbs says

you're shooting straight. I guess I believe you."

Chubbs and Darrell both laughed simultaneously. "Hell, we're all gonna need each other this Monday when school starts. Ain't none of us on the football team or knocking the girls off our doorsteps!" Said Chubbs.

Darrell's smile straightened into just a line across his face. "I know I'll be a target. I was on the damned news every night for a month, at least. I can't believe you never saw any of it. Where the hell did you move here from—ice-frozen Alaska or something? Hell, I thought the entire country had heard!"

The trio headed toward the pier to fish. Each carried a pole in one hand, and a small tackle box in the other—standard equipment for a man or boy walking near the pier in this small coastal community. "So, Darrell—you got yourself a girlfriend?" Kyle asked.

Chubbs laughed out loud, followed by, "Can you think of any girl that would be seen with him? Hell, they're all scared he might go psycho and kill 'em!" He looked over at Darrell and smiled.

Darrell reached around Kyle and punched Chubbs on his bicep so hard they could all hear the crack. "Don't say it again, Chubbs, I fucking dare you. Ain't nothin' funny about it."

"Sorry." Chubbs rubbed his arm as he looked towards the end of the pier, checking out how busy it was. "Hey, ain't that your dad and the preacher?" He pointed to the end of the pier.

"Son-of-a-bitch..." Darrell's shoulders slumped, dragging the grip of his rod and reel on the ground. "...why does he always have to be here? Sometimes I wish Reverend Gabriel wasn't so Christian."

"What do you mean by that? Of course, preachers is gonna be Christian. That's their damn job!" Chubbs responded.

"We can go to the 'point' if you'd rather?" Kyle asked. "Makes no difference to me as long as I get a line in the water! There's fish everywhere out there!"

Kyle and Chubbs laughed, but Darrell remained quiet with a stern look across his face.

"I ain't lettin' that son-of-a-bitch run me off of the pier. He don't own it, and we don't have to talk to him."

The three made the turn toward the pier entrance and started the long walk toward the end, looking for an open spot to drop their lines.

***

Jay and Gabriel both came to fish almost every day. Sometimes they would walk together while other times they met by chance.

Gabriel had been trying his best to lay ground-work for Jay and his son, Darrell, to patch their broken relationship. The reverend had stated many times to his wife that, "My heart aches to see the wall erected between them. At times, I feel the Lord moving mountains between the two, and yet other moments, those mountains seem to crumble quickly into flat ground."

Gabriel had spent many hours praying and thinking of ways to help Cat, Darrell, and Jay move forward and closer. "Gloria, Darrell's poppa's sudden entrance back into his life has brought on angst mixed with rebellion—and just as he was entering his coming of age." Gabriel said to his wife. After all, it was a constant topic of discussion between them, since they were practically Darrell's grandparents now.

***

Jay glanced back toward shore, and out of the corner of his eye, he spied Darrell. He was with his friend Chubbs and another boy it appeared. Jay shook his head in disgust followed by a snicker.

Gabriel noticed Jay turn back and heard the scornful laugh. Gabriel's face bore a look of wonder. One that almost begged the question of what drew it from Jay's mouth. He casually turned and spotted Darrell immediately.

As Gabriel cast his line out again, he turned to Jay. "Jay, when are you gonna accept your boy has reason to resent you being here? That boy endured a lot of pain brought on by your past choices." Gabriel set the butt of his rod into a holder on the pier and focused his attention on Jay. "This game of ignoring each other doesn't do nothing for either of you. You see that don't you? You're not an ignorant man." He waited for a response.

Jay looked as if he were thinking his answer through. He slowly turned the handle on his reel, drawing the bait to return towards him. The clicks were spaced out several seconds between each, causing an emphasis on the silence between them.

"Gabriel…" Jay thought again how to proceed. "…there are things you don't understand because you just don't know about them. I'm not sure the time is right to bring them to light for us to try and conquer them." He squinted through the brightness of the sun to look at Gabriel's reaction. "You're right though, that boy has a lot to resent about me and his life with how I treated him, but I have reasons for resentment too. I'm trying to work through them, but it's just not time to publicize." Jay turned his gaze back out to the water, reeling his line in a little quicker, the clicks sounding closer together. "It'll come to light though—mark my words. I'm not sure any good that will come from it, but it will come to light, my friend."

Gabriel cocked his head to one side as if the statement brought a sudden and quick sting. "I don't know how to process what you just said, Jay." Gabriel began reeling his line in also. Both of their reels clicked at different speeds, the sound mixing together seemed to add tension between them. "I try and understand you, and I pray every day that God can continue to reel you in closer to him, much like these reels are pulling our lines closer." Gabriel looked sideways at Jay. "I just don't understand all the wall building between you two. Guess the good Lord is designing it that way for a reason." He shook his head as his empty hook peeked up over the railing of the pier. "Seems like this silent drama you're living is as pointless and meaningless as this bait-less hook. Ain't gonna catch nothing with it—good, nor bad.

2

Jay was using his spare time getting things in his life back in order, such as working on applying for his driver's license and collecting furniture for his apartment. The usual things one needs to restart a life after living homeless in the streets. It was a challenge getting used to the responsibilities of living under a roof again. Jay knew it sounded crazy to others, but it wasn't an easy change to accept.

Jay found beginning from scratch was more difficult than he'd imagined, even with friends helping. Being accustomed to what was necessary to stay alive when homeless was far different from living up to the expectations of people who were now vested and involved in his life or personal business.

Ben and Gina were busy rebuilding and remodeling an old two-story house which stood next to the one they now lived in. They were both built on a piece of beautiful property that sat perched high on a rocky edge overlooking the bay. The project house next door was to be their new restaurant, which they generously made Jay a full partner. They even advanced him a sizable sum of money, so he could get his life squared away.

They needed his help to get the business open; but were kind enough to give him some leeway to re-acclimate back to a secure and steady way of life.

The whole scenario made Jay feel awkward, but he was grateful. He also tried to avoid Gina because of the curious feelings he still felt for her. Having his estranged wife, Cat and Gina bumping around together inside his head and being best of friends now, wasn't mixing well with him. Especially with all the pressures of being under everyone's thumbs. He still struggled with how to react with Cat, now that he knew for certain the circumstances of Darrell.

Cat still denied any affair, but he knew better after seeing the picture on the wall just months ago. He figured Sheriff Roy was unaware he was the father of Darrell. The entire thing just pissed him off. *How could Cat have pulled it all off? How could she look me in the face—the lying bitch?*

Jay felt the pull again to dole out judgment and punishment as he had in his past, but he continued to push those desires deeper within.

***

Jay lived in a small apartment on the second floor of a large home recently remodeled into four separate apartments. There were two upstairs and then two down-stairs. The two upstairs apartments each had separate outdoor wooden stairwells leading up to their entryway's doors. Jay's on the left side and the other stairs on the opposite side of the structure both facing the parking lot. A large, shared patio deck jutted out past the walkway, which connected three of the second story walls.

Jay wished they were separated completely. He enjoyed privacy with no surprises.

He hadn't met any of the neighbors' downstairs, the apartment next door to him was still vacant. He was, however, happy there wasn't any noise to hear through the walls. Jay was able to keep all of his windows open wide to feel the breeze that blew in from the bay. Being across the street from the ocean, he could hear the sound of the small waves splashing against the swampy shore.

His place was small and modest compared to his friend's new

home, but at least he didn't have to share it like his wife had to with Gabriel and Gloria Watkins—and Darrell, the little bastard.

Ben asked Jay to get his commercial driver's license reinstated because he needed him to be able to drive a box truck to pick up supplies. Essential things like fish and supplies for the restaurant from other coastal towns.

Jay showed excitement to get back on the road. It was a job he was comfortable doing before. He hoped that since all charges had been dropped, it shouldn't be any problems being able to drive again. There was no news about it yet, and he was getting antsy.

Cat questioned if it were a healthy choice for him to drive because of his past, but he dismissed it.

Jay still had some feelings for her, but with the time which passed along with the fact she bold-faced lied to him—her opinions on what he should or shouldn't do were of no consequence. He would continue to be deceivingly kind in his responses to anyone showing concerns though.

Jay was supposed to go out and have dinner with Cat this evening. As he stood in front of his open window that filled his living room, he took in the view of the storm coming inbound from across the horizon.

Jay poked at his teeth with the toothpick while he attempted to calculate if it would be hitting about dinner time. His nose took in the scent of rain and determined to cancel dinner, at least going out to a restaurant.

If he could convince Cat to have dinner in his apartment instead of going out—he might be able to seduce her and get some relief from the newly awakened urges that previously had laid dormant for the past three and a half years.

"Would I be visualizing Cat? Or would I secretly be picturing sweet Gina?" Jay spoke aloud as he stood at the window.

He smiled a wicked grin, thinking to himself. *It didn't much matter anyway. The evening's end would hopefully empty those urges invading my brain with a sweaty bang in the end, either way.* A naughty laugh escaped his mouth with the image created by the thought.

The ideas stirred up memories of his past. The dark secrets in his head that ruled him at one time. Recollections of trinkets from his history. Times-gone-by that came close to swallowing him alive. The thrill of memories long forgotten along with most of their mental intensity through all the time spent merely surviving.

A bright flash of light exploded out in the bay, followed by a sudden thunderous boom jolted him back into the present. The storm was moving at a faster pace than anyone forecasted, even himself.

The raindrops began to splatter against the window. Fresh moisture misted Jay's face in no particular sequence as waterdrops sporadically penetrated the screen when they would collide with it. The storm was already here.

Jay knew his plans for spending the evening with Cat would not happen. He felt his groin ache in the torment that was certain to well up inside him for another night. The childhood name for such an occurrence dropped into his memory from nowhere.

Blue balls.

He laughed aloud even though he found no humor in his circumstance.

The rain began to penetrate the windows so strongly he resorted to shutting them down before the floor became soaked. Again, he let out a snicker as he made the connection with being shut down himself.

He grabbed Ms. Cela's Good book and moved over to his reading chair.

He swore to himself the power her book held was life-changing—it was transforming him into an old woman like her, wasting time reading a book full of things that can't be proven and even harder to sell.

For some reason he couldn't explain, he missed the old gal along with her preachy words. He layed back in his chair, reminiscing of Ms. Cela and that toothy grin she always wore. Caring eyes and warm touch with her frail and boney hands.

<u>3</u>

Mitzi B felt excited about their move to the quiet little town of Apalachicola, Florida. It was, however, intermingled with fears, dread, and sorrow.

There were fears, of course, of the unknown. Mitzi grew up and lived in Hoover her entire life. The dread was of starting over and finding new friends who could be trusted. She knew that would be a struggle as she was always careful with whom she shared. Her sorrow was for the lifetime friends she would be leaving behind.

Mitzi B's mom had left her Dad before she was even born. Her parents weren't married for very long.

Mom told her how Dad was married to his job and held no desire to make time for a wife. She'd said the passing years gave her the maturity to understand their circumstances, that she knew my Dad would virtually abandon them at home.

Mitzi's mom, Joyce, gave up a career as an attorney's paralegal for a man who could not give up any part of his career for her. Let alone a new baby. Joyce packed up their things and moved north to her parents in Hoover, about forty minutes south of Birmingham, Alabama. It was far enough north of Apalachicola that Joyce's husband wouldn't become a bother to them.

For some reason, now eighteen years later, Mom decided to leave the comforts of home and move back south to Apalachicola. Back to where Dad, who barely sent birthday cards to either of them, still lived and worked. The entire idea was baffling, but her mom told her of the coast and sold the whole idea that it would be exciting to spend her senior year of high school being the vibrant new girl in town.

Mitzi was certain Mom wasn't being entirely honest, but ever since Grandma and Grandpa died in the car wreck, Hoover no longer held much to keep them there.

She would miss her closest of friends but didn't want to cause any troubles for Mom. She'd seen the lost looks in her mom's eyes. She tried to be excited when her mom told her about the job offer in Apalachicola with a famous crime attorney's firm.

Mom would be aiding the famous Ethan William Kendrick. This attorney freed Eddie Vanderloff, the renowned bank robber charged with a triple homicide, including a bank President and two employees.

The robbery happened in the early seventies up in Tallahassee and made the national news. Authorities attempted to tie the theft to a dozen others throughout Florida, but Mr. Kendrick tore the prosecutor's theory to shreds in a televised trial. The whole event embarrassed the state's prosecuting attorney so badly he resigned.

"Mitzi..." Her mom pleaded. "...I know it sounds completely crazy, but he wants me. He chose me out of a whole line of paralegals, and the money will go so much farther down there than here." Her mom batted her eyes at her, just like Mitzi did to her time and time again when she wanted something. "He's famous and intelligent, and I can learn so much." She pleaded.

"But, Mom! He became famous by getting a murderer freed! Is that what you really want?"

Joyce nodded her head. "I want to get out of this Birmingham area, and I want to further my career. It's not often a woman, especially one my age, gets an opportunity like this."

"What about Dad? From what you say, Apalachicola is small. Remember? 'You couldn't hide there any better than you could hide a French fry on an empty paper plate from ants at a picnic'— your words." Mitzi smiled, knowing her mom's mindset; it was no use pointing out any downsides.

They both hugged, cried, and then smiled through their tears. "It's a whole new era for us, Mitzi! You'll see!"

"Does Dad even know we're coming?"

"Nope. I guess we'll surprise him!"

"Well, that will be an uncomfortable moment at the market!" Mitzi smiled at her mom. "Oh, hey Daddy—which cereal do you recommend? The cornflakes or Captn' Crunch?" Mitzi winked at her mom, who broke into laughter out loud when she pictured Roy's shocked and rattled face at seeing his daughter.

"Yes, Mitzi B, that would be an uncomfortable trip down the cereal aisle, but one I hope I'm there to see!" They continued to laugh together.

"How soon is the big move? I do have time to have a going away party with my friends, don't I?" Mitzi asked and then scrunched her nose up.

"Of course you do, as long as we can get it set up by next Friday! I have to report to work a week from this Monday. We need to enroll you in your new school!" She looked hesitantly at her daughter.

"I already have an apartment set up for us with a great upstairs view of the bay! At least that is what the real estate man says!"

"Apartment? I have a bedroom of my own, don't I?"

"Of course you do, and it's just across the street from a beach!"

"Wow! A beach with no friends to go there with—what high school senior girl could turn her head on such an offer?" She coyly grinned at her mom before turning toward her bedroom. "I guess I'd better go pack. I wouldn't want to miss out on such a great thing!"

Joyce watched her daughter sonder down the hallway as she wore a look of selfish confusion. She questioned herself quietly under her breath. "Am I doing the right thing? Would Mitzi fit in and make new friends? Good friends? Was it right for me to make my daughter give up everything so I can start over fresh? And was it a good thing to go to work for an attorney able to get the worst of the worst out of trouble?"

Joyce walked to the garage to get the packing boxes from her car. There was a lot of work to be done in a short period. That first Monday at work would arrive sooner than later.

***

The car and small trailer were loaded, and a group of Joyce's and Mitzi B's friends were standing out in the yard. Hugs, tears, and good-byes were shared.

The news crushed Mitzi's friends. Everything happened so quickly. Summer flew by so fast, and now the first day of their senior year was next week.

"Mitzi B, I'm gonna miss you. Let's grab her and runoff, Carrie! You just can't go!" Melanie cried. "It won't be the same without you."

"We're only six or seven hours away at most. Visit me on a weekend. We're gonna live across from the beach! I love you Mel and Carrie." Mitzi B wiped her eyes, but the tears just returned as quickly as she smeared them away.

"Now Joyce, you just call if you need anything at all. Bob will bring me down right away to help."

"Thank you, Jayne. I know you would. I think we got it handled." Joyce reached out and hugged her friend and then pulled away to call out to her daughter.

"Come on, Mitzi. We need to hit the road so we can get there before dark."

Tearful last hugs and a crowd of waving hands through the rear-view mirror sent them off on their new adventure together.

Mother and daughter were making that first adventurous step into the unknown, together.

At seven p.m. sharp, Joyce's Volvo 245DL pulled into the parking spot reserved for Apartment 4.

Mitzi B threw open her door and hurriedly climbed out to look around. "Mom, let's go across the street and take a quick look at our beach!" Mitzi was cooped up too long in the car and needed to expel some energy investigating their new digs. "Hurry up, Mom. We can take luggage up after we get our feet wet!"

Joyce couldn't move quickly enough to satisfy her daughter. "I'm hurrying. I'm hurrying!" She answered with excitement. The two scurried across the street and over the small berm, only to stop suddenly in their tracks.

"Mom? Where is the beach that you showed me the picture of?" Mitzi's frown washed across her face with the question.

Joyce looked both ways, up and down the bay. Her face began to wear the same frown. "I don't remember the bay being so—swampy." She stood, trying to recollect back eighteen years earlier. "I do know that there are beautiful beaches on St. George Island, though."

"How far is that from here?" Mitzi questioned as she turned and started walking back towards the car.

"It's a short drive if my memory serves me right. I'm sorry, sweetie.

"Let's see what the view is like from the apartment. We'll go check St. George out tomorrow, I promise."

The two girls made the trek up the wooden stairs, each carrying a suitcase in each arm.

"The key is supposed to be under the doormat, sweetie."

Mitzi dropped her bags and lifted the mat to reveal nothing but deck boards underneath. She glanced back up to her mother, standing over her, then rolled her eyes.

"Well, that is where Mr. Hodges said it would be. Check above the door on the ledge or in the mailbox."

Mitzi stood up and reached above the door, running her fingers across the top ledge until she bumped something that suddenly fell. It made several clinks and banging sounds that quickly disappeared into the distance below them.

"Crap, Mom! Is this how every day is gonna be here now?" She scoffed as she headed down the stairs, keeping her eyes open for signs of the key that she'd knocked off. Mitzi quietly spoke aloud to herself. "I hate this damn place already. I'd rather have my friends back home than a swamp beach in this crap-hole town. Next, I bet good ole' Dad will show up, gun drawn and ready to shoot us as trespassers." She shook her head back and forth with each step she took.

"Honey, stay calm. I can't hear what you said, but I'm sure it's not pleasant. Do you want me to come help search for the key?"

Jay heard voices outside for the first time since he moved in. "Hmm, are there women outside?" He said to himself.

He got up from his reading chair, where he'd been delving into his Bible Ms. Cela gave him. He laid it down on the small wooden table beside his chair underneath the reading lamp. Jay grabbed a shirt, poking each arm through the short sleeve while approaching his front door. Opening it up, he stepped out onto the deck and stopped to listen for the voices.

"Any luck, Mitzi?" Before she got an answer, she set her bags down and walked towards the steps.

Jay walked the width of the house around to his neighbor's side of the structure. He came around the corner just in time to startle the woman who stood close to the stairwell.

Joyce was just about to take the first step downward, and as she reached for the handrail, a man with an open sleeveless shirt rounded the corner.

"Oh, my Lord…!" she screamed out as she began to stumble.

Jay quickly rushed up and grabbed her arm, impeding the stumbling fall she was about to take. He pulled her towards himself with his firm grip on her bicep.

Joyce's first reaction was to try and pull away, believing an assailant was attacking her. "Run, Mitzi, run!" Those were the only three words she could spit out as she caught a glimpse of the man's tattooed arms and chest. She continued to push him away as she batted at him with her free hand.

"Hold on, ma'am! I'm not here to hurt you…" He began to loosen his grip as she was now far enough from the steps not to tumble down them. "…I'm sorry, ma'am. I thought you were about to fall. I'm the neighbor…" He held his hands back, trying to show her he wasn't attacking. "…I live on the other side. It's okay…."

She'd stopped fighting the moment her daughter reached the top step with a shocked look on her face.

"Mom! Are you alright?" Mitzi's voice cracked as she struggled to catch her breath from her fast run up the stairs. Her eyes immediately saw the image of the scary tattooed man that stood near the corner of the house.

"Mitzi! When I screamed to run, I didn't mean run up here!" Joyce grabbed her chest and took a couple of deep breaths as Jay stood back, looking both of the women over.

"Mom? Are you okay now?"

Her mom drew another deep breath and stepped closer to her daughter near the top step. She reached again for the handrail. "I believe everything is fine. I was just not expecting anyone to come around the corner." She glanced at the man and then back to her daughter.

"Mitzi, this is our neighbor…" She returned her attention to the gentleman. "…I'm sorry, sir, my name is Joyce Bonham, and this is my daughter, Mitzi."

Joyce held her hand out to shake his. "I am so sorry that I tried to hit you. I have to say, Mr., you scared the hell out of me." She tried to smile as she continued, "We're your new neighbors, it seems. I didn't know our separate entries were connected up here, so I wasn't expecting to see anybody."

"No problem, ma'am. My name is Billy Jay Cader. I prefer Jay, though. I'm glad to meet you, and I'm sorry I gave you a scare." He shook her hand and then held it out towards her daughter. "It looked like you were going to tumble down the stairs—which is why I grabbed your arm."

Mitzi cautiously held her hand out, not convinced that everything was okay.

"My daughter dropped the key, and it fell through the cracks. It's been a long drive and filled with some frustrations."

"I can help you look for your key or call Bob Hodges, the maintenance man, to get you another."

Mitzi held the key out, like a prized award in front of them. "I found it, Mom."

"Well, I can help carry your things from your car then. It's a lot of stairs after a long tiring drive." He smiled.

"That would be great…" Her mom answered at the same time her daughter responded.

"Not necessary, we got it…."

Jay looked at the daughter and then back to Joyce. "Well, it's the least I can do after damn near scaring your mom to death." He winked at Joyce and gave a quick grin to Mitzi.

The women walked down the stairs with Jay behind them, watching the lady's hips wiggle with every step they took, both going down and then back up. They then emptied the car and made two trips back up to their front door.

Mitzi pushed the door open and searched for the light switch, unable to find it.

Jay rubbed up against her and reached his arm around to the right side of the door. The move made Mitzi step back quickly, looking uncomfortable. He ran his hand up, flipping the switch, bringing the living room light to life. "There it is, just about the same spot mine is. Kind of an odd spot to put a switch, in my opinion."

Mitzi felt a chill go up to her spine as the neighbor's demon etched arm, and then chest brushed back against her. After she was behind him, she looked at her mom, giving her a quick impression of vomiting.

"Thank you, Jay. I appreciate your help, but I think we can get it from here." She edged into the room next to her daughter as she gently nudged Jay to the side.

He seemed to take the hint and smiled. It was a slightly devilish smile, but he backed out of their door to the outside. "It was nice to meet you, ladies. I apologize again for the scare. Just holler if you need anything else. I'm just around the corner!"

As they closed the door, both Mother and daughter eyed each other with looks of tension. "Chills, Mom. That's all I have to say." Mitzi's body quivered. "We have a gosh-damn serial killer living next door to us..." She playfully pushed her mom back from her. "...and your new damned boss is gonna get him off scot-free when they find our decomposed bodies up here under our beds—muahaha...."

"Mitzi Burks! Don't you dare say anything like that again? What if he can hear us?" Joyce said in a hushed tone.

Mitzi snapped back. "Don't you ever call me by my last name either. Not a name I'm necessarily proud of wearing. That's why we go by B. Remember, that way everyone just assumes I'm a Bonham, like you!"

"Sorry, I'm just so tired, I hope we have beds here. The way the day has gone, I wouldn't be surprised if they weren't delivered yet." Joyce walked down the hallway, flipping lights on in all of the rooms. "There is one in my room, at least!" Joyce exclaimed.

She continued to the end of the hallway. "Yes, ma'am, you're taken care of also." She pulled the sheets back to check them out. "The bedding is clean! We can go to bed now, so we'll be ready early in the morning to find that beach in the picture!"

Mitzi studied the layout of the house for a moment. She scrunched her forehead a couple of seconds after obviously doing some calculations.

"I don't like it, Mom."

"What don't you like now, Mitzi, girl?"

"If our layouts are close to our creepy neighbor's…" She looked from one end and back to the other. "…that put's a bedroom next to mine on his side. The guy could be lying next to me with only a thin wall between us. That's a creepy thought." Her nose scrunched upward.

"Mitzi! I asked you not to talk like that! These walls may be thin enough to be able to overhear conversations. Shoosh, for crying out loud!"

"Do you hear what you just said, Mom?" Mitzi held her hands, palms up toward the ceiling. "You even think the walls are thin. You know—like the one separating my bed from the creepy tattooed guy on the other side. And you think I'm gonna be able to sleep?" She gave her mom a questioning look. "I'm sharing your bed with you tonight, and I won't take no for an answer."

Joyce stood in the doorway to her room, eyeing her bed. "Tonight only, dear. I don't want you punching me through the night, or hear you complain if I crowd your space."

It was a restless night for both. The two girls heard every pop and creak of the old two-story house.

After meeting their neighbor, Mitzi believed every noise was creepy Jay stalking around hidden passageways between the walls.

It was close to two in the morning when Joyce began shoving her daughter to the edge because Mitzi flailed back and forth so much. The sheets tugged back and forth as if they were in the middle of an old school-gym-class game.

Mitzi woke up at three a.m. in a pool of sweat. She stumbled out of bed to open the window for fresh air, but suddenly saw the wooden deck just outside the window. "Oh, sure, open the window and make it an easy home invasion and rape for creepy Jay—I don't think so!" Her words were spoken in a whisper as she flipped the shades down and crawled back into the moist bedding.

Mitzi completely missed the shadow on the deck that quickly moved away from the window.

Jay glanced back at the drawn shades that stole the view he was enjoying only seconds earlier.

There will be other nights. Jay would move slowly and earn some trust before trying to window peep again. The school locker-room catchphrase fell into his memory once again. He chuckled along with the pain that followed in his groin.

Blue balls.

4

Joyce's alarm went off too soon to suit either mother or daughter. She reached over to the nightstand to push the snooze button, her stretched out arms letting her know she would not be able to go back to sleep. Joyce also knew she shouldn't. She'd promised to take her daughter to St. George Island, and she also needed to do a drive-by at Mitzi's high school and her new office. Joyce enjoyed her preparedness. She'd raised her daughter to be the same. Ten minutes early is twenty minutes late. That was their motto.

Mitzi must have felt her mom's movement because she too mimicked her mother's stretches. Like mother, like daughter.

Mitzi looked over at her mom, noticing her being awake. "Well, we made it through our first night without being murdered by Jumpsuit Jay." She half-smiled at her mom.

"Where did you come up with that nickname? Or dare I ask?"

"I'm sure that is what he wore daily before Mr. Kendrick got him his murder reprieve on a stupid technicality! You think it was black and white—or orange?" She lifted and turned so she could see her mother's face. "I'm going with black and white because his skin art would make the orange appear blasé, don't you think?"

Joyce could never figure out where her daughter's sense of humor came. It certainly wasn't from her side, and she didn't remember any humor at all in her ex-husband. "Where do you come up with these ideas?"

Mitzi laid back down with a flop. Her ears perked up for a second when she heard a whistle. "Oh my gawd, Mom! Is that a teapot whistling?" Mitzi suddenly felt a sinking ache in her stomach. She would generally think it was hunger, but today it was the thought of a possible serial killer next door— if she could hear his teapot, it was possible he'd heard every word she'd spoke.

Her mom sat up with a sudden burst of energy also. She looked to her daughter with guilty fear. She whispered, "See what I mean, Mitzi? How are we going to face him now? He's our neighbor for gawd's sake, and he's done nothing but offer us help." She pointed her finger. "Don't you feel guilty now?"

"Mom, the first lesson in criminal justice, is never to admit guilt! I'm going to have to defer all questions to my lawyer—the famous Ethan William Kendrick!"

Her mom pushed her so hard; she nearly flew off the bed. "Okay, Miss smart-ass, get dressed in your swimsuit. We have a beach to find along with my office and your school. That's our mission today. Hopefully, we can avoid Mr. Cader on our way out this morning."

"We have our stairwell, and he has his, so if the stalker doesn't trespass again, we won't run into him!" Mitzi retorted.

"I think you are going to end up being the attorney of the family, young lady!"

They both fell back onto the bed, laughing before Mitzi hopped up and headed for the shower. She did give the room a once-over, looking for any peepholes that may have been added by the "neighbor." She found none.

They found Mitzi's school right away. It was going to be within walking distance. The building appeared to be reasonably new.

Mitzi looked out of the car window. "So, this is my final high school home. It sure does look small in comparison. I hope they have room for me, or then again, maybe I don't. I wonder if they use pen and paper here yet?"

"I didn't realize you were such a snob, Mitzi. Don't look too far down that nose you're wearing. You might see that it points toward the sky fairly quickly." Joyce wanted her daughter to be aware of the attitude she was showing. Joyce held no fears her daughter would have any real issues fitting in. Mitzi always blended in well with others.

"Well, Mom—let's go see where you'll be doing your time throughout the day. At least you have good legal representation!" She giggled at her mom's expense.

Joyce's office wasn't too far from the high school. It sat on the second floor of a refurbished brick building on U.S. 98, less than a block from the Franklin County Courthouse.

"Look, Mom, there's a neat little coffee shop we can meet at after school and work every day!"

"I imagine that would be a good place to hang out and work on your homework while you wait for me to get off." Joyce winked at her daughter. "See, things are already looking better than they did last night."

The two girls headed out in the Volvo east on Market Street, which took them straight across the John Gorrie Memorial Bridge to Eastpoint, Florida. From there, they headed south on Island Drive crossing over the bay again to St. George Island, via the Bryant Patton Bridge.

It was a beautiful Saturday with the sun shining brightly. Mitzi stared out through the open window with the wind blowing her long curly reddish-blonde hair. Her mom's light brown straight hair was blowing back and forth through her ponytail. The water shimmered with light, and the scent of the ocean made everything feel fresh and electric.

Thirty-five minutes later, they were cruising Gulf Beach Drive looking for a place to park at a public beach.

Mitzi's eyes didn't stay still for more than a second at most. Her mom enjoyed the view of her daughter's happiness in seeing things she'd never seen before.

The two pulled into a parking lot on the northeast part of the island. The wind was blowing gently, and the waves splashed up the shoreline in steady pulses of two-foot-high walls of water. As the two dropped their bags and blankets, kicking off their sandals—the waves seem to call Mitzi, beckoning her to the shoreline where they came rushing up to meet her.

Mitzi stood at the water's edge, raising her hands and spinning her wrists back towards her body as if she were directing the waves to come and bow to her. "Hmmmm…humm a na…humm a na…hummm…she called over and over in the same chant as she continued reeling in the waves. Calling out to the whitecaps as their reigning Queen, through her motioning arms and silly incantations, the ocean seemed to answer back in submission again and again.

Her mom stood watching in fascination at the way her daughter was reacting to the ocean. Mitzi's smile and child-like demeanor appeared as if the experience reverted her back in time to a ten-year-old girl.

The rhythm her daughter contained as she performed to the waves—painted a sereneness Joyce never before saw in her. She smiled, unable to move her eyes away.

Mitzi turned to search for her mom, and when she spotted her, waved wildly, motioning her to join.

Joyce took a mental snapshot of the moment. She studied her daughter and her surroundings so she would never forget this single snippet of time. She reminisced for a moment—if she were to lay dying alone sometime in the future—she would be able to ignore any pain while finding comfort recalling this exact mental photograph of her daughter.

She carefully absorbed every minute detail. The sun shining above poked through the puffy cloud-filled azure blue sky. Glimmering sparks of light bounced off of the rolling bluish-green waves. It was a beautiful moment as the waves appeared to be obeying the magic of her daughter's child-like sorcery. There were small shimmering strands of her strawberry-blonde hair blowing across her face that seemed to be enticing the water-world to bow at her smile. Mitzi became a mermaid goddess in this nanosecond. Joyce felt a tear trying to eke out, and as she reached to wipe it away gently, she was reeled back to reality in a flash.

"Mom! Come here! Let's wade together for my first time into the ocean!" Her mouth was stretched as wide across her face as possible. Her beautiful white teeth glowed with the grin she could no longer control.

Joyce looked as if she'd never felt more alive—Mitzi noticed it right away through the smile her mom wore as she jogged over to grab her hand.

In those moments, it would be hard to imagine either of them believing the decision to move south was a mistake. Giggles between the two were loud and rowdy as the car doors swung open in the parking lot of their new home.

The voices again drew Jay's attention to the ground below. He was lying on a lounge chair, catching some sun with his book in hand. He turned just in time to see the scantily dressed women leaning back into their car, gathering towels and such. He looked down towards the foot of this lawn chair, noticing the rising movement in his mid-section.

He tried to ignore the whole scenario, but the urge was too strong and drew his gaze back through the railing bolsters at the fleshy bottoms still wiggling just outside the car.

His inquisitive fascination with Ms. Cela's Bible continually gave him the desire to read more in-depth about Jesus and the times and wisdom that was between the covers. But he answered the devil's call because his invisible shackles which held him to his dark side could not be broken. He wasn't entirely satisfied that freedom from his wicked side was what he truly wanted.

The more he pushed those dark urges away, the louder the voice inside his head called out to rebuke his good side.

The devil most assuredly knew his way around the act of temptation. Jay believed he was tempted as Jesus had been in the desert. It wasn't probable that it was just coincidence two young women chose the apartment next door to live. Two women alone without male companionship.

A shameful grin washed across his lips. The footsteps from the staircase blended with the sound of laughter on the other side of the building.

Blue balls, again was the thought that popped into his head.

***

It was Monday morning and the first day of Mitzi's last year of high school.

"Mom! Does this look okay?" She hollered to her mother as she walked through the doorway. "Honest answer. First impressions are lasting, especially when they're truly first impressions, like…." Her excitement was adding to her nerves. "…like I've never been here before kind of the first impression…."

"Mitzi. Wow! You look incredible. You got some sun! Does it hurt?" Joyce reached out to touch her shoulder. "Do you want some Aloe Vera lotion?" She asked. Her daughter immediately shook her head no. "Okay, if you're sure. And you're right—first impressions are important. How about me?"

"Mr. Kendrick is gonna wanna leave his wife if he's married! You look more like my sister than my mother! Holy crap!"

The two giggled together.

"Mitzi, we have to get you there early. We need to fill out paperwork and schedules, and then I have to be at work by ten til nine. No later!"

"Seriously, you look great, Mom. I'm proud of you. I'm also sorry for the hard time I've been giving you. My room is fine. I didn't hear any moaning or muffled screams of help through the wall! After you go through your introductions with Mr. Kendrick and his team—be sure and give him my condolences that we failed to bring him a new client today." Mitzi laughed as she poked her mom on the side. "We're both still alive and kicking!"

"You just never quit, do you?" She shook her head back and forth as she held out a small egg biscuit. "Here you go, some quick nourishment to push you through your day."

Joyce and Mitzi quickly walked to the front doors of Apalachicola High. Upon opening the doors, they saw trophy cases on either side of the walls. Banners were bearing the school's sport teams mascot. "The Bull Sharks." It was a profile of a black shark with its dorsal fin just above a wavy blue line and its sharp, spikey teeth sticking out of a rather vicious grin.

"Now, that reminds me of our neighbor! He must have graduated from here." Mitzi looked closer at the banner. "Nope. No tattoos on this shark!" She then looked over at her mom and laughed. "I wonder if he was the captain of the killing team, um, swim team?"

Joyce punched her daughter in the arm. "Give it a rest, Mitzi. The punchline is getting as old as the punches to your arms." She shook her head as they walked into the front office.

"Welcome to Apalachicola High School!" The secretary greeted them with a smile and a wink. "Do we have a new student today?"

"Yes, ma'am, this is my daughter Mitzi Burks." Joyce glanced at her daughter through the corner of her eye with a daring look of, "don't you say a word" glare.

"Hmm, any relation to our Sheriff Roy Burks?"

"Yes ma'am, but my daughter has somewhat of an estranged relationship with him, as do I, as his ex-wife. We've just moved here over the weekend from Hoover, Alabama. He doesn't know we are here in town yet, and we'd like to keep it that way for the moment." She smiled a stern smile and nodded. "Oh, and my daughter likes to be addressed as Mitzi B. My name is Joyce

Bonham. Bonham is my maiden name. Mitzi likes people to assume the B stands for Bonham, instead of his. I hope you understand." She pulled her daughter close to her and smiled at the secretary.

"I imagine we can live with that for now. It's, of course, not a…common kind…" She looked up from the paperwork she was filling out. "…of a thing, but I'm sure we can make an accommodation. I'll just make some notes on her records." Her lips pursed for a moment, and then she looked back up to Joyce. "We're not expecting any problems between Mitzi B and Sheriff Burks, are we?"

"No, ma'am. We just haven't made the time to work out the details. We just arrived in town Friday evening. I start my new job with the Ethan William Kendrick firm…" She glanced down at her wristwatch, "…in just about thirty-five minutes, so if we could try and speed through some of the processes—I could, of course, set up a time to go into more detail later."

"That will be okay, as long as we get the home address and emergency contact numbers and such."

"Mitzi B will be no trouble at all, Mrs.—what did you say your name was?"

"Mrs. Tammy Hatley, I'm the secretary to the principal here. His name is Charley Bingham. I'm Just filling in for our counter-secretary."

"Well, thank you, Mrs. Hatley. I appreciate you tweaking the rules a bit on this hectic first day for us." Joyce glanced over to Mitzi and winked.

"Do you have Mitzi B's records from her previous school?"

"Yes, Mrs. Hatley, I do." She dug the folder from her bag and handed it over the counter.

"Follow me if both of you would please, and we will check your classes needed against the openings on the schedule." Mrs. Hatley got up and motioned toward the swinging door.

***

Joyce walked up the outside stairs to her new workplace. She couldn't help but think walking these steps daily along with the steps at home— would take no time at all until she sported some very shapely legs, along with a pretty tight body for someone in their late thirties.

"Welcome, Miss Bonham! It is wonderful to meet you finally!" The voice was warm and genuine, coming from the lady that appeared to be in her early fifties. "You are a sight for sore eyes! I hope you're ready to dive right in!" She grinned. "Of course, we realize we're going to be bringing you up to our speed, so don't worry. Mr. Kendrick has said nothing but wonderful things about you after you met with him. He is unfortunately out of the office and just left for Fort Walton Beach an hour ago." She motioned her around her desk toward the hallway. "He has a deposition to take, and he didn't want to throw you directly into the fire on your first day." She walked down the hallway, looking back at Joyce as they passed a couple of closed doors. "He's sweet that way…" She stopped momentarily. "…is it okay if I call you Joyce? By the way, I'm Addison. Addison Charmane, but please, just call me Addi. Everyone does!"

"Joyce will be perfect, Addi. Your name is beautiful. Rolls off the tongue with such ease."

"Why thank you, sweetie." She looked back and smiled as she held out her hand and pointed to a closed door. "This one is yours, Joyce. Your nameplate, what do you think?"

Joyce turned to face her new office door. On a walnut door with a smoked glass pane, backlit by a prominent window inside, was an attached gloss-black nameplate that read, 'Joyce M. Bonham-Paralegal' etched in silver bold-faced lettering. "It's perfect! The excitement of seeing the inside is eating me alive!"

Addi reached over, putting her hand on Joyce's shoulder. "Honey, I just know you are gonna be the perfect puzzle-piece fit here." She turned the knob and slowly swung the door open.

Inside was a large window that faced a side street just off of the central business highway where the firm sat. The shades were open, letting the sun fill the entire space. Her office was more significant than the area in her and Mitzi's living room. A beautiful old ornate table-desk sat in the middle, perpendicular to the small leather couch that sat against the window.

There was a matching credenza behind the desk that held a full-length bookcase on top, full of what was surely law books. The wall behind was old brick mixed with what appeared to be chunks of horse-hair plaster that still held tightly to the bricks in scattered spots on the wall. The rest of the walls remained bare, surely for her to pick out things to hang on them.

"This is far more than I imagined! It's quite beautiful. I don't know what to say?" A tear fell from her eye and rolled down her cheek as the experience set in.

"I shouldn't tell you this yet, so don't repeat it, but I think you deserve hearing it." Addi paused and leaned in. "Ethan has been going on about you since he met you. He's gone through your file several times. Each time I've entered Ethan's office, your file has been open—and he goes on and on about your potential."

"My potential? What does that mean? I'm just a paralegal. I feel very confident in my abilities as one, but potential is a strong word for such a position. Along with such a large and ornate office? I'm standing here, feeling as if I've entered a dream world or possibly the wrong firm."

"I'm about to explain more, honey, but you cannot let on when Mr. Kendrick returns. Can you promise me?" Addi peered intently into Joyce's moistened eyes.

"I can't imagine what you're going to tell me, but yes, I can keep a secret. I'm just a bit scared to open myself to hearing such clandestine confidence, but continue, please."

"Well, Mr. Kendrick hinted to the fact that if your value to the firm is as he imagines it will be…" She leaned in closer and spoke just above a whisper even though they were the only two in the office. "…he plans to offer some college law classes to you. In the future, of course." Addi held her finger to her lips as if to shoosh her from repeating any of this.

Joyce stood in the center of her office, having no idea what to think or say. She'd been here less than fifteen minutes and already received one of the biggest bombshells ever dropped on her shoulders in her entire life.

"Addi, why on God's green earth, did you tell me this? I can't live up to this expectation. I haven't…" She choked on her words. "…I haven't so much as opened a client's file yet, and now I have a possible law school education hovering over my head?" She turned, reaching out each hand and clasping Addi's shoulders. "Are you trying to give me a heart attack to keep me from joining the firm?" Her lips tried to widen into a smile, but they remained a quivering straight line between her cheeks.

Addi pulled her into her arms. "I can see what Mr. Kendrick's spied in you right off the bat. He's a talented judge of character. I've never seen him miss a call." She pulled back and looked directly at Joyce. "No, I'm not trying to get rid of you, I'm trying to make certain the confidence instilled inside of you—matches the confidence that you exude outwardly. I plan on seeing you in that office of yours well past my retirement, honey. And I ain't goin' nowhere in a hurry!" She let go and smiled again at Joyce as she slowly walked towards the door. "I'm going to leave you here to let everything gel. Mr. Kendricks asked me to let you know he would be back in the office by Wednesday morning. He plans to take you to lunch to get better acquainted and to see what your thoughts are of the firm so far.

5

Mitzi survived her first four classes. Lunch break was minutes away, and she already made plans to eat with a possible new girlfriend, Violet Emerson.

The bell rang, and the hallways were already full by the time Mitzi B stepped through her English Comp 2 class and into the chaos. She was clueless about how to get to the lunchroom. It hardly mattered because she was caught in the flow of classmates heading in a direction she wouldn't be able to change, even if it were wrong.

"Mitzi B! Over here!" Violet waved wildly as she jumped above the kids in the hallway so that Mitzi would be able to pick her out of the moving crowd.

Mitzi turned toward the sound of her name and quickly saw Violet. She smiled. "I see you, Violet!" She hollered. As she got close, she made one more cut through the river of kids. "Excuse me, sorry!" She dashed to the beginning of the hallway where Violet stood.

"No offense, but I can't believe this tiny town could have so many kids! I guess all the adults in town are sexually active and very fertile! At least they were fifteen years ago, or Catholic and no use of contraception."

Violet laughed at Mitzi B's hysterical observation.

"Where do you go for some quiet time at lunch?" Asked Mitzi.

"I'm not hungry, you?"

Mitzi shook her head no. "I have to skip lunches to keep my

butt nice and firm!" She winked and giggled.

"Let's go out to the south lawn. People spread out, and there are benches and tables enclosed by a stubby wall where we can sit." Violet grabbed her hand and began to lead the way. They walked out the side door, and she pulled Mitzi along the stubby wall close to the end of it. There were groups of friends scattered in different settings around the area.

"So—how's the first half of your first day?"

"Great question! I wish I could answer it easily. My classes seem like they won't be a problem. Some of the boys, however, might be a challenge." Mitzi giggled.

"Yeah, well, that problem is surely universal no matter where your butt lands." Violet answered.

Mitzi nodded in agreement. "Yes, but I've been in the same schools with the same friends my entire life until now. The change to a new school my senior year is sorta daunting!"

"You'll do okay. It seems like you're pretty easy going with strong confidence!"

"You're falling for my bullshit charade..." Mitzi poked her on the arm. "...now I know I can control the masses through replicating my spell that baffled you!"

"Girl, you got spunk. I like it. I think you and I are gonna get along fine." Violet poked her arm in return.

They continued the various conversations as Mitzi fanned her eyes across the area. "So many faces, so many fears are overwhelming me. I can't believe I've got you believing I'm not scared shitless, because I am."

Across the south lawn, positioned behind Violet, sat three friends around a concrete table. They were horsing around punching each other as if it were a game. Mitzi noticed one in particular, right away. He stood out above the other two even though he was also sitting. "Violet—nonchalantly scan the crowd right behind you on the other side of the lawn..." She grabbed

Violet's arm. "...hey! I said casually! Who is the kind of strawberry-blonde-haired older-looking boy with the other two punching each other?"

Violet slowly moved her head around as she scanned for the description Mitzi gave her. About three-quarters of the way around, she spied who Mitzie was asking about. She whipped her head back. "Oh my gawd, Mitzi B!" Violet held her hand over her mouth as she gasped. "Stay away! His family is bad news. He almost killed his dad just a few months ago!"

"Hmm. A boy with a built-in reputation of danger." She rubbed her lips with her right thumb and pointing finger like a sleuth would as he closed in on his mark.

"I'm serious, girl. His dad killed that boy's brother about four years ago and then went on the lam. He came back, and that's when he saw his dad with his mom—BANG!" Twice with our preacher's shotgun!" Violet's eyes were wide open, with the whites showing all the way around.

"Ew, Violet! That look's not good on you!" She nailed her arm to make her drop the wild-eyed look.

"Why are you asking about Darrell, anyway?"

"Hmm, Darrell, huh? I kind of think—Darrell..." Mitzi grabbed Violet's cheeks in each hand and straightened her face directly in front of hers. "...is a damn hot lookin' guy. That is why I'm asking."

"You need schoolin' Mitzi B, no doubt about it. It's a damn good friggin' thing I befriended you! And, stay away from Darrell!"

The last four hours drug. Mitzi's mind was anywhere, but whichever class she was sitting in. She sat in her previous hour class with her chin rested between her hands that sat propped from her desktop.

I wonder how I can meet Darrell, without looking like a desperate boy-starved new kid on the block? Each time she said his name in her head, she almost gave an 'awe' out loud. *I will be keeping my eyes peeled for an opportunity to bump into you—Darrell...awe.*

The bell rang, and Mitzi B didn't hear it. She was in la-la land until her desk got bumped by a kid rushing by. It almost toppled her head off of her hands.

Mitzi's walk to the coffee shop was dream-filled. She could hardly wait to share her day with her mom. But, then again, maybe she shouldn't give too much away. How could she keep quiet? Her mom would see right through her fantasy-filled eyes. She'd never been mesmerized by a boy so quickly. Especially one she hadn't even talked to or met. She knew she needed to remedy that.

Her thoughts turned to Violet's warnings. She was kidding her or playing a trick on the new kid. That kind of drama of murder and attempted murder between family members only happened in books and movies. No way things like that happen in smallville Florida! Regardless, Violet's stories of Darrell would NOT be divulged to her Mom. No way!

She looked up and laughed. At first, she was confused, but quickly realized she walked past her mom's office, which meant she'd also passed their meeting spot. "The Coffee Caper." Mitzi turned around and backtracked several shops until she saw the coffee cup on the window, with a super-hero type cape wrapped around it.

How totally silly of a logo for a coffee shop.

She found a table towards the back and impatiently waited for her mom.

She daydreamed some and studied the people inside and the ones who walked past the front window. That was when she saw three boys saunter past the window.

"Oh my!" It came out of her mouth before she could cup her hand over her lips to block it.

It was Darrell and the other two boys from school!

She quickly scooted up to the cashier's counter.

"Miss!" She called.

"Yes, ma'am?"

"My mom is going to be here from the law firm next door any minute looking for me. She's a pretty brown-haired lady in her thirties. She'll be the one with the worried look across her face when she doesn't see me sitting in here..." Her heart was racing, trying to get her sentence out before the boys were too far down the sidewalk. "...would you tell her I was here and will meet her at home. I'm gonna meet some friends for a few minutes, and I'll walk home. Thanks!" She fulfilled her daughterly obligation and was out the front door and headed to the right in a flash.

She knew she probably looked like a stalker as she wriggled in and out through the few patrons walking on the sidewalk.

It was her lucky day! She noticed a piece of paper fall out of Darrell's back pocket. She quickly bent down and picked it up. Darrell just happened to look back, possibly realizing he'd dropped something.

"Hey, I think that's mine!"

Mitzi looked up as she lifted the folded note to his hand. "I know. I saw it drop out of your pocket, and I was gonna give it to you." She smiled.

Darrell looked over at Chubbs then to Kyle and then back at Mitzi. "So, you were checkin' my ass out?" He tried to shoot her a serious look.

"Well, now that you mention it..." She climbed back up off her knee. "...it is quite an ass! In fact, it's the nicest ass I've ever seen between two other asses! Kind of the cream of ass in an Oreo cookie! That analogy would make more sense—if your friends were both brown, of course."

Darrell laughed aloud as Chubbs and Kyle looked blankly at each other as if they'd missed the fact that they were the punchline.

"Mitzi B is my name..." She held her empty hand out this time.

"...nice meeting such a sweet ass on my first school day here." She turned and bent over, feigning tying her shoelace, which was not untied. "Take a gander at mine! I've heard it said that it was sweet as Tupelo honey but jiggled like firm lime Jello!" She spun around and caught a shocked look that was slipping into a smile.

"I...um...I..." Darrell's speech began to revert to his past stuttering. "...I'm...Darrell and...." He wiped his sweaty brow.

"Did my sweet ass choke you up and make you speechless?" Her smile was warm even though her words were a little sharp with sarcasm.

"Sometimes, Darrell's words get all twisted up. Don't happen as much lately, but...." Chubbs was in defensive mode.

"Hey, I was just havin' some fun playin'. I didn't mean to upset you—Darrell. For real, your ass is nice. I left a cup of coffee on the table at the 'Caper' just to come out here and tell you that. Honest!" She smiled and turned back toward the shop, slowly walking away. She suddenly turned back abruptly. "Maybe see you at school tomorrow? With any luck—I just might let you brush against it!" She slapped her right cheek and then quickly turned and walked briskly back toward the coffee shop.

With any luck, he didn't see me blushing, and I'll beat my mom back before she knew I was gone.

She swung the door open and looked around at the tables looking back to see if her coffee still sat in her spot.

"Hey there, Mitzi!"

She turned back to see her mom just inside the door.

"Mom! You're here! Has your new boss made you a judge yet?" She smiled and rushed over to hug her.

"Are those new friends outside on the sidewalk?" She lifted an eyebrow.

"Yeah, sorta. It was a good day. Maybe even better tomorrow? How about you?"

Her mom reached for her hand as she let the door close. "You wouldn't believe me if I told you, sweetheart!"

The bell on the coffee shop door clanged as it shut.

"Let's go celebrate this first day, what do you say, Mitzi?"

"Perfect!"

They turned back around and opened the door to leave and walked down the sidewalk to a little diner a block or two down the road.

Mitzi spied what looked like the paper Darrell just dropped. She coyly bent down and picked it up, turning to block it, so her mom couldn't see. She nonchalantly tucked it into her back pocket as they walked in.

"Are you the litter patrol now, Mitzi?" Her mom curiously smiled.

"I think it was one of my new friends. It looked familiar."

"Boy or girl?"

"Oh Mom, come on. Let's just sit and read the menu."

"I've got to use the powder room, sweetie. I'll be right back, grab us a table and some menus." She kept walking toward the back.

Mitzi squeezed into a booth, grabbing the folded paper from her back pocket as she scooted. She quickly unfolded it and held it up to her face. The handwriting was sloppy. *That meant it was a boy.* She laughed aloud. She read it in a whisper to herself after looking around the room to make sure he wasn't sitting in here.

I know you ain't into the ladies that much, but did you see the new girl yet? WOW. I hope I can bump into her. She is really beautiful and those green eyes!

Mitzi sat motionless with a queasy butterfly feeling in her stomach. It was an excellent queasy! She couldn't believe he was already talking about her at some point today. It was surely a sign! She reread it just to make sure she wasn't mistaken.

"Damn!" She quickly covered her mouth with her hands and scanned the room. Unfortunately, she started from the opposite side that her mom returned.

"Excuse me, Miss B?" She held out her hand for the note. "I think I'd better take a look at this news you've received. Especially if it's going to have this kind of effect on you!" She continued to hold her hand out, wiggling her fingers in a give-it-to-me gesture.

She slowly picked it up and handed over the evidence. "Remember, Mom, you work for the defense's side. I'm holding out for a not guilty because of insanity." She sheepishly looked at her mom for the reaction. "I might just be insanely infatuated—I rest my case!"

Her mom let a smile escape from the corner of her mouth. She looked up from the note and toward her daughter. "Seems you have an admirer. I suppose he was one of the boys from earlier? The cute red-headed one, I presume?" She smiled. "Seems innocent enough for now, besides, we girls need an ego boost occasionally, don't we? It seems we both have gotten a confidence booster today." She slid a menu toward her side of the table and scooted a fingernail under the edge to pick it up.

"Really?"

A couple of seconds slipped past before Joyce responded. "Really, what?"

"Mom! I hate it when you pull this crap on me—and you know it!"

She smiled. "And you know I dislike hearing boyish words roll off of your tongue so easily!"

"I'm sorry, just spill the beans for gawd's sake. What happened today? Did Mr. Attorney ask you on a date or something?"

"Shoosh." Joyce held her finger to her lips. "Mitzi B, you have to be careful with that boisterous mouth of yours. I have an image now that I need to maintain." She leaned in and started whispering as she glanced around the room. "This job maybe even bigger than I imagined. I don't want to lose it from my daughter's loose lips before I even get settled into my...oh...I don't know..." She fought to hold her excitement to a quiet indoor level. "…own private office with a black leather couch and huge desk in the middle of a…basketball arena for an office!" She let out a sigh and leaned back in to whisper again. "I didn't even find my private powder room until eleven a.m. when I stepped out to ask where the lady's room was in the office."

"Wow, Mom, that's great! I'm happy for you. Seriously, you really deserve some happy times. I'm sorry Dad was such a dick to you. Oops. I mean such a…"

"Dick is right, Mitzi. I know I shouldn't talk him down to you, but you're right on both accounts. I deserve—we deserve to start living a better life on our own. Promise me you'll share in this, along with me."

"Don't start getting' mushy, Mom. I only like butter soggy mashed potatoes on my plate. Not my sleeves." She cracked a smile.

"I love you, honey."

"I know, Mom. I love you back—more."

6

Chubbs punched Darrell in the ribs. "I can't believe you like that new girl. She was makin' fun of us."

"She was makin' fun of you and Kyle. I believe she was complimenting the hell out of my ass!" Darrell laughed. "I'm gonna see if she wants to hang with us at school. We got room for another!"

"Maybe she's got a couple friends, Chubbs?" Kyle asked Darrell. "One that likes studly guys like me and one that can put up with you!" Kyle said as he pushed Chubbs back down in his chair. "There are girls that like chubbies like you!" Kyle laughed, finding his joke hilarious.

"I got your chubby right here." Chubbs grabbed his crotch and squeezed it.

"Come on, grow up. I'm serious. We need some estrogen added to the mix in here. I'm drowning in testosterone, and most of it belongs to you two." Darrell thought for a second about the way he worded his last statement. He shook his head in disgust and got up from the bench quickly as if one of them farted.

Both Kyle and Chubbs broke into laughter. "Drowning in it, huh?" Kyle asked and then laughed even louder.

"You know what I meant. This is our last year, gang. I've finally crawled out of the cave I grew up hiding in. Let's put on our cool and have a fun year. Who knows where we'll be next May when it all comes to an end, and the real world takes over." Darrell held his fist up high, challenging his friends to lift their fists in unity.

The three young men cracked their fists together to show solidarity. They weren't sure what it all meant yet, but they were a coalition of sorts.

***

The second day of school couldn't get here soon enough, according to Mitzi. She held big news to share with Violet. She slipped on her favorite outfit and spent an extra fifteen minutes in the bathroom until her mom shooed her out. She kept checking herself out in the mirror. She giggled to herself as she looked at the reflection of her butt. She knew it would be the topic—at least in Darrell's mind now.

"Honey, what's the special occasion?" A couple of seconds passed before Mitzi poked her head through the bathroom door.

"Really, Mom? Today is even a bigger day than yesterday, remember the note you booked into evidence?"

"Oh yeah!" She recalled. "The handsome red-headed admirer!"

Mitzi sighed. "Yesterday, I was just a random faceless plane flying around in a cloud of countless others, blending in and waiting for approach." She paused for the dramatic build-up to her punchline. "Now though—I'm Air Force friggin' One, buzzing the tower that holds the pilot who wants to inspect my ailerons." She giggled. "You know, to make sure they're in tip-top flight status and ready to approach the runway for a smooth, safe landing!"

"Oh, Mitzi, girl. Where do you come up with this stuff?" Joyce paused as she took in the beauty and personality of her daughter. "I'd worry if you weren't so damn smart and level-headed! You are gonna make some lucky guy the luckiest man in the world someday." She touched her daughter's chin softly. "Just take your time, sweetie, you don't want to take off too fast—unplanned flights can lead to a crash and burn situation." Joyce shook her head and then checked her own backside out in the mirror.

"See where I get it now? The vanity I mean." Mitzi smiled with a chuckle as she slapped her mom's backside and then did the same to her own.

Violet was waiting in the new meeting spot. Her face lit up as soon as she saw her new wing-girl at Apalachicola High.

"Have I got mission status to tell you about what happened?" The smile that filled Mitzi B's face tickled Violet's interests.

"Tell me! I can't wait to hear everything. Don't you dare tell me this has anything to do with dangerous Darrell?"

Mitzi slowly turned as if she were going to walk away in the opposite direction. "Okay, if you want to judge me…" She twisted back around to see Violet's reaction. "…I wish you could have been there and seen me in action! I was absolutely superior!" She walked back toward Violet, obviously unable to keep walking away.

"I'll admit, he's hot, but…" Violet spat out with a voice of relent. "…oh, what the hell, give me the scoop! I need someone to live vicariously through. It might as well be you and danger-boy! Nobody is lining up at my door to take your place." She smiled with a subtle pouty face and stomped toward Mitzi.

"There she is." Darrell's eyes glowed. He looked over at Chubbs and Kyle. "Remember, smooth and cool as cucumbers. No stupid moves!" He turned and slowed his forward movement toward the two girls.

"Watch…watch…out…ff..for the stutter." Kyle laughed as he mocked Darrell's final act yesterday.

Chubbs stopped in his tracks and watched Darrell's reaction.

"Kyle! That's the kind of shi…shi…bullshit move I'm talking about NOT doing. I'll kick your ass right now if you'd like? Or you can be a good wingman." He held up his fist toward the sky. The other two fists came to meet with a smack. "That's what I'm talking—hey, how about Mitzi B's friend? Either of you two Oreo asses interested?" He chuckled as they got close enough to Mitzi B to say hello. "You girls doing okay this morning?"

Mitzi just finished filling Violet in on the note and their interactions on the sidewalk yesterday. "Well, since you've decided to play nice this morning..." Mitzi stood up and walked over to Darrell. She stepped up very close into his personal space and looked squarely into his green eyes.

Darrell's breathing quickened, loud enough she could hear it and feel the exhales.

Mitzi looked down and grabbed his left hand, looking at it for a couple of seconds as if she were studying it. She started to lead it back down as if she would let go but instead brought it around behind her and slowly pushed it against her shorts and then pulled it from the back of her hip forward. She brought it back in front, still holding it. "...there you go, Darrell." She looked into his eyes again briefly then let his hand go. It dropped to his side quickly. "You've brushed my sweet ass." Mitzi let the silence linger between them other than the sound of Darrell's heightened breaths.

"Now, can we drop the shit about our bodies and just be friends? We have an entire year to see what becomes of you and me." She smiled, then looked over at Chubbs and Kyle, who stood dumbfounded. "No more shit from you two, got it?"

Chubbs was the first to respond. "Darrell! I can't believe she just forced you to touch her ass! Is she fuckin' awesome or what? Friends for life, Mitzi B!" He laughed out loud, breaking the silent tension between everyone.

The first warning bell for class rang out loudly.

"You two wanna sit with us at lunch today?" Darrell looked surprised he was able to spit the question out.

Mitzi B looked at Violet. "Your call, Vio?"

"I suppose it would be okay, the groping show is over, right?" Violet stared at the boys and then returned her eyes to Mitzi.

"I think we've worked through all of that!" Mitzi sighed as she gave Darrell a wink. "I think we can consider it done now, can't we?" She grabbed Violet's hand and tugged it as she began walking to class.

Darrell hollered. "We'll be at our table on the south lawn!"

Violet leaned into Mitzi, giggling. "That was so damned smooth. No, that was unprecedented awesome smooth for Apalachicola High. You just made the school buzz line."

Mitzi gave her a soft punch in the arm. "Good! That was my intention. We'll both be the talk of the community. Any news is good news!"

7

Jay checked his mailbox as he did every morning now that he owned one. He was hoping the news about his license would finally arrive. He knew Ben was probably getting concerned.

This sitting around "re-acclimating" to being housed was getting old. Jay was used to spending his time foraging for the day's meals or searching for a safe out of the way spot to bed down. He was becoming bored, and when he looked down at his belly, it displeased him.

"Aww, at least it's quiet here during the day—no giggling to distract me or the constant running up and down the noisy wooden steps."

Jay opened all of the windows and exited through his front door, a full cup of coffee in hand. He made his way to the deck area and looked out across the bay. It appeared to be a promising day—one made for fishing on the pier. There would be no Darrell to get under his skin. School was in session, and surely since it was Tuesday, Gabriel would be making house calls or getting his sermon ready for Sunday.

The curious lure for Jay to walk around to his neighbor's side finally overtook him, and his legs slowly carried him across the wooden deck.

The first thing he noticed when he rounded the corner was that their windows were closed tight. He imagined the air was steamy and moist inside. The small window air conditioner units were not enough to keep up with the heat and humidity of the trailing days of the Gulf summer.

Jay set his cup on the railing and then peered into the ladies living room window. He cupped his hands around his eyes to block the bright morning sun that made it hard to see inside. There wasn't much to see. He stepped back and continued to walk entirely around to their front door.

He heard someone stirring down below and decided to meander back to his side. Jay didn't want anyone causing him trouble by making complaints. He was sure most people knew who he was and his background. A visit from Roy was the last thing he wanted. The thought of that arrogant cheating prick stepping foot at his door uninvited caused his veins in his head to pulse. He knew Roy would enjoy ruffling his feathers from the safety of hiding behind his shiny little sheriff's badge.

He sat back down on the deck and hiked his feet up on the railing. He thought a moment about how long it'd been since he walked to the Big Apple on the Bay restaurant site to see the progress. Hopefully, after the mail was delivered, he'd have an excuse to go. He wanted to talk box trucks with Ben. And he also pictured what he thought Gina would be wearing on such a beautiful start to the day. She would be dressed provocatively, he imagined. She had the tight body for it and probably golden tan by now. The thought brought on an image of her lying half-naked, all oiled up on a towel on the beach.

His daydream had caused a bodily reaction again—causing him to look down to his lap. He quickly decided to go inside and relieve some stress. He'd check his mailbox in a bit.

***

Darrell sat at the cement table on the south lawn alone. He asked his partners earlier to give him a few minutes with Mitzi B before they showed up. Darrell also asked Kyle to look for Violet and see if she could stall a few minutes too. Being extremely nervous, his legs began bouncing up and down, but other than that, he appeared relatively calm.

Mitzi walked up behind Darrell and slid into the bench across from him. "What's up? Where's the gang?"

His body jerked from being startled. "Hey, Mitzi B, you caught me off guard!" He smiled and tried to slow his legs from shaking. "Honestly, I asked them to give us a few minutes. They're always hanging close by, and I wanted some quick alone time to get to know you."

"Hmm, I didn't take you for the old-fashioned type." Mitzi chuckled. "I'm glad, though. Maybe we'll have to get together after school and go down to the pier or something. You could show me the area. I live close to the pier."

"Anywhere but the pier. That place gets crowded. Walking on the boat docks is pretty cool, though." Darrell caught himself staring at Mitzi's green eyes.

"It's okay. I like looking into yours, too. You've got really cool brownish veins mixed into the bright green. You have the color of eyes that girls would kill for." She looked down as if she embarrassed herself and was trying to hide her smile.

"Okay, Mitz—it's gonna be difficult for me to keep a calm and cool persona going if you're gonna be so…" Darrell snickered. "…so, everything opposite of what I expected a gorgeous girl to be." He looked down quickly and then peeked up at her reaction.

Mitzi responded quickly, "I'm a comedian when I'm nervous. It draws attention away from the focus on me, or at least it feels like it does. It's my alter ego of defense—and I can't believe I've already shared such a personal secret with you. You're dangerous, aren't you?"

"What do you mean by dangerous?" His face showed a curious look.

"Oh, nothing. I've just heard that some are leery of you.

Something about trying to shoot your dad." She reached across the rough cement tabletop and placed her hand on top of his. "Is that true? It's okay if it is—I mean, you'd have to have a good reason. You don't seem like the kind of guy who would just go off on a crazed binger." She kicked his leg under the table, playfully, to lighten the mood. "We all have a history with things we'd rather others didn't know." She reached across and held his other hand, pulling them both closer across to her side. "I want to know more about your past and fears. You drew my interest immediately." Mitzi cocked her head a little to try and get a better view of Darrell's eyes again.

Darrell looked up, returning the lengthy eye contact. "I have a confession too." He winked at her. "I was attracted to you the minute I saw you across the hall in the crowd. I wrote Chubbs a note about you—the one you picked up on the sidewalk yesterday evening. I just knew you were gonna open it. I could have killed Chubbs for flipping it back and forth with Kyle." He laughed. "I grabbed it back from him and thought it was safe. Then, of course, I ended up dropping it. I about crapped when I turned around and there you were picking it up."

Mitzi giggled. "I bet you did!"

"Yeah, I guess I have an alter ego, too. I guess mine is talking about asses…"

"Asses!" Mitzi busted out laughing as they said the same word in unison.

"Well, you two seem to be breaking things in!" Violet grinned. Chubbs and Kyle were standing right behind her.

Darrell leaned into Mitzi's ear and whispered, "Meet after school at Capers, and we'll walk down to the docks." He touched her shoulder with his hand and gave her two quick squeezes and then turned and started walking away before she could answer. About ten feet from them, he turned and called out, "Chubbs! Kyle! Let's go." He smiled at Violet and then continued, "see ya later, Vio! Thanks!"

Violet looked out across the lawn and called back. "Later, boys." She grabbed Mitzi's hand and pulled her up. "Vio? I guess you gave me a nickname earlier, and it's sticking." She smiled. "I've never been given a nickname. I like it!"

"Another stupendous day, Vio! And to think I didn't want to move here! Go figure."

"Glad you did, Mitzi B. I'm gonna call you Mitz if that's okay. I like you as a single syllable girl! I mean, what's the B even stand for?"

"Don't wanna talk about it now. I love the single-syllable name, though. You'll have to try and make it stick on me, Vio!" She laughed.

8

Mitzi B opened the door to Capers at three forty-five and grew a humongous smile as she spotted Darrell already sitting at a table close to the front on the left. He stood up as she moved toward the table.

"You didn't stand me up?" She smiled flirtatiously.

Darrell reached back to the table and gave her a cup of something. "Wasn't sure what your drink of choice was, so I went with a popular one for the area—Pepsi-Cola, okay?" He handed it to her.

"I'm a Pepsi-Cola kind of girl. Thanks! You didn't spike it, did you?" Mitzi winked, devilishly.

"Uh, no, not today. I don't usually get my friends trashed until the second date. It is to go, though, so that we can take 'em and head to the boat docks now before it gets too late."

"So. Hmm. Is that what this is? A date?" She took a sip of her Pepsi through the straw, playing with it between her tongue and lips.

"Well…" Darrell said quietly, almost under his breath as if he'd made a blunder.

She reached and grabbed his hand softly. "Cause if it is, I hold hands on the first date." Mitzi tilted her head to catch a look at his big, green eyes.

The sound of the bell clinked as the door slammed to a close. The two turned left down the sidewalk, hand in hand.

Mitzi realized they were walking right in front of her mom's office, but she didn't care today. It was easier to say sorry later than to ask permission any day. She even looked up and smiled, holding her free hand up, giving a thumbs-up, and then a wave to the upstairs window. She wasn't sure which window was her mom's, but if she were looking out and saw them, it would work better later for her on the forgiveness side of things.

Darrell turned his head away from Mitzi B's face and appeared to look intently at the crowd of people fishing on the pier. Once they passed, he returned watching Mitzi B as she continued to talk.

"See anybody you didn't want to see?" She asked.

"What do you mean?" Darrell responded.

"It was pretty obvious you were searching for someone. An old girlfriend, maybe? Or worse yet, a current one?" She leaned forward of their steps and turned so she could see his eyes squarely. "I told you I was interested in you. I wasn't just sayin' it for conversation." She stopped walking and gave his hand a quick tug, and Darrell stopped and looked at her.

She continued, "I'm new here. I only know four people in this town, you being one of them, and I don't know any of the other three very well either." Her eyes became fixed on his. "I don't know what I've stepped in the middle of here. Maybe nothing—or maybe it's way more than I'm ready for?" She turned and began walking again. "That's why I'm here with you, Darrell. At some point, I wanna just sit and look at you and talk. I want to listen, and I want to understand." She looked from the corner of her eye again before she continued. "I don't know how getting to know someone works around here, but that's how we do it up in Hoover, Alabama."

"Wow, that's a lot to respond to and walk at the same time." He grinned. "I can't remember what order you asked, but I'm gonna say this—I've been here all of my life, I've never had a girlfriend—as stupid as that sounds—so the answer is no, I'm not looking for an old or current one on the pier." He paused. "And yes, I imagine that's the same way it works to get to know someone here also." Darrell stopped walking this time and spun her a hundred and eighty degrees, so she faced him. "I just wouldn't really know for sure. I've been basically a hermit all my life."

He started walking again without turning away from Mitzi's face. "I was looking to see if my poppa—I mean, my dad was out there fishing—and no, I wasn't looking for a girlfriend. I wouldn't need to. I'm a total idiot for telling you this, but why would I need to look when I was hoping I'd found my first one with you." He started walking more quickly. He thought to himself. *I should run. I'm sinking here. Because my heart is racing, and also because I know my face and neck are as red as my hair is.* He thought of trying to run from any rebuttal Mitzi may have that would make him hurt. But Darrell fought the urge and kept walking at a slightly brisker pace. Mitzi managed to keep up, holding his hand even tighter.

She wore a beaming smile for the rest of the walk. They crossed the floating ramp to the docks, and Darrell led her around the small store and toward the end where the big Charter boats were tied in their slips. At the very end sat a lone picnic table.

"Here we are—our secluded bistro on the bay." He let Mitzi slide in and then asked, "Do you want me to sit across or beside you? Your choice."

"Let's go with across, so we can see each other better."

"Damn, I was afraid you'd say that. If we're going to get into deep personal stuff this evening, you have to promise not to sit and stare too hard." He nervously grinned, followed by a sigh.

"You're not here for an interrogation. We're here to talk and search each other's souls. I am curious, and maybe we could get rid of the elephant on the picnic table first."

"You wanna know about my father, don't you?"

"Well, that does seem to be the obvious elephant. I haven't got much boyfriend experience, but I'm pretty sure as much as they might like to have shot their dad at one time or the other—it was left at the thought process and not the implementation part." Her forehead was scrunched, showing the concern in her face. She tried to lighten the subject, but after looking at Darrell, she realized she was falling short.

"It's a long story. I mean, it goes way back." Darrell's mood changed instantly. "Are you sure you want to hear any of this?"

Mitzi grabbed his hand again and nodded. "I want to…" She gave a hesitant smile. "…and I'm kind of dreading it…" She squeezed his hand. "…but I think you really need to tell me. I think it'll help your heart feel better if you do. I'll keep it locked up. I promise."

Darrell lifted his leg and swung it over the bench. "I gotta pace a little. You can sit." He kicked the dock with the toe of his shoe. "I don't even know where to start. I guess I'll start with a sick game he used to make us play every Friday night when he came home from the road." He paced back and forth in front of Mitzi. "I don't remember how old I was when it first started, but I remember counting the days from when he left, so I'd know when he would be home. I remember my older brother would do anything in the world to protect me."

Mitzi watched his face. Looking into his beautiful green eyes when she could. He was nervously moving around so much that she didn't get a lot of chances to see them. "It's okay, take your time."

"He used this damn jar. An old Mason fruit jar. We weren't allowed ever to touch it when he was away. It contained little wooden tiles inside that held different kinds of punishments etched on them. Things like hit, or slap or—much, much worse. There was one that said grace on it." Tears began to peek from his eyes as he dug into his memory. He would wipe them, but it didn't seem long before he was running his fingers over them again. He would lift his T-shirt and wipe his face with it.

"The minute we heard the low rumble of his truck rolling up the long drive, we knew to get ready for the judgment. He always seemed to come in with the same mood. I don't ever remember him being angry, though. It was just like part of his schedule. He just assumed we had sinned and done wrong while he was away. It was his and the damned jar's job to settle our scores. My brother Billy would try talking to me beforehand. Telling me, he would try to take the worst punishment—or trade me his grace tile, if he was lucky enough to get it."

He tried to look at Mitzi to see how she was taking his story, but his eyes were just too blurry from the tears. It didn't matter how much he wiped them clear.

Mitzi got up from the table and touched his shoulders with her hands. She leaned in and spoke in a whisper, "You can stop if you need to. I am so sorry you lived through this kind of hell." She squeezed his shoulders and rubbed them. "Where was your mom when this was happening. Didn't she try to stop it? Or maybe runaway with you?"

Darrell guffawed. "She was always drunk and passed out in her bed. I don't really blame her now, but I hated her back then. Poppa was a lot bigger than her. There wasn't nuthin' she could do except escape this awful shit anyway she could."

Darrell spun around slowly and buried his face into Mitzi's shoulder. He put his arms around her and began to squeeze tightly.

"It's okay, Momma. It's okay. I don't blame you. Billy will fix it. He'll fix it for both of us. He's gonna kill that motherfucker." Darrell let out a loud wail and buried his face deeper, squeezing even more. It was like Darrell had become another person right in front of her. He'd regressed back to his childhood for a moment.

Mitzi wasn't sure what to do except to comfort him. "It's okay, Darrell. Let it out. I'm here for you, sweetie. I'm sorry." She hugged him closer and rubbed his back while he sobbed.

There was a sudden loud noise in one of the bigger boats a few stalls down. It sounded like a tackle box, or something heavy dropped on the dock or boat deck.

Darrell pulled away and turned around toward the sound that snapped him back to reality. He spotted what looked like a fisherman climbing out of his cuddy cabin. The man looked over toward them and stopped what he was doing. "You okay over there, ma'am? Do you need help?"

"I'm okay, sir. We're just making up from an argument. Sorry to bother you, we'll move on away." Mitzi let go and leaned down to Darrell's ear. "Let's go walk, it'll help, and we can find another place with fewer people."

As they walked past the man's boat, Darrell stopped briefly. "Sorry for bothering you, sir. It's been a bad evening, but we're getting' through it. Thanks for checking on her. I appreciate it."

The man leaned toward them from his boat. "I'm glad you're working it out, kids. I didn't mean to chase you off. Hang in there and treat each other with love and respect."

Mitzi smiled through her tears that smeared her make-up across her face, "No problem. Thank you for your concern and wise advice. You have yourself a good evening."

They walked off slowly, holding hands. They were leaning into each other every little bit. As they walked the ramp and onto the ground, Darrell stopped and pulled Mitzi around and put his hands on her waist. "I don't know if I wanna talk about this anymore tonight. I'll tell you more, but it may need to be done in little bits. I didn't mean to cry like a baby."

"No, no, no, Darrell. No worries about that. I want to be here for you." She moved her hands from his side and lifted them, touching his cheeks. "I am here for you. I want to be your special friend that you call on, whatever time or need it is." She gripped his cheeks with her hands, pulling him closer to hers—stretching up on her tip-toes until her lips met his. She lightly ran her tongue across the outside of them and sucked his bottom lip into her mouth.

Darrell's hands softly grabbed her waist and then lightly slid them down—maneuvering around her back—slowly lower until he was gripping her hips. As Mitzi's tongue penetrated his mouth, investigating deeper, swirling around between his lips and then the insides of his cheeks and teeth—he pulled her into himself with his firm grip. Their pelvises were rubbing together.

Mitzi let a low moan escape her mouth between the moments of kissing and breaking for air. A long quiet sigh followed it as she pushed her lower body harder into Darrell's. She'd never before felt a boy's privates become firm and warm. She liked the way her body was reacting almost too much as she started to run the fingers of her left hand around his belt buckle. The tingles she was feeling inside her body gave her a fear she wouldn't be able to ask him to stop or, for that matter, stop herself.

The moment came to a jolting halt less than a minute, due to the abrupt voice that yelled out from someone walking past. "Good gawd, get a room. My family don't wanna watch that shit."

Darrell and Mitzi quickly backed away from each other as if they'd been caught red-handed, fingers in the cookie jar. They were red-faced with blushes as they looked around for the heckler, seeing only a family of four walking away from them down the sidewalk. The apparent father turned and eyed them before flipping them the silent bird.

They looked at each other, their eyes still showing the whites, and Mitzi was the first to break into uncontrolled laughter. Darrell followed in quickly as they slapped at each other in play. "I've never done that before," Darrell whispered.

"Me neither." She pushed him away, but suddenly pulled him back into her arms. "You are, dangerous Darrell!" She gave him a big hug and then pushed him again as she looked down at his pants for a quick second. "Wow! That's all I can say. I'm pretty sure we shouldn't have started this." She grinned at him coyly.

"I better get you home." He quickly turned away and tried to adjust himself nonchalantly. "You sure you've never done this before? I mean, I'm not judging. I'm just curious."

"Never. I kissed a boy a couple of times, but that was it. I promise."

The two walked back toward the pier area. Several minutes later, Mitzi pointed to the two-story house that was her new home. "There it is, home! The second floor, one on the left. You can't come up, though. I'm not ready for my mom to meet you just yet." She pushed on his side as she leaned over to look into his eyes. "You do understand, don't you?" She waited for an answer and then expected a goodnight kiss.

"You've got to be fucking kidding me, Mitz!" Darrell stopped suddenly as if he'd seen a UFO hovering above her apartment. "Oh, shit..." He just stood in his tracks with a blank stare looking toward the upper deck.

Mitzi was stunned. She searched for words to try and spit out of her mouth. *How could he talk like this to me just minutes after we shared such an incredible and close time?* She kept searching for something to happen that would explain the instant change in his mood. Ten seconds passed as slowly as twenty minutes felt.

Darrell was just standing, his eyes staring up at the man on the deck, returning the glare down at him.

Mitzi was standing with her knees beginning to quiver, staring at Darrell, waiting for him to say something to her and explain himself. And then she found the answer to her question with very few words spoken. The words that rained down on them from above.

"Just what the fuck are you doing, son? You leave that little lady the hell alone and get back to suckling on your momma's tit."

Jay's son-of-a-bitch dad was at Mitzi's mom's house. *What the hell was going on?* "Mitzi? Please tell me you don't live next door to my dad. Please." His shoulders slumped.

"Creepy Jay, is your dad?" Mitzi's body went limp as a curtain of black dropped from her head downward. In seconds she hit the ground hard and rolled out flat as a pancake.

Darrell dropped to the ground, not knowing what to do. "Get her mom, you son-of-a-bitch. NOW!"

Jay moved slowly around the corner toward Joyce's door, thinking to himself with each step. *That little fucker is finally showing some testosterone. Almost too bad he ain't mine. He's got more balls than his sheriff daddy does—and without the damn badge.* He knocked on the door, and it swung open almost immediately. Joyce was standing there with a disparaging look. "What do you want, Jay? I'm waiting for my daughter to get home."

"Joyce—your daughter needs your help out front on the lawn. I'll call for the ambulance."

She shoved through, pushing Jay off to the side. He wasn't expecting her to move so quickly and almost fell due to being off-balance. Joyce was down the stairs and to her daughter's side in no time flat.

Jay looked over the railing of the deck at the sight of Darrell and Joyce, kneeling next to Joyce's daughter. He took that as his cue to slip inside their apartment. Jay quickly scouted the area out visually and deciphered whose bedroom was whose. He opened cabinet drawers quickly, and when he opened a drawer up full of frilly panties—he ran his hands through them. He saw a bright blue see-through pair with lace on them and snatched them up quickly, tucking the pair into his pocket.

He then turned to explore Mitzi's room and quickly rifled through her drawers. He walked into the bathroom and rummaged through the dirty clothes hamper, spying what looked like a young girl's pair and pocketing them too before heading where the phone was. He dialed 911 and reported a girl passed out by the street and gave the officer the address.

Jay appeared at the doorway and pulled it closed and headed down the stairwell to the ground. He had done all of this in a matter of three or four minutes.

"Police and ambulance are on their way ma'am," he stated as he rushed up to their side as if he'd been hurrying the entire time.

"Thank you, Jay! I appreciate it. Mitzi seems to be coming around." Joyce then turned to her daughter, "It's okay, sweetie, I'm here with you and help is coming." She fanned her with her hand.

"She's gonna be alright, isn't she ma'am?' Darrell asked.

Joyce had been so concerned with the shocking news of her daughter needing help that she hadn't even noticed the young man kneeling beside her. "Are you the one that found her?"

"Well…" Darrell hesitated, remembering that Mitzi wasn't ready to introduce him to her mother. "…sorta, I'm a friend from school and was walking her home from downtown. I didn't want her to be alone."

Joyce looked up as Darrell climbed to his feet. He'd snuck a quick squeeze on Mitzi's arm as he got up.

"Thank you for being there for my daughter…" She looked back down as her daughter stirred. "…I'm not sure we would have found her if you hadn't of been there."

"Mom? What are you doing here? Where's…" Mitzi slowed her speech as she searched for words and thoughts, trying to figure out what had happened and where she was. "…where is…."

"Honey, it's okay. You passed out for some reason. You haven't taken anything or been drinking, have you?" Joyce asked.

"I'm…um…" Mitzi squeezed her eyes closed tightly momentarily as she slowly raised her hand to her head. "…I don't…I…remember being at the docks…."

"By yourself? Mitzi! No, no, no. My gawd, Mitzi. We don't know this town well enough for you to be running around alone." Joyce's voice cracked several times from the fear that was conjuring in her mind at her daughter's words.

"Sounds like the ambulance or police are about here, ma'am." Jay stepped over toward Darrell. "Son, you better mosey on away from here. You don't want no trouble, ya hear?"

Darrell leaned into his dad's personal space and spoke quietly but with a distinct firmness. "If you don't want me to finish what I started with the shotgun—you just better leave these two women the fuck alone. Do you understand that? I'm not afraid of your cowardice ass anymore." He reached over and stuck his finger in his dad's chest. "I'll first shove a Mason's jar up so far that when I kick you in the nuts, it'll shatter and leave you bleeding like gator bait in the swamp. Nobody would even miss you or care, especially Momma." Darrell gave him a stare as if he was serious.

Jay leaned in closer. "It's good to see you don't stut…stutt…stutter…no…no more. You're finally becoming a man a dad could be proud of. Now, get on outta here, boy." He smirked and let out a small chuckle.

Darrell turned and began walking away. Once he had gone about twenty feet or so, Jay shouted out, "I'll keep my eyes on 'em, I'll take good care, don't you worry." Jay turned and began listening to what the ambulance techs and deputy were saying. Jay began to respond to questions he overheard. "Deputy, I was up there on my deck and heard what I thought was a couple of voices. She was already on the ground, and someone was kneeling beside her, trying to wake her up. That's when I recognized who it was and ran next door to get her mother. Then, of course, I dialed 911 as quick as I could get to the phone."

"So, where is the other person that was with her?" The deputy asked.

"He was here just a minute ago. Not sure where he went? Is the girl gonna be okay? Jay questioned.

The ambulance technician removed the blood-pressure cuff and looked to the other technician. "Blood pressure is 141 over 92. I'll give her a minute and retake it."

"Has your daughter been suffering any kind of anxiety or nervousness lately?" Asked the tech.

"No, everything has been good as far as I know. The first week of school here, as we just moved into the area, but no problems I know of." Answered Joyce.

"I suggest we take her in and watch her overnight. Would that be okay?"

"Anything that you suggest is what I'll do. Mitzi is alright, isn't she?" Joyce asked with a fearful look on her face. She rubbed her daughter's shoulder.

"I think she'll be fine, ma'am, but I'd feel better letting the doc give her a once over."

"Can I ride with her?" Her mom asked.

"You're going with me, Mom!" Mitzi cried out.

"Yes ma'am, that would be fine."

The techs lifted her onto the gurney and began to load her into the ambulance.

"I'll lock your house up or watch it for you if you like Ms. Bonham?"

Joyce looked over and smiled. "Thank you, Jay, just watch it; please, I don't have my keys with me."

"I can get 'em for you or keep 'em until you get back and lock the door if you point out where they are?" Jay replied.

"They're in my purse on the kitchen table, should be towards the top. Thanks again. I'll come to get them when I'm home." Joyce smiled again at him. "Thanks for being so neighborly." She got help stepping up inside the ambulance, and once the doors were closed, they took off with only the lights running.

Deputy Cloud tipped his brown circular rimmed hat toward Jay. "I think we're done here for now. You live just upstairs, next door if we have any further questions, sir?"

"That I do. You just come see me if need be." Jay responded

with a bit of a smirk. "Sheriff Burks knows who I am." Jay turned and walked toward the outside steps up to his and Joyce's apartments. *Hmm, I got a little more time to dig around now.* Jay shoved his hand inside his pocket and felt the silky- smooth panties he'd poked inside. Tonight, his mind was already racing with the thoughts of using his trophies in ways to help excite himself. There would be no time to read Ms. Cela's book tonight. He had an apartment to roam around in and treasures to fondle. Jay had never moved up the stairs any faster than he did tonight.

9

"What's wrong, Darrell? Why the long face?" Cat walked up close to her son as he sauntered through the back door, heading toward the back room. "It seems like I never really see you these days."

"Just school and stuff, Mom. Ain't no need to make a deal out of it."

"Well, I didn't realize it was a deal that I was making. I just miss seeing my son, that less than a couple of months ago was always close by my side. Feels like I'm losing you to maturity too damn fast. Pardon my language." She tried to smile.

"I was bound to grow up sooner or later. I guess since mine was later, I'm just making up for the lost time. I'm eighteen, Mom. I'm getting' my own life now. Doesn't mean I love you any less." Darrell had paused in the doorway. "I sure wish I had more privacy too—this quilt doesn't really give us much of that."

"Well, I'm not spying on you, if that's what you're implying." She answered defensively.

"Just sayin' that a man needs more than a thin blanket to give him the privacy he needs. What if I want to have a friend over, and there you are on the other side of a blanket? You think that's not gonna create problems for me?"

"You know, son, ever since you man-handled that shotgun…" Cat wasn't entirely sure she wanted to broach the subject of her son's recent changes, but she continued. "…it almost seems as if you've suddenly outgrown your britches. You may be eighteen, and that might be when most boys put their feet down firmly and demand their manhood..." She took a deep breath and let out a slow sigh, attempting to calm herself. "...but just remember it wasn't that long ago that you were showing some pretty strong signs of still being a boy. There's no need to go racing into something that your mind isn't as ready for as your hormones are telling you." She waited for his response, nervous about how she had worded it.

"My hormones are none of your damn business anymore. If you like, I can get a job and look for a place to move out. Something maybe you oughta think about doing instead of feeding off the Watkins goodwill." He turned away from her. "It's been over three years, after all." The door slammed, and she swore she could hear the swoosh of the quilt flailing in the air on the other side of the wall.

"Well, that went well," Cat said under her breath as she stomped her foot.

"I saw your son-of-a-bitch, husband, tonight too," Darrell yelled through the door.

Cat reached, turning the doorknob before barreling into the room. She swung open the quilt and stood boldly in its opening.

"See, no fucking privacy." Darrell spat the words out as coldly as the spring water flowed from Duckbill Springs.

"Darrell! That language will not be tolerated in this house! This home is the Watkins home, and we are guests in it."

"Momma, we were guests in it three and a half years ago. We're squatters now. We've staked out our digs and refused to better ourselves enough to live on our own. Even that son-of-a-bitch that killed my brother lived on his own the entire time he was gone and still does now." Darrell was red-faced mad.

Cat could tell that her son was angry because something must have happened between Darrell and Jay. The look on her face showed that she was hurt but somehow knew this discussion was really aimed elsewhere rather than at her. She backed up a step. "I love you, and I'll think about what you've said. Maybe we should be moving forward." She wiped a tear from her eye. "Maybe I have resorted to letting my comfort with the Watkins keep me from reaching for the stars for us." Cat let the quilt fall closed, only her calves down to her feet showed. "I'll sleep on it, Darrell. I'll pray about it. I'll search my heart for God's answer as to what direction I should go." Her calves turned, and Darrell watched from his seated position on his bed.

"I was hoping that you and your father would work through things and reach an understanding—maybe even work things out and be close." A sniff could be heard through the curtain as he watched the back of her legs move toward the door. "I know now that that isn't going to happen, and I need to process that."

"He's an evil and sick fucker. No other way I can put it. He hates me. I see it in his eyes. He gets pleasure from making me suffer." He paused a moment, waiting for a response that didn't come as the door opened slowly. "He's no different than he was before. He just don't have the power of the Mason jar anymore to hold over us—that's the only change in him. He's Satan."

Her legs disappeared from under the quilt into the other room as the door slowly came to a creaky close.

Darrell heard her soft footsteps head toward the front of the house. He knew she was going to the front porch to watch the moon and contemplate what he had just dumped onto her lap.

He was correct when he told the man on the boat at the dock. It had been a rough evening from that point until this one. He laid back in his bed, still fully clothed, and prayed to God that Mitzi would be okay. He also prayed that God would grant him the power and the plan to keep Mitzi and her mom safe from the evil damned demon that had made his lair next door to their new home.

Cat sat quietly on the porch swing, not knowing what to do or which way to turn. Her face was flush, and she fanned herself using a paper that she found on the swing.

Ms. Gloria walked out through the screen door to see Cat sitting alone with a look of despair across her face.

"Oh, Miss Cat..." She strolled over and sat down beside her. "...do you mind if I sit and chat with you for a minute or two, honey?" She didn't wait for an answer and rested her hand on top of Cat's. "I believe I heard your son hollering at you tonight. It sounded as if he came home with a load of angry baggage. Is there anything you'd like to talk about and get off your chest?" Ms. Gloria leaned in and reached around Cat, giving her a big hug.

"I don't know what to do. Darrell came in with fire inside him. He says he had a run-in with Jay." Cat looked over at Gloria. "He also called us squatters for overstaying our welcome. He told me even Jay maintained his own place to stay after being on the run up to and including now." Her eyes spoke her next question before her words could form the sentence. "Are we overstaying our welcome? I've tried to help out with chores and extra money with my paycheck from the grocery store, but It's just not enough to pay rent and utilities, food...."

"No, no Cat! You mustn't think that way." Gloria assured her. "We love having you and Darrell here. This is your home for as long as you like. You're family, sweetheart!"

"I appreciate you and your husband. You are my family." She hugged Gloria with everything she had. "You've been so good to us, from the moment you took us in. I don't know how I'll ever be able to repay you."

"That's all I'm gonna hear of that, Cat! You just shush that kind of talk!" Gloria sounded serious. "Don't make me go get the man of the house to explain these things!"

Cat smiled and instantly released some of the tension she was holding inside. "I just worry about Darrell now. He is changing so much. I just pray he is changing for the better and not the worse. I think back at just how Jay changed and if I actually noticed it, or if it snuck up on me." Cat's eyes appeared very tired, and she had some dark circles forming around them. It was apparent to Ms. Gloria that Cat had been suffering some worrisome times lately.

"I can see these worries have plagued you." Gloria got up and headed inside. "I know just what you need. I'm going to brew a couple of cups of chamomile tea! It always helped put my mind at ease when stressful times dwelled around my soul!" She gave a little laugh as the sounds of the screen door opened with a squeak. "I think Darrell is just beginning to grow into his maturity. Sure, he's had the appearance of a grown young man, but now he's gettin' more than just the testosterone. He's growing into some man-sense. I bet he just doesn't know how to deal with it." She continued inside and waited for Cat as she pulled herself up from the swing to follow.

"How come you always seem to know exactly what to do or say in these situations, Gloria? You seem to always have it together."

"Oh, I have my times at bein' a mess, Catrina. But in my kitchen, everything has its place. I know just where to look to find what I need." She tilted her head toward Cat and smiled as she lit the gas stove burner. "A young boy is kinda' like a kitchen. There are the tools inside him to deal with most of whatever he needs—he just don't know where they are. Darrell's had to live with that frustration of not knowing and always having to go to you to help with his needs. You see where I'm going here?" Gloria smiled as Cat vaguely shook her head. "You see, now, he's gettin' older and learning where all the tools are in the kitchen. Now, he's needin' you that much less, 'cause he knows if he can't go right to the drawer—Darrell knows he can find it on his own."

"I'm starting to see what you mean. I'm hurt because he needs me less, while I need him more, and he's able to find what he needs without help." She smiled, but it contained hurt from the thought of the truth of this conversation. "He's feeling the occasional frustration of not immediately knowing but enjoying the challenge of doing it himself. Which makes him lash out when I suggest I can do it for him." Cat nodded at her perception of what Gloria so clearly illustrated.

"Yes, ma'am. There's friction from every angle. You hurt his pride, well—your little red-headed boy is grown up. And that hurts. But it's God's way. You'll have to step back and be there when he asks—but be there in a way that you're not invading his individualism of growin' into a man. Hard stuff, Cat, as a mother. 'specially when you two had to be so close because of your background and circumstances." She reached over to Cat and pulled her into a hug. "It's gonna be all right, though. And Gabriel and I are right here for you, honey. Through the thick and thin of it. This is your home, and we'd like you to think of us as your Godparents. In a way, we are, because God put the four of us together for a reason, honey." She rubbed Cat's shoulder until the whistle of the teapot sounded. "Looks like it's tea-time in Apalachicola tonight!"

<u>10</u>

Jay enjoyed being able to snoop around Joyce's and Mitzi's home. He was learning the layout and looking through every drawer in the apartment. He laid down in each of their beds, smelling their pillows and inhaling their scents. It was amazing to him how different each of their things smelled. As he laid in Joyce's bed, he rolled over to the side and pulled the covers down. He remembered stuffing her panties into his pocket and reached in to pull them out.

The mere sight of them conjured up urges that began to seduce him to take risks. Risks he usually would think better of, but surely, they would be gone for the night. As he pulled her soft sheets over himself, he shoved the lacy undergarments to his face and inhaled deeply through his nose. Jay's eyes pressed tightly closed as he imagined Joyce's naked body lying beside him in fear, wondering what he would do next. It had been a long time since he'd been this close to a woman. And she wasn't even in the room, yet her scent was overwhelmingly intoxicating.

It wasn't long before he let out a moan as his muscles instantly lost the tension they were holding. There was wetness under the sheets, and suddenly he realized what he'd done.

Panic set in as he quickly threw back the sheets. He cleaned himself and quickly tried to put things back like they were. Deciding not to draw any attention by having them miss any of their things, he returned the undergarment to its drawer. After taking in one last long breath of the aroma—he buried the last of his treasures which he'd plan to keep, back into the dirty clothes hamper in the bathroom.

He rushed back into Joyce's bedroom and rechecked her bed, tightening the sheets as smooth as he'd found them before pulling the comforter back into place. Jay fluffed the pillows and looked around once again to make sure he'd left no sign of being there. Flipping the light switch off as he exited her room, he re-checked all his previous steps through the house.

"Phew," He said aloud. "That felt like the husband of a cheating woman almost caught me." He smiled to himself. "What a night. Damn shame I couldn't keep any trophies, though. That smell just makes a man feel alive and invincible!"

He pulled the door to their apartment closed and strolled around the building toward his own apartment, stopping at the deck and looking out at the bay. There was a breeze tonight, and he could hear the clinking and clanking of the fishing boat cables blowing in the wind, along with the light banging of the boats against their dock bumpers.

The sounds from the dock mixed with the sudden rush he felt after realizing what he'd just done in his neighbor's bed and panicked and it took his memory back to the time he'd found Ms. Lila Pasternack dead in her bed. Seeing the sweet old woman who'd taken him in way back as a young runaway just lying there brutalized. The adrenaline he had just felt was much the same as back then. An overwhelming panic and burst of uncontrollable nervous energy raced through his veins.

The sounds of the fishing boat noises now reminded him of his shattered boyhood dream of owning one. He had been getting so close to being able to make it a reality. Dashed at some bastard's dirty deeds to such a fine old woman and stealing from him to boot. Not only that, but then having to pay for his losses with ten years of hard time.

He knew he deserved so much retribution and more. "Damn! I wish I could find those bastards. They're probably out by now if they're still alive."

He sat down on a chair and let his anger brew as he relived those days of past—those hard time days of the past. Beaten, raped, and almost killed. By men just like the sick bastards that killed Ms. Lila and stole his life. Being raped by prison inmates, and at such a young age, changed Jay forever. He knew it. It's what made sex dirty to him. It's what made sex brutal to him. There was no love possible in that dirty act.

He stood up and kicked the chair across the deck as he looked one last time toward the docks before entering the humble apartment that he shared with nobody. Nothing, but his memories of how he got here. Even the relief of tension that he'd enjoyed only twenty minutes earlier was stolen from him through those bastard's taunts within his memories.

"Even freedom comes with prison bars of one sort or another." Jay reached down, opening the cabinet door beneath his sink and found the bottle of Jack Daniels just sitting there. "I think you need some company tonight, Jack. It looks like we'll be the only ones here tonight." Jay pulled a single glass from the cupboard and reached for the freezer door to grab some ice-cubes.

He poured a tall shot over the ice and then screwed the lid back tight. As one hand set the bottle down, the other lifted the glass to the light and he studied its medium brown color. He lifted it to his nose and sniffed in its aroma.

"It's not as fragrant as a woman's treasure, but it'll have to do." He raised the glass as if to toast to ole Jack himself as he clinked it against the bottle.

"Here's to you Cat, I can drink but you can't, you can get laid I'm sure, but I can't. A hell of a trade-off. Together we'd make quite the pair again. But then again, you're a cheatin' and lyin' no good...."

Jay lifted the glass to his lips and tossed its entirety down in two quick swallows before setting the ice-filled glass down on the counter.

He peered over to his reading chair that sat dimly lit under the floor lamp. On the table to the left side of the chair sat the only activity he had left tonight—Ms. Cela's good Book.

Was there a point in reading it? What the hell else am I gonna do?

Jay slid the bottle back under the sink cabinet, and after closing the door, he ambled over to his chair and picked the Bible up as he plopped down.

One of these days, I'll have this whole thing read, along with Ms. Cela's words of knowledge. Will I truly be saved by then? Doubt it.

11

It was Friday and the last day of school for the week. Darrell hopped out of bed, quickly getting showered and ready to run through the door.

He was hoping Violet had heard something from Mitzi. He hardly slept with all that had happened. Darrell practically ran the entire way.

"Chubbs! Am I glad to see you?"

"What's the excitement, Darrell?"

"Have you seen Mitzi or Violet yet this morning?"

Chubbs scratched his head as if it took that action to decipher Darrell's question. "No, I haven't seen either of them, why?"

"I was with her last night, and she blacked out..." Darrell stopped to catch his breath. "She lives next door to my dad! I think the whole thing overwhelmed her. The ambulance came and took her and her mom to the hospital."

"You're shittin' me!" Was Chubbs' reply.

"I was hoping she would be here today. When she blacked out, she fell backward and hit the ground pretty hard."

"What were you two doing together? You guys a thing now?"

"Have you seen Kyle?" Darrell responded.

"Just me—and of course, two hundred and twenty-eight various walking hormone and estrogen carriers, but no Kyle either. I was beginning to think maybe the alien seedpods had hatched and took you back to the mothership." Replied Chubbs.

"Ha, ha. Funny in a stupid kind of way—but not today." Darrell turned to head into the building when he felt a sudden overwhelming relief.

Around the west corner of the building came the new girl who had stolen his heart and then scared the shit out of him. She was walking with Violet and Kyle, smiling as if nothing had ever happened.

It was all he could do to keep himself from dropping his backpack and start galloping across the field in slow-motion like the movies. And then pull her into his arms before spilling to the ground and rolling in a blur of smiles and tears.

Instead, he kept his cool and meandered toward them, Chubbs at his side.

"Are you okay? You had me worried." Darrell calmly asked.

"Yeah, got a bump on the back of my head, but I'll survive. We need to talk, though, when we get a chance. Lunchtime?"

"Sure. Everything good, or do I need to dread lunch?" Darrell tried to muster a smile.

"No worries, mate!" Mitzi smiled. She leaned into his ear and whispered. "Did my ass feel as good as it looked, last night?" She pulled away quickly and smiled as she recollected his hands firmly grasping it last night by the docks.

Darrell smiled and nodded to her in agreement.

The morning seemed to move extra slowly for Darrell. His mind racing about the night before, focusing on the good parts.

"Darrell, can you answer the question?" Mrs. Summers repeated.

"I'm sorry, Mrs. Summers, I need you to repeat it."

The class broke into a burst of laughter.

"For the third time now, I asked what year did Ponce de Leon arrive in Florida, and to whom did he claim the new territory for?"

Darrell sat blankly for a moment, he had just read his history book in his second-hour study hall, but his mind was scattered. "Um—he claimed the territory for…" He looked around the classroom and smiled. "...the Spanish crown and it was where St. Augustine is now. April 2, 1513, was the year." He leaned back in his chair, relieved.

"You are correct, sir. Now, please stop daydreaming and pay attention. There will be a test on this material Monday. I expect everyone here to do well. The bell is about to ring, so gather your things and study this weekend, class! But have some fun too. The weather is calling for swimming!"

The bell rang, and as Darrell rose from his desk, Mrs. Summers walked toward him.

"Darrell, I just wanted to say how proud I am of you."

Darrell looked with an air of question.

"You've come such a long way from last year. I have high hopes for you. You had me worried last year, but you've matured and grown so much socially. Keep it up!" She held her hand up, begging for a high-five.

Darrell raised his hand and tapped Mrs. Summer's palm with his. "Thank you, ma'am. I appreciate your encouragement." He smiled awkwardly and turned toward the door. As he exited, he looked back, giving another quick smile to his history teacher.

As he sat under the tree at the far side of the south lawn, he couldn't help but stare into Mitzi's eyes. The green in them seemed even brighter and bolder today. The wind gently blew strands of her strawberry blonde hair across those beautiful eyes, and she would run her hands in front of them, retrieving them back behind her ears. The breeze almost made the act futile.

"You scared me last night, Mitzi. Why am I so attached to you so quickly?"

"I feel the same way about you. It's like we were already connected before we met. I've never felt this way about anyone else. It's kind of strange and scary."

Changing the subject for a moment, Darrell asked, "What time did you get back home last night?"

"It was one a.m. when we crawled into bed. Mom said I didn't have to go today, but I wasn't gonna miss seeing you."

"Did she ask you any questions about who I was?"

"I'm sure she will once I get home today. It was too late, and she was as tired as I was. She begged me to sleep in her bed with her, in case I got sick or something. She tosses and turns more than I do!" She giggled. "Neither one of us really slept. I'm dragging ass today!"

"Mitzi." Darrell hesitated and adjusted his body from his seated position. It was partly because of comfort, but mostly because of where he was leading the conversation. "You and your mom have to be careful around my dad. I hate to even call him that." He reached over and touched her arm, she answered by scooting in closer to him. "He's dangerous. I don't trust him." He fidgeted. "I wish I had succeeded in killing him. My brother lost his life trying, and believe me, the world would be safer without him."

"He is creepy, Darrell. There is something ominous about him." She pulled herself into his arms. "You're nothing like him—it's like he's not really your dad. You don't even look like him. Do you look like your mom?"

Darrell couldn't respond because he never heard the entire question. He became lost, staring into her eyes and reliving the kiss they shared the night before. His heart pounded within his chest as if it would burst at any moment. He raised his hand to her cheek to pull her into another kiss. Mitzi responded by bringing her lips to his before his hand ever touched her face.

Their tongues danced inside each other's mouths as they twirled and twisted together like lovers searching desperately to make that ultimate connection.

Their passion was dangerous. It was unstoppable.

Darrell's hand moved to cup her breast, and as it connected, he firmly squeezed and felt her nipple harden.

Mitzi pulled back as she began to moan. Her heart was

thumping. She pulled away and glanced toward the school and noticed several students looking their way.

"Darrell, we have to stop, they're watching us."

Darrell turned and saw as several of the students then stood up, each clapping their hands in applause.

He turned to Mitzi. "I'm sorry. I can't control myself when I'm around you."

"It's okay. I can't either. It's not just your fault. I guess we're just going to have to be strong." She moaned a deep sigh. "We will be the talk of the school now!" She laughed and looked toward Darrell's crotch. "Are you ready to face the judgment—or do you need a few minutes?" She giggled and gave him a shove, knowing what she'd done to him. "Those things must be a real job to control!" She looked into Darrell's deep green eyes and licked her lips. "I know a warm spot to keep it in one of these days."

Darrell had started to get up from the ground but changed his mind. "Um, yeah, I'm gonna need a couple of minutes now. Thanks, Mitz." He smiled. "Doesn't seem to be something you have trouble controlling though. All it takes is the sound of your voice."

12

Joyce opened the front door of the office and stepped through slowly.

Addi immediately noticed something seemed to be amiss with Joyce. "Are you okay today?"

Joyce hesitated a moment before answering, "Yes, Addi, I'm fine. I'm just a little tired today. I was at the hospital until about twelve-thirty this morning with Mitzi."

"Oh my, she's okay, isn't she?"

"She's got a pretty good bump on the back of her head, but she's doing okay. She demanded to go to school today…" Joyce let a serious tone enter her voice. "…I'm fairly certain I know why—I just don't know his name yet." She frowned.

"Awe, I see. Mitzi is a beautiful girl, and at that age, I'm sure everything will be okay. This is a quiet and safe town!" Addi tried to reassure her. "I do have some news though, and I hope it will work out with your schedule—although, I'm a little worried now after hearing your news."

"Yes?" Joyce replied. "Go ahead and just give it to me."

"Ethan needs you over in Fort Walton Beach by tomorrow afternoon."

"Seriously? I mean, I can be there by then, of course."

"I can keep an eye on Mitzi for you if you need it? She can come here after school until I get off."

"I can figure something out. Her father actually lives here, we don't talk much, but he does live here." She smiled. "It might be time to let him know we're here in town." She winked at Addi. "And let him know it's time to play daddy again!" Joyce headed toward her office. "I'll work it out Addi, is there anything pressing this morning I need to attend to?"

"No, ma'am. You're free to go search out the ex! Good luck!"

Joyce's office door clicked to a close. She immediately sat and opened her purse to get Roy's number. *This should be a joy and a huge surprise to him. I wonder how he'll take us living here?* She thought to herself.

Roy picked up the phone receiver and held it to his ear. "Hello, this is Sheriff Burks, what can I do for ya?"

Joyce remained silent for a moment as she drew in a deep breath. "Hello, Roy. Are you in a good mood this morning?"

"Joyce—I saw my check has cleared, so it can't be child support you're calling me about. Mitzi needs a new car or prom dress?"

"Now, Roy. We have asked very little of you. There's no reason to puff up this early in the conversation. After all—" Joyce let the silence fill the space between them over the phone line for several seconds. "…we may be sharing occasions of work together now." She let her sentence settle in before she continued.

"Just what the hell does that mean?" The silence lasted about two seconds before Roy responded to her statement.

"Mitzi and I live here in Apalachicola now." Again, she waited.

"What the fuck?" He drew in a deep breath.

Joyce could picture his cheeks reddening, and his brow furled into wrinkles. She imagined his feet crossed on the top of his desk were now spilling to the floor. And quickly, as he more than likely damn near fell out of his chair.

The silence was interrupted by sounds that complimented Joyce's imagination of his response.

"When the hell did this happen? And why?"

"It happened when I got a great job offer. Mitzi and I couldn't just remain stagnant in Hoover forever now that my parents are gone."

"Why here, Joyce. It didn't work out back then, and it sure as hell won't work now."

"We live here, Roy, I'm not asking to move back in and relive the crappy life you offered me back then. Mitzi and I are fine and not begging for you or your gawd damn money. But you are her father."

"Am I?"

"You son-of-a-bitch!" **CLICK**.

Joyce couldn't remember the last time if ever, she'd been angry enough or childish enough to hang up on someone. But then again, she'd never been treated with such lack of respect from anyone. Short of that piece of crap, Roy. The thoughts inside her mind exploded immediately. *That worthless bastard couldn't have cared less for me or the baby of his I was carrying back then. I can't believe that son-of-a-bitch would sink to the level of accusing me of cheating on him. Lord knows, I had ample opportunity. Some because of my appearance, but some as a way of screwing him. What better way to stab a knife into a dirty cop other than banging his wife and then bragging about it across this little Peyton Place. I never took anyone up on the opportunities. I tried to make our marriage work—the gall of that asshole. I'm not leaving Mitzi with that dickless piece of work. She would be safer staying alone next to creepy Jay at our own house. It's just overnight. Right?*

There was a tap on Joyce's door about thirty minutes after her call to the asshole.

"Yes, come on in, Addi."

"Do you have everything worked out for your trip?"

"I believe so. Can I ask you to give her a call while I'm gone? That way, she knows I've got eyes on!" She smiled. She's eighteen, so I hate to have her babysat. I have to say though; I'm a little nervous about meeting Ethan in Fort Walton. What if I can't perform up to what he's built me up for in his mind?"

"You'll do fine. This case is one of his lighter ones, a good one to learn on." Addi smiled with confidence. "Joyce, don't worry. He doesn't bite. Ethan knows you're not yet accustomed to our style. He chose you because he knows your qualities—you're hungry, and you're willing to learn. Here's your hotel address. You'll be staying at the Breakers, and it's on the beach! Here is Ethan's hotel suite number. Give him a call after you get checked in. The reservation is under your name. All expenses paid, so if you spend a dime—get a receipt!"

"Thank you so much, Addi. You're an angel—wish me luck!"

"You don't need luck, Joyce!"

***

Joyce's Volvo pulled up to visitor parking at the High School. She stuck her long slender leg outside the door, her high heel planted firm on the asphalt before she pulled herself out of her car.

From the window of his office, Charley Bingham watched a gorgeous blonde woman climb out of her car. He wasn't married and the look in his eyes gave away the fact he could appreciate the beauty of long-legged woman. He watched intently as her long legs strode up the sidewalk toward the front entryway.

Charley timed his exit from his office with precisely the moment the fine-looking woman entered the front and walked toward the receptionist.

Joyce was about to say hello to Mrs. Tammy Hatley when Charley stepped up to the counter.

"Hello, Miss..." Mr. Bingham held his hand out toward Joyce. "...I'm the principal here, Charley Bingham—what can we do for you today?"

Tammy gave a quick eye-roll as she scooted out of the way, remaining seated in her task chair on wheels.

Charley squared up with the counter as he noticeably sucked his gut in as far as he could.

"Hello, Mr. Bingham, I'm Mitzi B's mom. She's a new senior this year, and I need to have her brought down, so I can talk to her for a few minutes. I hope that's not a problem?"

"No ma'am, not a problem at all. And your name is...? He straightened his tie and looked briefly at Mrs. Hatley.

"Joyce Bonham. I hate to add to the interruption I'm causing, but I have an appointment I should be headed to shortly, can we try to call her down soon?"

"Mrs. Hatley—could you look up what class..." Charley looked at Joyce again. "...Miss Mitzi is in right now?"

"English, Ms. Harper's class, Mr. Bingham."

Charley turned back to Joyce. "I'm headed that way anyway. I'll just walk with you and show the way." He side-stepped Mrs. Hatley and pushed the swinging gate open. He put his hand in the small of Joyce's back, leading her toward the door. "This way Ms. Bonham."

Mrs. Hatley let a quiet guffaw slip as she rolled her eyes again.

Joyce led the way through the door, feeling the heated stare at her ass from Mr. Bingham's lust-filled eyes. She was suddenly annoyed. He in charge of so many young, pretty, female students. Was that a good thing?

"Hey honey, how are you feeling today?"

"Mom! What are you doing here?"

"I have to go to Fort Walton Beach today..." Joyce observed her daughter's reaction.

"So? What does that have to do with me?"

"I'll be spending at least one night if not two. Mr. Kendrick has a client he needs me to work with him on."

"I'll be okay. I'm not a kid anymore, Mom. Just leave me your number at where you're staying, and I'll call if I need anything."

"You're okay with being alone at the apartment?"

"Mom, the doors lock, and my dad is the damn sheriff. I think I'll be fine."

"I tried calling your dad—it didn't go over so well. He's less than thrilled that I live here, not sure how he feels about you yet. His number is..."

Mitzi interrupted her mom. "Mom! 911, anybody can remember that number. Remember? It's new for emergencies."

"Well, your dad's home number is on the refrigerator, along with his office number. Just in case the new 911 doesn't work."

"I'll be fine. I need to get back to class, Mom. See you either tomorrow or Sunday, then?"

"I'll call and let you know. I'll leave a message on the machine if I don't get you." She eyed Mitzi. "I'm counting on you to behave. You may not be a kid, but you're not an adult yet, either. Be safe." She started to lean toward Mitzi's forehead to kiss it, but Mitzi dodged her and turned toward the classroom door. As she opened it, she turned back toward her mom and winked. "I'll be fine. Enjoy your trip and impress the hell out of him." Mitzi pressed her lips together as if blowing a quick kiss that no one could see.

Joyce stood, watching her daughter disappear back into the classroom as the door quietly banged closed. She turned to observe her path to return to the office.

Miraculously, Charley appeared around the corner. "Awe, Ms. Bonham. Are you lost?"

"No, but if you like, you can lead the way out."

He sidled up beside her, as they walked, he tried to slow down a half a step behind her. She noticed and slowed to match his pace.

As she said good-bye and headed for the doors, she could feel the return of heat from his stares, making it uncomfortable to walk. She knew her tight skirt outlined each jiggle she made with every step. He was undoubtedly enjoying quite a show at her expense.

13

Mitzi rushed out to where Darrell was sitting at lunch. She was very excited about the news she was busting at the seams to share.

"What are you doing today after school, Darrell?"

"I don't know? Do you have any ideas? I'm just glad it's the weekend. I was hoping we could go to the beach or something."

"I have a better idea than that!" Mitzi's face was beaming.

"Okay, Mitz—I'm all ears?" Darrell hadn't seen her with this kind of excitement.

"Guess who has the house to herself tonight—and possibly tomorrow night too?" She reached over and touched Darrell's leg. Her thumb brushed closely to his crotch as she squeezed his thigh.

Darrell's body reacted instantly. "Are you kidding me?"

"No, I'm not kidding you. We could stay at my house all night and catch a bus to St. George tomorrow morning! We can get to know each other practically the entire weekend!"

Darrell's mouth widened into a grin as his mind began letting the scenario play out the possibilities. And then, the smile dropped to a frown.

"What just happened here, Darrell?"

"Um, remember last night? Remember, who just happens to live next door to you?"

Mitzi paused for a moment as if in reflective thought. She suddenly smiled. "Pardon my language, but—" She paused.

"Yes?"

"…fuck him. I'm eighteen and legal, you're eighteen and legal.

Screw him! He has no power over us."

Darrell was slightly shocked by her statement. "I guess you're right. The most he could do was tell your mom when she got back—or rat me out to mine."

"Eighteen, Darrell." She smiled. "Besides, it's always easier to ask forgiveness than permission!" Mitzi winked and moved her hand a little closer to where she shouldn't.

"And you call me dangerous Darrell." He laughed. I believe I'll call you malefic Mitzi!"

"What the heck does that mean?" Mitzi asked.

"It means a bad influence! Which is exactly what you are!" He smiled evilly as he took his hand and persuaded hers a little closer to where it shouldn't be.

Mitzi looked down at their hands and then moved her eyes upward until they met his. They stood quietly, just staring at each other, speaking without words.

Each was surely imagining what would happen tonight being together—alone—with no supervision or anyone to stop what they may not be able to stop on their own.

Mitzi leaned into Darrell and moved her lips next to his ear. Her breath lightly blew into his ear canal, causing him to quiver suddenly. She whispered, "Do you have some condoms you can bring?"

Darrell's heart raced. "I've never had anyone ask me that before. If you're serious, I will get some."

Mitzi pulled back, looking him squarely in his gorgeous green eyes. "I'm serious. I'm a virgin. I want to be smart."

Darrell responded after choking on his gulp. "I'm one too. And I'm not ready to be a father. I am ready to learn together with you if you promise not to laugh at me."

Mitzi pulled him back into her body and reached again with her lips to his ear. "I won't laugh." She ran her tongue around the inside of his ear.

"You are definitely malefic Mitz."

Lunchtime was over and each parted way, off to their next class—drawing them nearer to the weekend.

14

Darrell told Mitzi he had to make a stop at home and then the drugstore. "I'll be over as soon as I can, be careful, Mitz, watch out for Jay. I'm going to use your stairway and try to get in without him seeing me. Close your blinds. I'll lightly tap on the door three times, then pause and then two quick taps."

"This sounds so clandestine! I'll be waiting for you." She winked a naughty but nervous smile.

***

Knock, knock, knock—knock, knock.

Darrell could hear music playing through the door. The song wasn't familiar, but he liked it.

The door slowly opened.

Darrell's eyes immediately locked onto Mitzi's mesmerizing green eyes. They were lost for a few seconds, but as he stepped inside, closing the door behind him, his gaze moved south. His stare stopped when they met the cleavage held by her frilly bra. Her breasts tightly pushed together, visible behind her shirt. She had light freckles across her white chest. His eyes continued downward as her hands reached out for his. He saw her bare stomach and belly button that was smooth and fleshy, just above where her scant cut-off shorts hugged her hips. There was an enticing gap between her tummy and the waistline of her shorts.

His pants bulged out in front of him, barely rubbing against the covered buttons of her shorts. Darrell ran his hand down her side and around to her belly button, running his finger in a small circle before poking it into the shallow crevice of her navel.

Mitzi moaned slightly. The temperature of her internal oven was set immediately to high-heat.

Darrell barely stepped inside the living room, and already, his hand began to search and investigate the gap between her stomach and edge of her shorts. His fingers reached deeper, and Mitzi maneuvered her hand on top of his and gently pushed Darrell's hand farther down inside her pants as she ground against him.

Mitzi, satisfied where Darrell's hand was headed, retrieved her hand and, with her other hand, began unbuttoning Darrell's shirt, pulling it away from his hard abdomen and chest. His free hand shot through the sleeve while his other still touched and searched inside the gap between her shorts and soft skin.

He reluctantly removed his hand and quickly pulled his arm through his sleeve. He placed his fingers up close to his nose and took in the scent. His heart pounded harder inside his chest, feeling it would explode. He knew he no longer had the self-control to stop or withdraw from this animalistic deed that was about to happen between them. He had no intention of trying.

Mitzi reached down and began unbuckling his belt, then unbuttoning his fly. She nudged him toward the couch, and as he sat, she knelt on her knees and began to pull his pants from each leg. Carnal instinct overtook her and caution thrown to the wind. She craved seeking to pleasure and to receive it also. This new desire was overwhelming and uncontrollable. She had no yearning to fight it, the drive was too powerful.

The song switched to the next song, which was slower than the first. "These Eyes" by Guess Who. The tempo and groove pushed them deeper into their romance. The lyrics continued, "These eyes, cry every night, for you. These arms, long to hold you...."

Mitzi pushed herself in close between his spread legs as he sat on the couch. She pulled his hand, which was just exploring beneath her panties, up to her face and ran her tongue around his fingers before taking each one inside her mouth. She slowly pulled them out, her lips wrapped tightly around them.

Darrell's head fell onto the back of the couch as he looked down his nose at the top of Mitzi's head as she playfully sucked on his fingers. The anticipation of what would happen next excited him in ways he'd never imagined. The gap on his tidy boxer shorts suddenly pushed open, exposing his erection.

The movement drew Mitzi's attention down to where she felt the activity. She looked up into Darrell's eyes, noticing his enjoyment before looking back down and touching her tongue where it had never been before.

Darrell released an uncontrolled moan as his hands naturally ended up touching her hair on either side of her head. It didn't take long before he caved into his self-control and released his tension with a drawn-out groan ending with a whimpering murmur. He'd never felt so instantly relaxed. His entire body tingled in a symphony of never-before felt sensations.

Mitzi reached around and undid her bra, freeing it to fall to the floor.

Darrell looked down and smiled at Mitzi and looking at her beautiful body, sheepishly asked, "Are you sure you've never done this before?"

Mitzi kept moving and answered with only one word. "Never."

Darrell laid his head back down against the couch, feeling spent but re-aroused. He was sweaty and breathing hard but ached to see what it would feel like to be inside her.

He lifted himself and reached out to touch Mitzi's face. "Let's change spots."

She scooted back and watched as he stood up in his nakedness. She crawled up onto the couch and sat in the warm moist spot he'd just gotten up from.

Darrell leaned down and kissed Mitzi deep in her mouth. He ran his tongue wildly throughout the inside of her mouth. He felt like a wild tiger with a driving hunger to be satisfied along with making his partner writhe in the gratification he would soon propel her to.

Darrell pulled back and ran his hands down to her breasts. He watched their moldability as he massaged and pushed them together. He leaned down and ran his tongue over her nipples, playfully nibbling on them as they grew harder.

Darrell suddenly leaned back on his knees and tugged her lacy panties until he pulled them past her hips, down her legs and into his hands. They were damp, and he could smell the scent that had given him the drive he was now so drunk with.

He pushed her legs wider apart and exposed what he had never seen before.

Mitzi cooed and squirmed as Darrell realized how his internal instincts drove him with the inherent knowledge of how to pleasure her.

Mitzi pushed herself harder and forcefully into him as he continued toying his tongue against her.

"Oh Darrell, that's it!" She screamed as she wriggled her torso uncontrollably, tears of pleasure pouring from her eyes.

Suddenly she let out a scream, and Darrell reached up to try and stifle it. He held his hand over her mouth as she quivered and shook, her legs bouncing and kicking.

When she began to quiet down and just lay against the back of the couch, her head where Darrell's had been, he collapsed his head onto her chest.

His erection screamed for more, but his heart was racing, and he felt as if they would both explode in unison.

Mitzi finally raised her hands and began running her fingers through his hair. "I want to feel the real thing, Darrell, but I can't right now. My body is tingling so much, and my heart—I can't breathe." She sucked in a deep breath and returned to melting into the couch.

There was the scent of sex mixed with sweat filling the room. Silence hung over them except for the sighs and deep breaths of air from them both. Their energy spent. Both sat up suddenly hearing someone walking across the deck outside. The room became quiet as they both perked with alertness, trying to listen where the footsteps could be headed.

Dried planks creaked and moaned with each slow and deliberate step.They looked at each other, the pleasure they just experienced, now became a frightening thrill of what may happen next.

Creeeak...moan...creeeaak...thunk. Silence.

15

When Joyce opened the curtains exposing the view of the ocean from her room—she was overwhelmed. It was the most exquisite sight she'd ever seen. She turned three hundred and sixty degrees and slowly took in everything the room held within.

There was a stocked bar, a bright red leather sofa, and a side-chair with matching ottomans—a black marble and glass coffee table with matching side-tables and a table desk where she could work. The bed was huge and faced the floor to ceiling window. She fell back onto the bed and soaked in the view from her reclined position.

Her drive had been uneventful and full of scenery. It had given her three hours to clear her mind as she traveled the gulf coastline. She was worried about Mitzi. Why had she passed out? Her anger had taunted her from Roy's reaction when she'd called him. Hell, what an asshole he'd been since she met him those nineteen years ago. Joyce had apprehensions about Ethan, her boss.

Why would he put me up in such an expensive room? For that matter, why did he seek me out for employment? I'm a good employee who is good at my job, but I don't really stand out above any other paralegal. Joyce sat back up as her thoughts continued to rattle her. *Sure, I hold dreams and aspirations of going farther up the ladder, maybe even law school, but how would Ethan know that?*

The drive had been beautiful but now she was unable to relax. She knew she needed to check in with Ethan and see what the plan was, but now she felt more uneasy about meeting him. Even more so with the time that had passed since Monday. *This just feels out of the ordinary and awkward. I need to motivate though.*

Joyce climbed off the bed and freshened up in the bathroom. She glanced in the mirror as she stood sideways, brushing the wrinkles from her short, tight skirt that Mr. Bingham had admired so blatantly this morning. She smiled at herself in the mirror. *I do look good. My body is something to notice, especially for a woman in her late thirties.*

She pushed her breasts together, rearranging the fit of her brassiere. After being comfortable with her appearance, she sauntered over to the phone beside her bed and called Ethan's room. Joyce suddenly let out a quick laugh. *All this prep and he of course can't see me through the phone!*

"Hello, Ethan." She paused. "Yes, this is Joyce…" Joyce smiled. "Yes, the drive was nice, actually beautiful…" She turned and glanced out at the coastline, and the dozens of umbrellas set up, adding color to the azure blue water and white sand. "I would love to eat some lunch and talk. Yes, that sounds wonderful. I can be down whenever you like." She paused, listening to what Ethan had to say. "Okay, I'll head to the bar and see you there. Thank you." She set the phone down on the cradle and walked by the mirror, checking herself out in the reflection through the bathroom doorway one more time before heading downstairs to the restaurant lounge.

***

"Darrell, go peek out the window." Mitzi whispered. "Surely, he's gone!"

Darrell quietly got up, now very aware of his nakedness as he turned to Mitzi, covering his genitals.

She spoke just above a whisper. "You've got to be kidding me,

Darrell. Are you going to play awkward and embarrassed now? After what we just did for each other?" She giggled quietly. "How can you be so boyish now?"

Darrell removed his hands from covering himself. "Boyish, really? What the hell does that mean? There, are you happy now, Mitz? Why don't you stand up and show me your stuff too?"

Mitz scooted to the edge quickly, not willing to give in to an unanswered challenge, and pushed herself up, so she was standing in front of him. She quickly turned away and looked at him over her shoulder. She jiggled her butt and smiled. "So, how's it look with no clothes? Better than that day on the sidewalk when you couldn't take your eyes off me?" She turned back to face him and purposely brushed her hand against his now soft but growing erection.

"I thought I was supposed to be checking the window? Now I'm going to be parting the curtains farther than I was planning!" They both stood silent for a second, listening for any sound outside.

"This is ridiculous, Darrell. This is my gawd damn house." She bent down and grabbed up her clothes and began putting them on.

Darrell just stood and watched, mesmerized by her beauty, and the look on his face showed he was new to the ease of nudity that Mitz was perfectly comfortable with.

Mitzi marched over to the window and pulled the curtain back. She quickly gasped out loud.

"What, Mitz?" Darrell jumped and quickly reached for his pants.

She looked back and smiled at the speed he was pulling them on. His underwear was still lying on the floor beside his shirt.

"Oh, Shit!" Mitzi continued and backed away from the window nervously.

Darrell hopped up and down as he shoved his legs downward through the pantlegs and pulled the waistband up, all in one fluid and fast motion. "What the hell?"

"Come here, quick." She motioned with her hand to move quietly.

Darrell tip-toed over with a serious questioning look across his face. As he got close to the window, she motioned him to pull the curtain open.

He slowly pulled the curtain back and leaned in closer to peek out.

Mitzi stepped back and grabbed his sides as she yelled, "Bawahahaha!"

Darrell about jumped out of his skin backward as he tripped over himself. He ended up on the carpeted floor, sprawled in a heap.

Mitzi stood and laughed until tears were rolling down her cheeks.

Darrell lay disheveled as he quickly tried to sit back up. He stared wide-eyed at Mitzi. "What the hell…?"

"I'm hungry—how 'bout you?" She smiled and walked toward him. "Or do you wanna get naked again?"

"I can't believe you, Mitz." He shook his head. "It's really not funny. My dad is a psycho. I'm serious. He could slit our throats and then eat lunch while we bled out before digging the holes to put us in. All without blinking an eye."

"I know, remember—I named him Creepy Jay before I even knew you. But, I'm not gonna let that asshole make me change my ways. Fuck him. I live here now, and now, that I've had a taste of his son…" She walked over and pushed Darrell back to the floor as he was getting up. "I'm not gonna let him steal you away from me with his creepy creepin' around."

"Mitz, you definitely are like no one I've ever met. And I'm hungry too. Let's go out. I'll buy." Darrell winked.

"You care if we ask Vio and the gang to go with us to the beach tomorrow? Vio has her license too. I mean, I have mine too, but Mom has the car." She smiled at Darrell. "When are you getting yours?"

"My mom doesn't have a car. Neither do I. I never really thought I needed one in this one-horse town." He was up on his feet and putting his shirt on. "I don't mind walking around here."

Mitzi looked at him. "You're not always gonna be here, are you?" She pointed down to the floor. "And, you not gonna put those boxer shorts back on? I was hoping to watch you again."

Darrell looked down and snagged his underwear, then turned and headed into the bathroom.

Mitzi was surprised Darrell was such a prude, especially after the way he seemed to know his way around her body.

She picked up the phone and called her friend, Vio.

"Sure, I think that will be okay." Mitzi looked over at Darrell as he exited the bathroom. "Do you mind if the gang meets us at the Coffee Caper? I told Vio about tomorrow, and she's in! I mentioned we were gonna grab a bite to eat, and Chubbs was over there. Kyle is on his way."

"I don't mind. The more, the merrier."

"Okay, Vio, we'll head that way in just a few. See y'all there."

On the way out of her front door, they both looked toward the deck area—no Jay.

"Did we imagine those footsteps, Mitz?"

"I don't think so. I think it was CJ. You know, Creepy Jay."

"I'll bet he's fishing on the pier with Reverend Gabriel. Kind of glad he's not out here. It wasn't pleasant the last time I saw him after you left in the ambulance."

"I'm sorry, we still need to talk and let you share about him and that jar. Maybe when we get home?" Mitzi grabbed Darrell's hand at the bottom of the stairs.

"Maybe." Darrell answered, knowing he didn't want to ruin their night by all that stuff.

16

Cat decided to be quiet about Darrell's actions. She didn't like the fact he wasn't coming home tonight, but she did realize he was eighteen and wasn't a young boy anymore. He was becoming a man, and he'd made her well-aware of that fact. All she could really do was pray and hope for the best. There was no need to get the Watkins involved.

She decided this early evening was perfect for a walk. She loved the bay and the docks. She wondered if Jay would be out on the pier. A nice walk down the boardwalk would do her mind some good.

***

"Yeah, I had no idea that Darrell's dad was our creepy neighbor." Mitzi faked a shiver through her body.

"Mitz, you are such a drama queen! And a damn good comedian." Vio poked her in the rib as they sat down at the table. "So, what were you two doing there, anyway?" She giggled.

Chubbs and Kyle looked at Darrell to see what his reaction would be.

"Yeah, sport! Are ya…" Chubbs put his pointing finger into his other pointer finger and thumb formed into a circle. He then moved it back and forth. "…you know, cave splunkin'?" He then elbowed Kyle's shoulder and laughed at his sophomoric joke.

"How would you know about splunkin'? It usually doesn't take place in the bathroom when you're alone, does it?" Darrell looked and cocked his head in a question. "Bet it sounds like this when you're in there..." He grabbed his cheek in a pinched grip and pulled it back and forth, making a rude noise.

"Well, only for a second, though!" Kyle winked at Chubbs and watched his face turn red.

They all laughed loud enough that the entire crowd in the restaurant looked over at them in disgust.

"Hey! My kid's here trying to eat. Don't make me come over there and show y'all kids some manners."

"Yes, sir. We are sorry for disturbing your family's dinner tonight. We'll keep it down." Darrell quickly responded.

Chubbs leaned over toward Darrell. "What the hell? Are you gonna go kiss his ass too?"

"You need to learn some respect, Chubbs. His kids are like eight and twelve..." He pushed Chubbs back. "Don't be an ass."

"I know it's Friday night kids, and y'all just started back in school. No harm. I just want to enjoy my dinner with my family without the rowdy teen talk." The father responded. "Not sayin' y'all shouldn't be kids and have fun—just be respectful of others around you."

"Yes, sir." Kyle piped up. He then looked over eyeing Chubbs. "You have to buy the beers now, buddy."

"What beers?" Chubbs asked.

"The ones we're gonna enjoy over at Mitzi's tonight since her mom's outta town!" Kyle chided back as he glanced at Mitzi, daring her to say no to the gang.

She looked at Darrell, and then answered, "Sure, as long as it's Pabst Blue Ribbon! And at least a case, there are five of us!"

"But you are all gone by midnight!" Darrell chimed in.

"Splunkin' time don't start until one a.m.!" Chubbs laughed.

"That's just your momma's time, Chubbs..." Kyle laughed. "Well, at least tonight...since we have to leave Mitzi's at midnight!"

The five broke into laughter. Even Chubbs was chuckling. "She told me the other night you really loved her granny panties!" Chubbs laughed even louder.

"Okay, okay. Enough already. Let's eat and get outta here and get some beers." Kyle replied.

Chubbs pulled out his wallet and thumbed through his cash. "I'll get the beer, but somebody has to buy my burger."

On the way out of the Caper, they all agreed to meet at Mitzi's but to tiptoe up the stairs so CJ wouldn't hear them.

***

Cat thought she saw Darrell and several others walking down the sidewalk away from the Coffee Caper. She smiled, seeing that he was out with several friends, and her smile read like she was happy that it looked innocent. She continued toward the pier and dock area.

Cat made the turn at the pier and began the walk out toward the end. The sun would be going down in a short matter of time, and she loved watching that happen from the very end.

It made her feel as if she were walking on water in the middle of God's vast creation. Tonight's beautiful clouds were high, and the 'green flash' at sunset should be spectacular.

She saw Reverend Gabriel and Jay about a third of the way out. They both had poles in the water and seemed to be talking tonight.

There were times when Jay would shut not only her out, but Reverend Gabriel also. She felt deep down inside that Jay was suffering tremendously. Cat could sense it, see it, and feel it in the air around him. But she had no idea what to do to help him. She supposed she shouldn't let it bother her. She thought when they reunited in the cemetery, there may still be some chance of a reconciliation of some sort, but that seemed to have left the realm of possibility.

She was sad at first, but now, she just didn't really care to see him. She wasn't really at a place yet in her life where she needed or even cared about having a man in it. She was just now losing the young man in her life a little more each day.

Darrell was pulling away and becoming a man on his own. Cat smiled to herself at that thought as she stepped closer to the two fishing.

"Hello, gentlemen. I hope I'm not buttin' in on a private conversation!" Cat smiled as she looked at the two and the beautiful bay that lay behind them. "Any luck this evening?"

Reverend Gabriel was the first to respond, "I've caught nuthin' but a great suntan, Miss Cat!" He laughed as he stuck his chocolate brown arm out as if to brag of his new golden skin.

"Why, Reverend—I do believe you've got yourself burnt to a crisp!" She smiled.

Reverend Gabriel chuckled. He often joked about his skin-tone. It was his way of relieving any possible racial tensions. The man loved everybody, no matter their color, sex, or faith.

"Jay, are you doing okay tonight?" Cat asked. She squinted a bit as the fading sun peeked through a beautiful pinkish-orange thick cloud.

Jay looked over, and his eyes spoke before his words even tried to begin. His dark eyes looked filled with pain deep enough to drown in. He looked lost. "I'm doing okay. Getting adjusted to the heat again. Waiting on my driver's license, so I can know for sure that I can do what Ben needs doing for the restaurant." He fired the response back so neatly that it sounded rehearsed.

"It looks like it's coming along. Are you going to take me there on opening night?" Cat smiled.

"You would want me too?"

"Jay, of course, I would. I'm worried about you." Her nervous habit dealing with pain came back as she instinctively reached where the cross and locket were hanging around her neck. She fidgeted with it between her fingers. It usually helped calm her anxiety or gave her comfort in painful times. "I don't always know what to say to you, it's like it's new again, but in a different way—but I don't want to see you hurting. That's what it looks like I'm watching when I see you." Cat forced a smile across her lips.

Reverend Gabriel had reeled in his line and checked his bait. He let out a little bit from the reel and then drew back to cast it again. Gabriel could overhear; she was sure. But the Reverend seemed to know when to talk—and when to fish. Cat continued talking to Jay.

"Why don't you let Reverend Gabriel watch your line and walk down to the end of the pier with me. We can watch the green flash together."

"Green flash?" Jay questioned.

"Oh, Jay. You're kidding me, right?" Cat asked.

"I haven't a clue what a green flash is, Cat."

"All those years together and you never asked? Or even heard? Now you have to put your pole down and walk with me while I explain!" She stepped closer and put her hand out toward his.

Jay glanced over at Gabriel as he turned and nodded in agreement. "You gotta' know about the green flash, Jay. The Lord didn't put it there just to be ignored! Git on outta here, son—I'll probably catch a whopper on your line just as soon as you step away!" He chuckled aloud.

Jay set his pole in the rod hole on the rail. "Thanks, Gabriel. I'll be back in a bit."

"No worries, son. Keep your eyes open, or you'll miss it for sure! It don't hang around long 'nuff to straggle." Gabriel snorted with a laugh.

Cat grabbed Jay's hand and pulled him away as they started to stroll toward the end.

"So, when the sun is setting…" Cat began talking to break the gap between them. "...there is a couple of seconds as the sun appears to hit the water's edge. You have to keep your eyes on it, or you'll miss it..." She leaned around to look into Jay's eyes. "...just as the sun and water appear to touch, the sun seems to change its color from yellow-orange—to green instantly. A brilliant green! But it only lasts one or two seconds."

"Two seconds of beauty, and then it's gone? That's kind of what my life with you feels like now." Jay looked away from Cat. "Do you ever feel like maybe it's too much effort for such a short moment of joy?"

Cat continued to walk beside him slowly. His hand loosened his grip, but she squeezed tighter, refusing to let his fingers escape. They both kept walking in silence as the sun crept closer to dropping into the gulf. The entire railing at the end was clear of people, which never happened.

Cat grabbed onto the top of the wooden rail with her free hand as they bumped up against it. "I did regret that moment of beauty for quite a while, Jay." She looked down at the slow waves rolling in. "When I lost Billy and you—I hated you. I couldn't regret the fleeting beauty because it brought me Billy for almost eighteen years, and it gave me Darrell. Darrell was all I had after that Friday night." She released Jay's hand when he tried again to loosen his grip. "It was a beautiful green flash when it began, though." Cat wiped her eye that held the beginnings of a tear. She then reached up again to her emotional lifeline, her necklace. She held it out in front of her and drew Jay's attention.

"Where did you get that?" Jay asked.

"The cross and necklace came from Ms. Gloria—she gave it to me on a special Sunday morning that I will never forget." She held the cross between her thumb and finger as the locket slid down the chain. "It was the Sunday I felt the Lord put his hands around my heart. It was the most beautiful feeling of warmth I think I ever felt. It was a green flash that has stuck with me for over two and a half years now. I can still feel it on a Sunday morning or when I start feeling lost."

"I had that feeling once. Not that long ago. But it didn't stick like yours. I guess my heart was just too cold—even for Jesus." Jay's tanned tattooed arms were leaning on the railing, the inked demons beginning to fade from the years, and exposure to the elements.

"So where did you get the locket? I don't remember ever seeing it." Jay was trying to change the subject, but he had no idea what was in store for him with his question.

Cat reached down and grabbed the locket and let the cross slide away down the chain this time. She used both hands to open it, and as she did, she felt the tears begin to poke from her eyes again. She held it out and pushed it toward Jay. She had to move closer to him, so he was able to see the tiny portraits the locket held. There was now little space between them. "It came from my mother. It was given to me when I was very young. It was put away until I found it again when Darrell and I were gathering the things that were important to us when we moved from the farmhouse to the Watkins." She took one hand and brushed the tears away. "It's the only thing of my mother's that I have left. Ms. Gloria helped me put these two pictures inside." She pushed it even closer to Jay, making him lean in to see.

As Jay leaned in, he could see the tiny pictures of Billy and Darrell. Emotions he thought he no longer held began to bubble up from deep within. Jay had felt unable to feel sentiment of this kind. He quickly felt anger and lust and hate, but this response that was making him feel like crying had been one he'd only faked in his past. He thought at this moment that he might not be able to hold back this passion. He felt little of this sensation at the sight of Darrell's picture, but he felt like he was drowning from the moment he caught a glimpse of his boy, Billy. The memory of his face had receded into the farthest reaches of his brain. So far, he seldom made any effort to travel there. Now here that emotion was with his boy's eyes staring at him. He was face to face without intention. His boy, Billy, was peering into his murderous soul, begging him to drop to his knees in shame for what he'd committed.

Jay's legs began to quiver at first. In seconds they erupted into full shaking. He felt them giving way as he clutched the railing supports.

Jay's body sank to the deck floor in unison with the sun, making its final seconds of descent into the waters in the distance. He managed to look between the pillars that held the railing up just as the sun quickly kissed the ocean. The green flash seared into his vision for the brief seconds it was etched into the ball of fire. And then the sun was tucked in for another night as it fell below the horizon.

Jay could only sit on his knees, crying to himself. He spoke no words, just painful cries from a man who never in his life before had been able to free his mental bondage enough to drain the pain from the anger that contained it.

Cat knelt beside him and rubbed his shoulders and drug her fingers through his thick black hair.

She never foresaw what power the green flash mixed with the tiny pictures held inside her locket would have.

Gabriel showed up a couple of minutes later after noticing the two of them.

After Jay assured them both he was okay but wanted to remain alone for a while, Gabriel walked Cat back to their home. Gabriel spent a good portion of the slow walk back, assuring Cat she'd done nothing wrong and that Jay had plenty of demons trying to maintain their hold on him.

"Satan has been housed inside Jay for a long time, Cat. Jesus is strong and can help him defeat his demons. But he must ask earnestly for his help. Jesus isn't going to take away his free choice. He will open doors for him to seek refuge, but he won't forcibly push him in. Jay has to do that on his own." He pulled Cat to his side as they walked, giving her comfort that no other would be able to at this moment. No other than maybe, Billy, but Billy was home with his Father and Master above.

17

Kyle was sipping his PBR and telling the gang where he was from, and his story. He had been the quiet one in his recent past. He, like Darrell, was coming out of his shell. No one knew that fact, because he was basically a new unknown to the area. Hell, they were all unknowns to each other.

Nobody would have ever recognized the Darrell today from the one only mere months ago. Chubbs and Violet were the only ones who had previous knowledge of Darrell—before the attempted murder of his "poppa," and Violet had been told growing up to stay clear of the Cader family by her parents.

"You guys are pretty awesome. I wasn't sure I could ever trust you or even if I wanted to try…" Kyle drank another deep swallow of his bottle of beer. "But you guys are pretty cool." He reached into his pocket and pulled out a small baggy with a greenish-brown leafy substance. "…now it's time to see just how cool you are!" He smiled as he checked each of their expressions out. "Who among us has ever smoked weed?" He pulled out his little cardboard pack of rolling papers from his other pocket. "Oh, come on now! None of you?" Kyle grinned as he pulled a paper out and nestled it between his thumb and middle finger, his pointing finger on top holding it in a curve-like trough. With his free hand, he pinched a couple of small piles from the baggy and laid them out in the paper trough. All the while, he kept talking. "This will take all of your tensions away and relax you. You will never feel like you're out of control of yourself. You'll just find simple things funny, and we will all have fun, I promise. Nothing scary."

The others looked back and forth at each other as Kyle focused on building the perfect vehicle to deliver them their first quality high. "Everybody's in, right? No stragglers!" He held the 'joint' in between his thin lips as he struck the match, watching the flame grow and then die down. The reflection in his brown eyes of the fire gave Kyle an eerie look. He was now the pusher. Kyle sucked the flame into the end of the joint. Drawing in the smoke and blowing it out until it was finally lit. He then sucked in a long drag and held it in his lungs.

Kyle passed the joint to Darrell, who glanced over at Mitz, looking for approval before he followed suit.

Mitzi smiled and nodded in agreement. As Kyle passed it and Darrell took it, he still held the smoke deep within.

Darrell put the cigarette to his lips and inhaled. He'd never had smoke in his lungs, and he immediately coughed and hacked as puffs of the grey smoke sputtered from his mouth.

The group laughed, and Kyle assured him that it was normal the first time.

Darrell attempted again, only taking a smaller amount into his lungs. He managed to contain his composure this time and looked at Mitz before carefully handing it to her.

Mitz pushed the small joint to her lips and inhaled just a little and passed it to Chubbs. He in turn started to hold the joint to his lips but hesitated. "This isn't gonna make me a junkie, is it? I don't want to live on the streets and rob people to get more of this."

Kyle smiled at Chubbs and then laughed. "No, you won't be a junkie. You don't have to try it if you don't want."

Chubbs sucked just a little in and started to hand it to Violet.

"Hey, wait a minute, let me have it for a second." Kyle took the cigarette from Chubbs and scooted closer to Vio. "Just lean toward me and breathe it in, Vio."

Kyle inserted the lit end into his mouth and leaned closer to

Vio, their lips almost touching. He then began blowing the smoke out from the unlit end and into Vio's mouth. She breathed it in and then held it in her lungs, looking into Kyle's eyes. He removed the joint from his mouth and passed it back to Darrell. "Shotgun!"

Minutes later, they all sat quietly around the living room. Darrell and Mitz on the floor leaning against the couch. Chubbs on the recliner and Kyle sat on the floor below Vio, who sat on one end of the sofa.

Darrell suddenly became talkative. He started telling them about his "poppa," Jay. Darrell told them about the sick game of the Mason jar and the punishments it held. He spoke about the Friday nights spent in dread of when he would hear the sound the diesel truck made pulling up the gravel drive.

It was a setting like kids sitting around a campfire telling ghost stories. Everyone's eyes were glued to Darrell, who remained calm tonight as he relived his past to his friends.

Mitz curled up next to him as she rubbed his back and watched him.

Kyle was the first to respond when Darrell finished talking.

"This son-of-a-bitch lives next door to you, Mitzi?"

She was silent as she nodded in agreement.

"We should drag his ass out and give him some of his own medicine!" Kyle responded.

"No, Kyle. You should all avoid him. He's dangerous, and I don't believe he's really changed. He killed my brother, and he wouldn't hesitate in doing the same to each one of you…" Darrell began to look agitated and in a different demeanor than he was just minutes earlier. "That's why I tried to kill the bastard when I saw him with my mom just a couple of months ago. And the fucking sheriff just let him go scot-free! He got away with murder."

Mitzi's muscles tensed at Darrell's last statement. She scooted away just a bit, causing Darrell to turn toward her.

"You okay, Mitz?" He asked.

She realized that she'd not let him know that sheriff Burks was her father. Her estranged father. Now, she wasn't sure how to respond? Mitzi just stared toward the window.

"Are you okay, Mitz?" Darrell asked.

A moment later, Mitzi responded. "I'm okay. I think the pot is just making me spacey." She looked over and smiled at Darrell. "I'll be fine. My head is just a little cloudy."

"Pretty good smoke, ain't it? It's Columbian Gold. Ready for another joint, anyone?" Kyle questioned as he smiled wide.

Silence filled the room as each looked at the other, everyone glassy-eyed.

Chubbs snickered, "I'm so damned hungry, I could eat a fuckin' donkey. That's what I am."

"I think we have some frozen pizzas; I'll go check," Mitzi answered as she got up to head to the kitchen. She used it as an escape from Darrell. She still didn't know how to tell him that the man who let his father out of jail was her estranged father.

Kyle reached into his pocket.

"No way, man. Not for me!" Darrell said.

"Did I upset you 'bout what I said? I mean, I know he's your old man, but damn!" Kyle asked.

Darrell shook his head no. "I think he thought he could waltz his way back into my life—no f'ing way. No, you didn't say anything wrong. I'm serious, though, he's psycho. Be careful around him."

"I guess I should be more thankful…" Violet chimed in. "I was raised by parents that never abused me. They gave me everything. I feel guilty about it now."

"I thought my dad was mean, but he was an angel in comparison." Chubbs echoed. "Now the SOB is just gone. He left my mom and me. Good riddance."

"My dad was gone before I was old enough to know. I never met him." Kyle said.

"I've never asked Mitz about the story on her dad. I wonder if he's still around?" Darrell questioned as he climbed up from the floor. "I'm gonna go check on her."

After Darrell left the room, Kyle scooted closer to Vio, pulling her legs into his side resting his elbows on her kneecaps like chair arms. "I may have to fuck with this CJ, dude. I hate to let a guy get away without reminding him of the people he's hurt."

Violet reached down and squeezed his shoulders as she leaned up toward his ear. "Not a good idea, Kyle." She whispered. "I'm starting to like you—I may wanna keep you around." She touched the tip of her tongue into his ear, making Kyle jump a little. He turned and looked up at her.

"I like the sound of that and the feel." He smiled.

"Well, shit. It looks like I'm a damned fifth wheel here. I'm gonna eat some of that pizza, and then I'm outta here!" Chubbs snorted. "I need to find a babe for me—any suggestions?"

"How picky are you?" Kyle chuckled.

"She can be either fat or ugly. Not both—unless there's two, one of each!" Chubbs snapped back before breaking into a laugh.

"What an order!" Violet answered. "But I'll keep my eye open."

Kyle laughed out loud. "You better keep both eyes open—you're not gonna wanna miss Chubbs' only opportunity!"

Back in the kitchen, Darrell walked over to Mitzi and put his hands on her waist. "Are you okay? You seem to have changed your mood."

She hesitated for several seconds as she put the pizzas in the oven. "I, uh…" She turned and looked at Darrell squarely. "Sheriff Burks—is my dad." She watched for his reaction but started talking before he had a chance to respond. "He's my dad, but we don't really speak—it's a twisted, long story." She stood silent, waiting for Darrell's reaction.

"You're kidding me? Seriously?" Darrell dropped his hands from Mitzi's waist. "Why didn't you tell me before?"

"Why would I have? I never even thought about it. I didn't put two and two together until tonight!" She began to tear up. "Why? Does it make a difference? He's not in my life. I never see him, hell, he doesn't even know we moved here."

"He doesn't know? Doesn't your mom talk to him? Apalachicola is a tiny one-stoplight town, you haven't bumped into him anywhere?"

"He hasn't been a father to me, like my entire life! No financial help to my mom, no birthday cards or Christmas presents sent to me...." Her eyes flooded. "He's to me—what your dad is to you—a big, useless nothing! A bad memory. The only difference between my dad and yours is which side of the law they're on." Mitzi slammed the oven door.

Darrell realized that he was being a judgmental asshole. "I'm sorry, Mitz. I didn't mean..." He put his hands around her waist again, but Mitzi pulled back. "I'm sorry. Should I leave?"

Mitzi remained silent as she let his words enter her thoughts. *Was it already over? Are we going to allow our worthless fathers who either did harm or ignored us—ruin the relationship we were building together?* She already knew deep down that she had fallen in love with Darrell. She knew he had troubles before she ever met him, thanks to Violet. Was Darrell already willing to throw her away because a man she didn't even know had been the one to let his dad out of jail without any prison time? It wasn't his fault. It would be the fault of the judicial system. Not her dad's, even if he was the sheriff. Her head began spinning.

Mitzi wasn't sure if it was the pot or the argument, or the fact they had too much baggage between them in such an early stage of their romance.

Mitzi needed to think it through. Her mom had always preached to take things slow and think decisions through thoroughly. She knew she needed to back away for at least the night before making any rash conclusions. They had both looked forward to sharing their bodies more—bringing pleasure to one another. That fit was perfect. But now, with this—this was a sign. A big 'ole stop sign.

She looked at Darrell and then to the floor.

The look on his eyes painted the picture that this wasn't a good sign, and he stepped back.

"I think we both need to think things through before we take that next step that we were headed to tonight. I wanted you tonight, Darrell, but now—if that step ever happens—I want it to be perfect, with nothing hanging over our heads." Mitzi looked up from the floor and at Darrell, who was standing, staring blankly back at her.

"Is this good-bye, Mitzi? Is this over—you and me?" Darrell asked with a somber tone.

"I'm saying we need to think this through. My mom has always told me to step back and wait if I ever have questions. I'm saying we need to take a step back until we know what we mean to each other."

Darrell took two steps back. "I know I love you, Mitz. I'm sorry for the way I reacted about your dad. I don't want this to end between us, and I'm trusting that you love me too much, too, to let us die. But I respect you wanting to wait." Darrell turned and began to walk away before he turned back. "I don't think we should let two people who mean nothing to us—kill something before it's had a chance to grow. I love you, Mitz, and I'll be there when you realize what you want and if I'm a part of it."

Mitzi knew she spotted wet eyes on Darrell as he walked through the doorway. She heard a small bit of chatter in the other room and then the sound of the front door closing. She put her head on the counter and began crying.

Violet rushed in and did her best to console her.

It wasn't long after that the pizza was done. Mitzi couldn't eat and ended up sending it with Chubbs, Kyle, and Violet.

"Call me if you need anything, Mitz. I'll check on you in the morning. You may wanna go with us to St. George, just to give your mind a rest." She hugged Mitzi.

Silence filled the apartment to a chilling effect. Mitzi B realized she was totally alone tonight. It would be the first time she'd spent the night alone—and an uneasy feeling began to overtake her. It wasn't fear, and it wasn't even that she missed her mom. It was the unknown of what her future now held. She thought she had everything roughly planned out like most girls surely do when they meet "the one." The one that feels certain inside right down to your bones. The one that makes you stay awake dreaming of the next time you would be near them. The one that could bring you to such a scary pleasure with just their touch. And now in the blink of an eye—the one that could quickly bring your world to a crashing halt.

Mitzi tried to sit quietly and read a book. She wondered why her mother hadn't called to check on her. She looked at the clock every five or ten minutes, feeling as if time were standing still. It was only midnight. She laid her book down and got up to pace the floor. She walked to the window and pulled the drapes apart quickly, hoping she would catch Darrell still on her deck. But he wasn't there.

Mitzi walked to the door and opened it up, stepping through the doorway to look at the crescent moon peeking from behind some grey-black clouds. In the distance, there was heat lightning. It was pretty, and when it lit the bay, she could spot the silhouettes of fishing boats either coming in or going out to sea. It was quiet, and the breeze was calm, with only an occasional light gust. The air was refreshing compared to the hot sultry day it had been.

Mitzi was taking in the evening ambiance when something caught her eye. It was a shadow of someone walking up the street towards her house. She drew in a quick breath and felt a chill run down her spine when she noticed just who the shadowy figure belonged to. CJ. It was Darrell's dad. Creepy Jay.

He glanced up and waved at her. Her hand went up to return the wave before she could catch it. She was certain it was a very awkwardly given gesture in return. Hopefully, he would just go up to his side of the stairs, and that would give her the chance to step back inside without looking as if she were avoiding him.

"Damn it." She quietly spoke under her breath. The son-of-a-bitch was walking past the point of his stairway towards hers.

"Hey there, Mitzi. Whatcha doin' out so late? Your momma know you're out?"

He was close enough she could see his smile. "Yeah, she knows. I'm headin' in, though."

"Well, don't go runnin' in because of me! I'd love someone to talk to tonight."

"Well..." Mitzi felt trapped like a mouse nibbling on the cheese set in the trap. If she stayed outside—the trap bar could slam fast on her neck. If she quickly went inside—the tomcat would know she feared him—a perplexing predicament. Jay surely didn't know her momma wasn't home, or did he?

Why, oh, why had she sent Darrell away? She needed him now.

18

"Beautiful night out here, little missy. I don't know about you, but I kind of had a rough one, for such a pretty night." Jay started the conversation the minute he hit the top step.

"Um, yeah—mine didn't end the best either," Mitzi replied, not knowing what to say to head inside her open door.

"Your momma may not like you leaving your front door open like that. What if she comes around the corner half-dressed?" Darrell winked and smiled.

"Mr. Jay…" Mitzi stood firm. "That's not your concern, now—is it?"

Jay stood blank for a moment, not knowing exactly how to respond to her bold stature. "Don't go ruffling your tail-feathers, missy. I didn't mean anything by it. I just had a rough evening and was trying to make a conversation. I don't talk to the ladies much anymore—except for Cat. My estranged wife, Darrell's momma."

"Well, it ain't right to be talking to a young lady about possible naked mommas. It just ain't right." Mitzi began to look nervous and fidgety.

"I had a rough conversation with Cat tonight too—down at the pier." Jay looked away and toward the clouds that were showing lightning through them. "She was telling me about the 'green flash,' and then she showed me a locket that I'd never seen before."

"What's so bad about a locket? And I don't know what a 'green flash' is?"

"That's what I told her! She thought I was crazy for never hearing about it." He smiled, and Mitzi noticed his teeth were kind of yellowed. She thought to herself; he would probably be a reasonably handsome man without those scary tattoos and yellowed teeth. Then, she remembered Darrell warning her about him.

"What about the locket?" She asked.

"It was given to her by her momma. I'd never seen it. When she opened it up—it had a picture of each of the boys, our boys. It made me sad. It reminded me of what a crappy poppa I've been all these years. And of course, the accident with Billy, my oldest boy."

"Is he the one you stabbed?" She felt an instant tinge of shock and awkwardness as she spit the sentence out without thinking it through and what the outcome may be.

Jay tensed a moment. She could see his jaw tighten. Mitzi began to worry what her stupid damn question would bring on. She already knew it was Billy he had killed.

"I'm sorry. That's none of my business. I spit that out before I thought. Please, forgive me." Mitzi looked into Jay's eyes and quickly looked away.

"That's okay, missy. I deserve much worse. I've made some huge mistakes in my life that have affected a lot of people. If it weren't for Ben and Gina over at the Big Apple on the Bay, I'd probably still be hurtin' people and livin' on the streets."

"Big Apple on the Bay? Ben and Gina? I don't have a clue what you are referring to, Jay."

"A restaurant that two of my friends from New York City are opening up here in a month or two. They were kind enough to make me a partner in it. They're the angels sent to save me from myself!"

"Interesting. It would sound like a story to hear, if it weren't too late to listen." She smiled, started to maneuver her way back inside when the phone rang, breaking the silence. "I gotta get this, Jay. Maybe we can talk about this some other time?"

She stepped inside the doorway and waved as Jay said goodnight, and she closed the door and latched it before answering the phone.

"Hello?" She was out of breath from running.

"Mitzi, sweetie? Are you okay?" Joyce asked.

"I'm fine, mom, just out of breath. I was outside on the deck, watching the heat lightning out over the bay."

"Outside past midnight and alone? My gawd, Mitzi! What if CJ came out there and found out you were alone?"

"I'm okay, Mom. I'm inside now, and the door is locked. No worries. So, how are you? I was wondering if you were gonna call at all? What's Mr. Kendrick like?"

"Oh, honey. I can't wait for you to meet Ethan. He is the nicest boss I've ever worked for, and he wants to help me begin law school and …" Joyce began talking a million miles an hour. "…he is just fabulous and nice. I think he's single and I'm certain that he has been checking me out. And…."

"Mom! Take things slowly! Remember? There's no hurry. Take the advice you've pounded into my head all these years! Lord knows I have."

Mitzi suddenly thought about Darrell. Her mind drifted back to this afternoon as she sat on the very couch where it all happened. Mitzi's mom was excited and talking, but Mitzi barely heard a word except for throwing an 'uh-huh,' or 'that's great' in here or there. Her mind was back on Darrell and wishing she hadn't thrown their special night together away.

"Well, I gotta go get some sleep, Mitzi. We need to be at the client's home by nine a.m., and that is gonna come way too early. I probably won't be home until Sunday night—are you okay with that? You'll be okay on your own another night? There's plenty of food in the cupboards and fridge!"

"I'll be fine, Mom. Enjoy yourself. Just don't rush anything!" She smiled as she slipped that into her mom's conversation before her mom could advise her the same. "Goodnight, Mom."

"Goodnight, Mitzi." And then the line went silent.

Suddenly, Mitzi felt re-energized. She and Darrell could have their night together on Saturday if she could convince him that she was ready.

And she was—ready. She was sure her soul had found its mate for life. She wasn't going to let her absent father or his crazy poppa ruin their relationship. Neither had been a big enough part of their lives to have that kind of control over them.

19

The Saturday morning sun shined into Mitzi's window just about the time her alarm went off. She hopped out of bed quicker than ever before. Running to the phone, she began pushing the buttons to call Violet. She was jumping up and down with the anticipation of her answering.

"Hello, Mrs. Emerson! Is Violet available to talk?" She began twirling the cord to the phone. "Yes, this is Mitzi."

"Wow, Mitzi…" Violet yawned into the phone. "Why are you calling so early?"

"Is Darrell going today? Please tell me, yes!"

"Oh, my gawd, Mitz…" Violet sighed. "…do you have it that bad for him?"

"I do, Vio. I do! I wanna make up with him, and I need the beach to do it. Promise me you will get him in the car with you guys! Promise me."

"I will do whatever it takes, Mitz. But you're one bat-shit crazy bitch! And you will owe me for this, girl!"

"If you can make sure this happens—I'll do whatever you ask! And, by the way, are you and Kyle an item too now?" Mitzi had a huge smile on her face.

"Mitz, he is such a good kisser. I didn't think he was ever gonna get there, but when he did…" Violet cupped the phone and looked around to see if her mother was nearby. "I've never felt like I did last night. I thought I'd peed myself! Have you ever…" She looked around the room again. "…you know, done anything other than kiss before?"

"Yesterday. Before you guys came over, I have so much to talk to you about. So, so much." Mitzi whispered as if her mother was in the next room. Of course, she wasn't. "Vio, could you spend the night tonight? My mom is in Fort Walton…" She looked around again as if she would get caught. "You and Kyle could stay over. My mom isn't getting back until Sunday, early evening!"

"We'll talk when I can talk if you know what I mean. See you in about an hour and a half." Violet responded, almost as giddy as Mitzi.

20

Jay woke to the loud giggles of girls and the stomping across the wooden deck. He sat up quickly and walked over to the front room window and peeked through the shades.

The sun was coming up and he was surprised he had slept so late after looking back to the clock on the wall. Eight a.m. It wasn't like him to sleep past six. He was obviously losing his street sense now that he had a home. That fact annoyed him. It made him feel less in control of himself and his circumstances. He'd already began to feel way too beholding to Ben and Gina. Sure, they were great people and had done more than he could ever be able to thank them for—but had it been at the high price of giving up his freedom? He had begun to think so.

His mailbox seemed to be one of the first on the route, so he threw on some shorts and headed out to check his mail. He hoped his license would show up soon. Jay walked down his steps and spied a nineteen seventy Chevelle SS parked in the drive. It was bright red and had shiny chrome Cragar wheels, five-spoke. It was the kind of car he'd seen in magazines and always wanted. He knew only rich people and their spoiled snot-nosed kids could afford them. He admired the beauty and muscle the car sported and could only guess who the owner was. It had to be Kyle's. He'd watched Mitzi's friends enough to spot who was who and who could be trouble. Kyle, the kid with the longer hair and attitude, was the kid who could bring trouble. He could taste it in the air when he was around.

Jay opened the door to the mailbox at the road and spied an interesting envelope. *Could this be the news I've been waiting for?* "Florida Department of Motor Vehicles. About fuckin' time." He quickly tore open the envelope and opened the letter. It also contained a license. "Son-of-a-bitch! I'm a legal truck driver again!" The smile across his face was ear to ear.

Violet peered out of Mitzi's front room window just in time to see Jay doing a little shuck and jive dance on the street by the mailbox. "Hey, Mitz! Come look at your neighbor out here!" She giggled.

Mitzi ran over and saw Jay dancing oddly by his mailbox. "Well now, that's crazy isn't it?" She laughed but turned quickly to Violet. "Darrell's coming right? We're going to pick him up?" The energy was barely contained within her small body.

Kyle leaned over to Violet. "She's as crazy as her neighbor is out there doing the dance. I think she must have gotten the really potent part of the weed last night." He poked Violet and then grabbed her and pulled her into himself. He looked into her eyes and smiled. Looking back towards Mitzi, he continued, "Looks like we're in tonight! Book a room for two at the Mitzi B Inn." He grinned and squeezed Violet closer.

"Let's get the hell out of here and go pick up Chubbs and Darrell!" Mitzi squealed.

"Um, Chubbs..." Kyle paused. "...decided he didn't want to be a fifth-wheel. He opted out for today."

"But that makes our group incomplete!" Mitzi replied. "We have to find him a woman!"

"He's okay today. He said he was ready to do some fishing at the pier, anyway." Said Kyle.

"Let's go, let's go, let's blow this pop stand!" Mitzi squealed again as she jumped up and down.

They piled out through the front door with beach bags and towels in hand and as they hit the bottom step heading for the car, they bumped into Jay.

"Sweet ride! She's a seventy, isn't she?" Jay asked.

"That's right. 454 cubic inches of kick your ass." Kyle responded with a dare me, stare.

"Well, she's a beauty…" Jay grinned a toothy grin. "You kids be careful out there. Looks like a great day for the beach." He looked over at Mitzi. "Your mom sleepin' in today? Haven't seen her lately."

"Yeah, she's good, gotta go Jay." And they quickly piled into the car. Kyle fired his Chevy up with a twist of the key and gunned it into reverse to the street. After backing out and lining up, he revved up the motor and dropped the clutch, laying rubber in first gear and chirping the tires in second.

"What a dumb-ass rich punk. And little missy—your momma ain't home asleep—her car ain't here; just like yesterday and last night." He shook his head as he rounded the corner to his door. Something on the ground caught his eye. He stopped and bent down to pick up a little wooden square. As he got it in his fingers, he rolled it over and stopped dead in his tracks and turned a complete circle as he spied everything around him with a keen eye. Jay's smile he'd worn from receiving his great news had now morphed into an angry glare. He looked down at his palm once more to double-check what the tile he clutched said.

WHIP.

He slammed the door after entering inside. "Just who the hell put this here? Darrell? Do you really wanna play this fuckin' game?" He spoke aloud.

21

Darrell was quiet and showed less enthusiasm as he climbed into the back seat of Kyle's car. He smiled slightly at Mitzi and said hello, but he seemed to lack true excitement at seeing her.

Mitzi was obviously hurt by his lack of joy. She knew she probably deserved some reprimand, but she wasn't going to give up today. She knew what she wanted and she would show him throughout the day.

"You look good today, Darrell. Can we talk later?" Mitzi quietly asked.

"Last time we 'talked' it didn't turn out so well. You sure you really want to try that again?"

"Kyle! Stop the car!" Mitzi yelled.

"What the hell…?" Kyle began to answer as he lifted his foot off the accelerator.

"Because I fucking asked you to. I want out." Mitzi screamed and then leaned up and turned to Darrell. "I'm trying to fix things, Darrell. If you're going to be a jackass and play games, I want out. I'll walk the hell back home."

"Wait a minute, Mitz. I'm sorry." Darrell glanced up at Kyle in the rear-view mirror. "Keep going, Kyle, we're gonna be okay." Darrell reached over and put his hand on Mitzi's leg and pulled himself to where he was facing her directly. "I didn't sleep last night. I couldn't think of anything but why I shouldn't just stop feeling the way I do about you, and just kicking this shit to the curb." Darrell stopped and remained silent for an uncomfortable, few seconds. It was felt by everyone in the car. "Guess what? I'm not strong enough to do that. My desires to be with you overpower my common sense. I wanted to be able to forget you Mitzi Burks." He stopped again as he collected his emotions. "But I love you damn it, no matter who your father is or what he did to my worthless piece of crap dad. I love YOU!" Darrell plopped back around and into his seat. "There, I said it. I hope you care for me half as much as I care about you."

Violet broke the awkward silence by clapping her hands as if she just saw the best part of a movie and it moved her emotionally. "Now, THAT, is what I'm talkin' bout!" She paused and then looked at Mitzi. "Your dad is Sheriff Burks? Holy shit! How in the hell did I not know that?"

Mitzi leaned over into Darrell and reached up pulling his face to hers. She looked squarely into his eyes. "I love you back. Even more than before." She put her lips to his and kissed him deep as her hand dropped from holding his chiseled chin, southward to his lap, which quickly made his trunks fit tighter as her hand landed purposely where it did.

Kyle gunned the gas as they continued across the Big Bend Scenic Byway Coastal Trail Bridge toward St. George Island. Windows rolled down, hair blowing wildly, the sun shining brighter by the minute—life had become full of teenage excitement, angst and hormones racing.

It was still summer on the forgotten gulf coast and life just turned damned grandioso once again, just in an unexpected instant.

Kyle cranked up the stereo to the sound of Joan Jett and "I Love Rock and Roll," as he stepped on the accelerator and roared across the bay. They all sang, "I love rock and roll, so put another dime in the jukebox, baby...."

22

Joyce woke up with a smile. She experienced a wonderful evening complete with sweet dream-filled sleep. She left the balcony sliding door open so she could fall asleep to the sound of the waves rolling in. A sound she always loved. She listened quietly as she lay in bed. Joyce knew she shouldn't be daydreaming about her new boss, but, my oh my. He was handsome, smart, and seemed to be an extremely caring man who was passionate about his career of helping people. What middle-aged woman wouldn't let her imagination run a little amuck? Her daughter was about out of the nest. It would soon be her time to shine on her own like when she was young just starting out.

***

Jay's blood was mixing with anger and excitement. On one hand he just received the news he was waiting for. Hell, his partner Ben was also patiently waiting for this news. But on the other hand, his past was coming back to try and intimidate him.

But by whom? It had to be Darrell. Or maybe Sheriff Burks—the son-of-a-bitch that cheated with his wife when he was out of town? Someone else in town that knew the story. There can't be anyone else that knows about the punishment tiles but them. Could there someone else he wasn't aware of? One of the damn kids his neighbor was playing around with? The long-haired rich kid, or the fat one? The list was getting longer by the minute. He hadn't noticed the tile last night. Could the culprit be sneaking around in the middle of the wee morning hours to play a prank? Perplexed was the feeling rolling around in his mind, jumbling with other emotions, like revenge.

Jay reached for the phone after looking at his clock and saw that it was nine. Ben would be awake and he needed to share his great news. Finally, he could be a better part of the restaurant he was partnered in. He could once again have a purpose instead of laying around doing nothing but getting fat and lazy. He could drive again, another form of freedom.

"Hello, Gina! I haven't seen you or heard that sweet New York voice in a while!" Jay paused. "Yeah, if he's up and around—I have some great news for him, well, you too for that matter, partner!" Jay listened to Gina's response.

"Tell you what, I'll just head that way and give you two the news face to face. Is that okay?" Jay glanced at his license as Gina was talking.

"Yeah, I need to get cleaned up and then I'll be by for a late lunch—right, brunch in restaurant lingo! See you by eleven."

Jay hung up feeling a tad better as he headed to the bathroom.

I have a gut feeling it may be that little rich prick, Kyle. I'm going to keep a watchful eye on him. Not being able to let the tile he found leave his mind, he stared at it in his hand one more time. *Somebody thinks they can fucking judge me? I've beaten all kinds of better circumstances than this little pain in my ass.*

***

The beach was full, but Kyle found a good spot to park where they could walk to a more secluded place he knew about. He was new to the area, but before school had started, he was a regular to St. George and loved scouting for awesome spots to be more alone.

Kyle appeared to be the quiet, ruffian type, but he had an artistic side to him also. He played guitar and loved to write and paint. None of his friends knew this of course. He wasn't ready to share that side of him. He was enjoying the bad-boy image he'd presented himself of late.

He'd been the nerdy kid growing up. Pushed around and bullied by others. His growth spurt hit late and when it did, he shot up overnight it seemed. His parents one day looked at him across the table and remarked how he now suddenly looked stocky instead of thin.

Violet grabbed Kyle's hand and they took off running and playing in the surf. It was as if they were the only two there.

Mitzi smiled as she watched her best friends let the waves roll up and splash on them as they held hands. What were the odds that the two of them could find their boyfriends so close together time-wise?

Darrell noticed Mitz seemed lost in her thoughts. He walked up behind her and put his hands on either side of her waist and pulled her back until his torso was rubbing against Mitzi's warm sweaty back.

She brought out sexual urges and carnal lust. He felt like a wild bronco ready to bust out of his stall and frisk with the beautiful mare housed next to him. He was uncontrollable. He was untamed and it overtook most all his other thoughts. It grew quickly to the point he'd surrendered into the new brazen desires that had sprouted. Mitzi was a hormone injection to his system. She breathed life and energy into him but also an eerie comfort of familiarity. He liked the feeling, but it also confused him.

"Are we just gonna watch them? Or are we gonna make our own love story?" Mitzi reached behind herself and ran her hand between her bottom and his swim trunks, rubbing and gently squeezing.

"Mitz, you are the most sexual person I've ever met."

"Is that a good thing? You realize that you bring this out of me.

I feel like I know just how to touch you to get what I didn't know I needed. Does that make sense? I never had these desires before. A kiss was always enough. Now, with you, I feel like I have this constant thirst that needs to be quenched. The more I drink, the more I need filled." She turned quickly and pulled him in close, mashing her lower torso into his. "I'm addicted. And you are my only supplier. I hope you can keep up with my needs." She looked up into his eyes and smiled a devilish grin. "Keep me filled, Darrell. Forever."

The words she spoke should have scared him and he knew it. But, instead, it warmed his body, heart, and soul. A relief settled into his entire psyche. This must be what it felt like when you met your soulmate. He drank it in, like sweet strawberry wine. Darrell tugged at her hand and he led her to the surf where Kyle and Vio were.

"Hey, we're gonna head down the shoreline for a bit and do some talking. See you in a while?" Darrell hollered.

"Yeah, talk man, that's what you're gonna do!" Kyle and Vio both laughed. "See you in a minute then?" He laughed again as they turned and left footprints that quickly disappeared as the surf washed over them.

About a quarter of a mile down the beach Darrell noticed that there was really no one around. There was some driftwood piled that appeared to have been there since the last big storm several months ago. He led Mitzi over to it and spread his towel out in the middle of some branches. It felt secluded and alone. He looked at Mitzi and winked. "Welcome to my beach house, miss."

She answered, "What a fabulous view, sir. The sounds of the waves have a luring effect on me."

They both sat, their legs wet and the sand quickly stuck to their extremities. Neither one seemed to care.

"Did you bring protection?" Mitzi asked, trying not to spoil the mood.

"Um…" Darrell hesitated. "No, ma'am. I had no idea I would need that this trip. I was planning on going solo today. You see, my girl broke my heart last night, so…" Darrell looked into Mitzi's bright green eyes. "…so, I wasn't planning on winning her back today."

Mitzi let her hands wander over Darrell's body. She started at his chest and with the tips of her nails she lightly ran them around his nipples and then down to his belly button. She looked back into Darrell's green eyes with a wanton desire across her face. "I just don't know if I can resist you. Should I stop?" She playfully asked.

Darrell's body obviously answered her question by the arousal she'd caused by her light touches.

"Well?" She asked again as her fingers ran across the waist of his swim shorts, dipping lower and lower beneath the fabric.

"Mitz, you have so much control over me. I shouldn't tell you this, but…" Darrell reached for her hand. "I can't tell you no. It's not in my vocabulary." He tucked her hand deeper into his trunks as he sucked up his stomach to give her hand more room to maneuver deeper until she found her target.

The waves crashed harder onto the shore as the two of them coupled together in passion. The heat of the sun beat down on their fragile toned bodies, but they were oblivious of anything but pleasing each other.

"Oh, Darrell…" Mitzi moaned as she scratched her nails down Darrell's thrusting back, her legs flailing wildly behind him.

The sweat beads on his forehead danced in circles before letting go and falling onto Mitzi's body in various places.

Mitzi climaxed first and Darrell followed quickly after hearing her scream his name over and over. He rolled over onto his back in exhaustion. He was spent completely and fighting to suck enough air in to fill his emptied lungs.

Mitzi lay beside him saying "I love you, Darrell"—over and over as tears filled her eyes.

They both began to hear sounds of someone coming their way down the beach. Darrell struggled to lift his head up and between the scraggly driftwood to gain advantage of seeing who it could be. "It's Kyle and Vio." Darrell said. They both struggled to get their swimsuits back on over their sand encrusted bodies. They giggled as they struggled to pull them over their sticky and sandy flesh.

As Mitzi began to climb up, Darrell grabbed her neck and pulled her mouth to his. He drank in her sweaty and salty lips, licking them and driving his tongue deep into her mouth. His world so filled with passion he knew he would explode; only this time—he feared nothing would be left of him.

If he died at this moment, he would have at least tasted the gift of becoming one with his first love and soulmate. This world was suddenly his and he reveled in its bounty.

23

Jay hit the top step of Ben and Gina's home at exactly eleven-fifteen and knocked on the beautiful glass double-door with sidelights on either side. The siding was ocean blue and the wrap around porch and trim were bright white. A typical south Florida architectural beauty.

He began to walk around the covered porch to the back when the door opened and Ben greeted him with a huge smile across his face. "Jay! It's so good to see you." He reached out and took Jay's hand in his and shook it firmly, then pulled him inside the entry way. "I've been wondering how you've been this week. We are moving right along with construction! It's been what—a week and a half since you've done a walk-thru?"

"Yes sir. It's been just about that long. I've got good news for you today." Jay smiled with pride as he continued, "I've gotten my commercial driver's license reinstated! I'm ready to drive for you."

"Perfect! We've got a van and a small box truck picked out but were waiting to go look more serious at them with you. You'll be the man driving them, after all!"

Gina walked around the corner and waved. "Hey there, Jay! How are you?"

"I'm doing terrific, ma'am. You wear the sun well." Jay said.

"What's all this 'ma'am' business? It hasn't been that long has it? It's me, Gina. Remember?" She laughed out loud.

"I'm sorry. What I meant to say was that the sun looks very good on you, Gina. I've been missing the sound of New Yorkers talking, all us southern bumpkins down here…" He guffawed.

"Come on in and sit at the table, brunch is just about ready. I cooked some of those scrambled eggs you liked. Brown sugar added to taste!"

They sat around the sizeable oval table which overlooked the water through a large bay window. Gina stood ready to serve them from the several covered dishes that sat beside plates of fresh fruit.

"This looks and smells terrific, Gina. You've outdone yourself." Jay smiled as he inhaled the scent.

"Ben and I have been experimenting with different dishes to serve at the Big Apple on the Bay. "We're hoping you will like some of them, so be honest!"

"What would you like to drink, Jay? Coffee, tea, soda, whatever you like, I'll fetch it for you." Ben asked.

"Actually, some iced tea sounds delicious. I'll see if New York-style tea can keep up with the south!"

"Iced tea coming up!" Ben walked through the doorway into the kitchen.

Gina leaned over the table, cutting a lump of meat she'd just uncovered. She was concentrating on it as she sliced thin layers. Her breasts jiggled ever so slightly catching Jay's sight. He tried not to stare, to fight the urge to imagine them unclothed. He looked away.

"That's quite a view you've got here. I imagine you enjoy sitting out on the back deck on cooler evenings." Jay turned back to see Gina continuing to cut the meat. *Damn, Gina still looks incredible. She has the hottest body I've seen in a long time. She could compete with the young girls that my neighbor's kid brings around, any day—beautiful, tight body with just the perfect amount of jiggle.*

Ben headed back in, carrying a tray with glasses full of iced tea.

"Jay tells me he has his renewed license now." Ben looked at Gina as he set the tray down and handed their company an ice-filled glass of tea.

Gina looked up toward Jay from what she was concentrating on. "Awesome! It won't be long until the restaurant comes together for our grand opening! We're both scared shitless—I have to tell you."

"It's gonna do well, don't you worry," Jay reassured her.

"My brother is going to try to make it down for the opening! He said he's looking forward to seeing you again, Jay."

Jay chuckled. "I bet he's surprised I'm not doing time! I know I am!"

"Now, Jay. That's all behind you and forgotten. Exonerated! A new chapter in a new book."

"Thanks to the Good book, right?" Jay asked.

"Yes, sir! Still reading Ms. Cela's Bible she sent with you?" Ben inquired.

"You bet. Every day and most evenings. Interesting stories. You could say that I may not be as bad as some of those highlighted in the Good Book." Jay smiled.

"Okay, boys. I think we're ready. I hope you taste some new flavors across your pallet, Jay. I have my fingers crossed!" Gina grinned.

"This spread looks fantastic. I'm certain it will tickle my taste buds! It sure has awoken my sense of smell."

The three sat around the table, sampling the differently prepared dishes, and talking about the grand opening plans.

"Any lady friend you've met that you'd like to bring Jay?" Gina asked as she cut a piece of marinated steak to poke in her mouth.

Jay laughed. "Well, now, I'm not sure there is a woman left around here that hasn't heard the worst about me and is more than willing to cross to the other side of the street when she sees me coming."

Gina looked at him, thoughtfully. "Jay, that's awful. Don't kid like that about yourself."

"I wasn't joking, ma'am."

Gina looked over at Ben with a sad frown. She looked back at Jay. "I may have to see about fixing you up. Can I cut your hair again and trim your beard that's looking a bit woolly?"

"Gina! My gawd! We've been through this once already." He looked at Gina, who looked at Jay. There was silence for a split second before Gina burst out laughing.

Jay looked at Ben and began laughing, who followed.

"It's these damned sweet, scrambled eggs that did it!" Jay rattled.

A moment after the laughter ceased between them, they all shared a reflection of their not-so-distant past. It was apparent in each of them, the memory that brought laughter again, also reintroduced a sober moment. It was in each of their eyes as the silence overtook the table. They each exchanged glances between one another. It was suddenly awkward. There was no harm intended by any of it, but it appeared the scab of that shared experience was still just below the surface, and no one had dealt with it since they'd reached Apalachicola.

It was a couple of minutes before the conversation slowly started back up. No one even knew who was able to break the silence and turn it back into a pleasant but vague and distant conversation. It just happened.

Gina and Ben shared quick eye glances between them, and Jay kept trying different dishes and telling them how good they tasted. The smiles began to rebound, but the previous jovial chatter seemed to dissipate from the room.

When they finished the meal, Ben showed Jay the back deck outside, and then they walked around the covered porch toward the restaurant side. They both looked at the new structure, which was also southern styled and looked very much like Ben and Gina's home. Simple but elegant. The color a darker blue than their home, but very much like a twin, a maternal twin as such.

It didn't take long for Ben and Jay to decide when to view the vehicles and what the next steps were that Ben needed Jay's help to complete.

"I need to do more to earn my keep, Ben. I can't just fish all day and expect a paycheck."

"I know, Jay. I'm working on it. I remember you saying that as a boy you always wanted to have a boat and fish for a living. Would you be interested in fishing for fresh catch for the restaurant? I could maybe lease a boat, and you could drive and captain a boat for us?"

"I would consider that, Ben. It could be a dream come true. We talking one with a cabin I could liveaboard?"

"Let's keep our eyes and options open, Jay. Robert said the real estate agent has a buyer for my home in the Bronx. I should have some cash I could invest. I'd, of course, need to talk to Gina about it."

"Yes, sir, I understand."

<u>24</u>

The ride home was beautiful. They all saw the 'green flash' that Jay told Mitzi about. Of course, she hadn't let anyone in on who told her about it. She played it as if she'd read about it or heard something on the television.

The roar of the Chevelle's 454 held a steady low rumble as they crossed back over the Coastal bridge. The windows open, and their hair was blowing. Each couple was smiling and playing hand searches on their partners in the dark interior of the car.

Violet glanced back and caught Mitzi's attention. They shared brief smiles, each thinking about what was to come later in the evening to them. Violet's eyes showed excitement mixed with uneasiness.

Mitzi must have sensed her apprehension and nodded to her an assuring smile. She knew Violet was a virgin also. Well, Violet was anyway. She replayed her romantic scene in the middle of the driftwood mere hours earlier. Mitzi sighed. It was a sigh of satisfaction and anticipation. She opened her eyes to see Violet still looking at her. Violet then looked over at Darrell. His head was laid back and as her eyes travelled down, she saw his hand nestled between Mitzi's legs.

Violet, embarrassed, turned back toward the front window of the car and watched the bridge pillars disappear into a blur as they flew past them. She also felt a stirring inside from what she'd seen. She glanced at Kyle and imagined his hand where Darrell's was on Mitzi. Vio let her eyes close briefly as she replayed the scenario.

She suddenly felt the warm touch snuggling in between her legs as she quickly eyed Kyle and smiled.

Kyle reached over and turned up the radio when he heard a favorite new song playing. It was the Rolling Stone's new title, "Start Me Up." It had a driving beat and got all their adrenaline stirred up.

"You make a grown man cry!" They all sang together, their off-key notes mixing with the road noise and wind. They all waited for the last lines of the song and intuitively broke into unison singing it loudly as they also laughed, "You made a dead man come...."

***

Jay's day had gone well with Ben and Gina. Their food was good, they were still friendly to him. Sure, there was the awkward moment between them at the table, but who could expect their past to disappear altogether at once.

Gina's talk about finding him a lady friend stirred up his physical frustrations, reminding him of the sexual part of relationships he was missing. It reminded him of his days driving his truck before things changed between him and Cat. He remembered anxiously getting home after the week on the road and racing Cat to the bedroom.

There for about a year or so, their passion for sex was very driven. She called it making love, but he really wasn't sure he ever understood that term. The things they did were unbridled and uninhibited acts of lust. Was that really love? He always just thought of it as that harshest of words. Fucking. People threw the word 'love' around as if it were dime store candy. If there were such a thing in this world, it had become so watered down it no longer held the same value.

Whatever it was, he did miss those days. Thinking about those shared evenings with Cat and his long weeks away piqued darker memories of those times also. A sudden thought that Cat's locket brought to the front of his thinking.

She'd talked about when her and Darrell moved out of the farmhouse and into the Watkin's home.

Finding her locket as she packed things that they wanted to take with them. He now wondered about his shop. What happened to the things in his shop? He had things meant for his eyes only in there. Things he now became worried about their existence.

Jay was fortunate the law had set him free from some of his past. But there was much more to his story he'd rather keep tucked away. Dark things that needn't come to light. Things he'd kept buried in his past. He now wondered again just who in the hell put the tile in front of his door. A memory of the past that was coming back. Someone knew things. What more did they know? Just who the hell was playing this new game with him? Jay now knew one thing for sure. He had to go make a visit to the farmhouse and get a look inside his shop. There could be things in there that could haunt the fortunate position he now held.

He thought for a brief moment. Surely, not. Did Cat find anything she shouldn't have? Did she know part of his dealings without letting on? Or Darrell? The little bastard seed of Mr. bigshot Sheriff.

Jay's mind was snowballing with paranoia now. If someone had been in his house watching him, his pacing and widened eyes would be a scary scene. Amazing how one little memory can take a volatile person straight to the edge of the cliff.

That was where Jay was figuratively standing at this moment.

***

Mitzi quickly noticed Jay's lights were on. He was home. "I think we should keep it kind of quiet tonight on the way up and when we're inside. CJ might start shit with Darrell if we're loud."

"Don't worry about me, Mitz. I'll be okay."

"Fuck, CJ. I'll kick his tattooed ass down the stairs and into a coma!" Kyle said loudly.

"Guys! This is my house. My rules apply. I don't want any trouble. My mom will never leave town again this year if she smells one small scent of trouble going on. I'm serious. It's late anyway, and I thought we all had plans of ..." She tried to turn her stern face into one of sexual mystery. "...you know, turning in early. We can be rowdy and loud tomorrow."

Kyle threw his door open and looked over at Darrell. "I'm sorry dude, I know he's your old man and all, but I wish he'd cross me. I really fuckin' wish he would."

"Kyle! I'm serious, I won't let you come in ever again, if you don't shut up." Mitzi said.

"Okay, okay, okay. I hear you." He flipped his seat back up and reached in to offer help pulling Mitzi out of the back. "I'll be good. Just for you."

"I know you'll be good. I know it has nothing to do with me, though, and everything to do with what you're hoping Violet will do for you. Just keep it down." Mitzi gave him a stern look.

Kyle glanced up at CJ's window and noticed the silhouette of him walking back and forth. "What a nutjob." He said under his breath.

Once they got inside, Darrell was the first to speak. "I'm gonna take a quick shower, anyone need the bathroom before I go?"

Kyle turned the television set on and pulled Violet over to the couch. "We're good."

Mitzi answered, "I'm getting a beer out of the fridge and then do you need help washing your back?"

She smiled a devilish smile.

Darrell grinned. "Sure, see you in a minute."

The evening progressed uneventful. Darrell and Mitzi slept in her room while Kyle and Vio slept on a pallet made of blankets in the living room.

The night held a lot of passion between the two rooms.

***

Jay woke up early and headed out to the deck with a cup of coffee. As he walked through the doorway, his foot kicked a small object and it scooted across the deck boards like a stone skimming across the water when one skips it.

At first, he thought nothing of it and then the thought of the tile he'd found yesterday hit his thoughts.

He walked slowly with his eyes glued to the ground, seeing if he could spy what his toe had hit. He was about to give up and count it as a fluke when he noticed an object caught under the foot of a chair near the edge of the railing. Jay set his cup of coffee down and bent over to pick up the small square.

"Gawd damnit!" He said loudly. He looked at his palm and then scanned the area looking for footprints or a sign of any disturbance on the deck. As he scanned the area he walked near the corner where his steps from the ground came up.

"Son-of-a-bitch!" He said even louder. Jay was filled with anger as he saw a Mason jar laying on its side, the metal ring lid propped up against the jar. It had obviously been purposely placed. He looked at the tile in his palm again. DARK, was what it read. Jay's mind raced with questions. *I'll be damned if it didn't look exactly like the writing on the tiles I made in New York. But that jar and tiles had been thrown away. Or had they? Was Ben and Gina or one of them alone fucking with him? What reason would one or the other have to do such a thing? They seemed like everything was fine when I was over there?*

He by-gawd had to figure this out. There was no amount of reading Ms. Cela's Book that could solve this problem. He would have to unravel this mystery and rectify it himself. Soon! Before it got out of hand. He thought to himself. When I find out who the person or persons responsible for this are—I'll make them rue the day they were ever fucking born. Vengeance will be mine.

Jay's anger caused him to stomp across the deck as he headed back to his door. On the way he walked over to his coffee cup and picked it up. He held it to his mouth and gulped. When the temperature of the liquid it held, burnt his tongue, he hollered again, "Son-of-a-bitch!" After blowing on his tongue a second, he dumped what was left in the cup, then reared back with his hand behind him and drew forward, hurling the cup end over end until it hit and smashed into pieces on the road.

Jay slammed his door hard after crossing the threshold into his living room.

***

Vio woke up feeling the floor rattle for a second. Kyle roused also, looking down at the morning erection that was lifting the sheet in his view. He smiled and looked over at Vio, who had also noticed the tent that Kyle had pitched.

She leaned over and kissed him, reaching down under the fabric, and lightly touched him. Vio gazed back up into his blue eyes. "Wow, just wow."

"You're holding everything I got, whatcha gonna do about it?" He grinned bigger and reached down grabbing her hand with his grip.

"Hey, you two." Mitzi quietly said as she walked into the room. "Was that you guys that made the walls rattle a second ago?" She was sleepy-eyed and rubbing her face.

Kyle held his finger to his lip, "Shoosh…" He ruffled his brow towards them. "Listen! He pointed towards CJ's part of the duplex. "I hear him stomping and cussing."

They all strained to listen.

Their faces began to match Kyles—that scrunched up look when you're perplexed.

They could hear Jay stomping and it sounded like muffled swearing.

"Somebody's having a melt down." Kyle grinned.

"Poor, Darrell," was all Violet could say.

Mitzi agreed. "I can't imagine the hell Darrell lived through with him. I don't know how he can even face that monster."

"I don't know how he keeps from killing him." Kyle interjected.

"Well, he tried to do just that—remember? The bastard is like a cat with nine lives." Violet said.

25

Joyce had never sat in on a deposition quite like the one she was attending with Ethan. She watched with amazement at the way he controlled the room and questioning, yet made the person being questioned feel at ease with him. She could see how he could squeeze things out of people before they really understood what they had admitted to—and still be smiling at him.

She sat quietly taking notes and writing down questions she would have him answer later, after the depositions were done.

All of this was over land and mineral rights on a piece of basically, swamp land. How could Ethan make something like arguing over swamp land sound so interesting?

Later, he would tell her it was about things possibly buried in that 'swamp land' that his client was concerned about.

She knew there was quiet savageness in the world and those that perpetrated those evils. She also knew that by our laws, you were presumed innocent until proven otherwise and everyone deserved fair representation and judgment. Being able to turn a blind eye was something she sometimes struggled with. Ethan would try to explain those things more thoroughly at the cocktail bar—again, later in the day.

Joyce knew one thing for certain after today. If she or some-one she cared for was ever facing criminal charges—she now knew who she would want representing them. It seemed that Ethan was ingenious in the entire process.

***

On the ride home, Joyce took her time and enjoyed the sight of the coast off to her right almost the entire trip home. She wrestled with her personal attraction to her new boss. She knew he also shared the attraction. Ethan all but laid it out like an opening statement. She enjoyed being pursued again like her younger days, but she now held the knowledge of what age can bring. She always preached "moving slow and thinking things through" to her daughter.

Oh, the mistakes she had made in her young days. She was certain most people held skeletons in their closets, but she could think of possibly more than her share in her past. Falling for the wrong guys, but blindly believing they would change. Or thinking that experimenting sexually was what every girl from her school did.

If momma only knew. It makes me wonder what I don't know about my Mitzi B. It also makes me wonder if I'll ever have to reveal any of my dark secrets to my little girl. She certainly hoped that would never be the case, although, she now worried about it as she was hashing out her thoughts and past while she drove home.

It takes so long to bury some things deep enough here in Florida. Things always seemed to float back to the surface around here.

She reckoned it was the same in other states too. Thinking of her darker past always made her feel somber about her mother and the way she treated her. She felt fortunate that Mitzi didn't treat her like she treated her mother. Mitzi and she were like best friends. She tried not to be too much of an old choke hold like her momma was on her.

She remembered revealing one of her most dreaded deeds that she was ever forced to own up to. There was no hiding a pregnancy in her day. She also remembered her momma telling her she would have to tell her daddy also.

Joyce quickly shook her head and realigned her focus on the road and scenery. There was no need to travel down that memory lane when she had such a beautiful path in front of her. She wondered if Mitzi had missed her. Had she just laid around and read books or watched television? Maybe had a girlfriend over so she wouldn't be alone? She'd left at roughly three p.m., so she calculated an arrival time of close to six-thirty. She'd take Mitzi out for dinner over at the Caper. Mitzi seemed to really like that place.

***

Jay was back out on the deck sitting in a lounge chair with Ms. Cela's book in his hands.

All of Mitzi's friends were gone and she lounged on the couch reliving the passionate moments with Darrell. She just knew she'd marry him one day not too far off. He was the man for her. No one could share the passion they felt together and not end up married and raising a family together. It just wasn't possible. She laid her head back on a pillow and closed her eyes. She'd opened the window earlier to catch the uncommonly cool breeze that was blowing in from the bay. Must be a storm coming. She could faintly hear the soft waves coming in. The sun was still up, but hidden somewhat with the thick puffy white clouds that lazily blew across the sky. They caused shadows to come and go through the blinds that were open slightly.

The quiet breeze took her back to where Darrell was lying beside her. He was running his hands across her belly and playing with the edge of her bikini. She knew what he wanted to touch. She ran her own fingers down to her panty line and let them softly dally across her tummy and then back and forth over the cloth that covered the spot Darrell had spent so much time playing.

It didn't take but seconds before her daydreams became acted out by her own hand. She parted her legs as she stretched herself out on the couch, adjusting her body so she could easily reach the spot that gave her pleasure. Continuing to rub her fingers back and forth she became more and more excited and focused on reliving her time with Darrell.

She imagined him doing the same and the thought brought on even more feverishness. Her hand pushed harder against her pelvis. Her fingers found their way underneath her panties. She began to moan with soft control at first, but as she continued, her moaning and sighs became less controlled and louder. She was too focused to realize just how loud she had become.

Jay's ears perked up, believing at first, he'd heard a bird of some kind, but upon fixating where the sound was coming from; he determined it was no bird making that sound. Birds cooed; they didn't moan. At least no bird he'd ever heard besides a chick. A chick that was enjoying something other than birdfeed.

Jay jumped up quickly, but quietly. He followed his intuition and cautiously edged up to the partially open window. He leaned in and peered through the shades just in time to see little young Mitzi pull her underwear down as she lifted her bottom off the sofa. Hiking her legs high into the air once her panties were past her butt cheeks; she then got one leg out and shook the other. The light fabric rolled down her leg like a horseshoe ringer around a stake. Mitzi lowered her foot and the panties slid off, landing on the floor beside her. She quickly closed her eyes and started giving herself pleasure. Jay couldn't believe what he was seeing. *Such a naughty girl.* He thought. *Such a wonderfully, sexy, naughty little tramp.* He lifted his head up momentarily looking around towards the Bay and the road, making sure no one was there to see him peeking. *Damn, why couldn't it be darker, so I wasn't so noticeable.* He had to concentrate on being quiet. Words of cheering her on or directing what he'd like to witness were sitting on the tip of his tongue ready to launch. There were other parts of himself ready to launch also. In unison with what he was watching. She appeared ready to blast off herself.

Jay knew he should leave. He realized his chances of getting caught were high. But what could she say? She couldn't tell her mom what he'd caught her doing. He reached down and moved his shorts giving himself room to breathe.

The clouds continued to darken the sun as the storm was blowing closer. The wind was cooling down quicker and as it blew the shades in Mitzi's window, they began to clatter. The sound didn't stop her from enjoying her actions. It seemed, if anything, to enhance them. Finally, as she drew very closely to climaxing, Jay could hold his words no longer. "Do it baby just scream and holler."

He quickly moved away from the window and he could hear the clatter of Mitzi jumping up. She quickly grabbed her clothes up and ran for the bathroom.

When Jay heard the door slam, he looked in one more time to see an empty couch and a pair of panties on the floor beside the couch leg. "Holy shit!" He said as quiet as he could. He quickly turned and headed back to his door. He opened and shut it silently as he let himself inside.

Had she managed to know it was him? Or was she so lost in herself that she might have thought she imagined it all? What should he do or how should he respond if she grew balls enough to confront him? He sat in a mental state of confusion for a few seconds. *Would she tell my little bastard son what he'd caught her doing?* That was when the evil grin passed across his bewildered face. *Maybe it was time all this quiet bullshit between us was over and out in the open. How long can we keep up this tired game of charades? Maybe I might just blurt out that I wasn't his "poppa" any fuckin' way.* Jay's nervous internal battle with his new situation continued to flood his thoughts. *Cat had been a cheatin' slut all along with sheriff Roy. That would put all this shit to an end. Yeah, if that hot little piece of strawberry fun says a thing, I'll just drop the hammer that'll shatter Darrell's world.* Jay's grin turned downward just a bit for a second. *Cat...just where in the hell would she fit into this? I'd always thought I'd like to give her another go, but shattering the little bastard's heart would put an end to that possibility.* Jay paced back and forth as the thoughts raced through his head. *Oh, the decisions to be made. All because Darrell's little young tart couldn't keep her hands outta her own panties. This game of chance don't even need a Mason jar...the ball was in "strawberry's" court.* He thought to himself. *She'll pick her own damn punishment.*

26

By the time Joyce got home, Mitzi was almost beside herself. The thoughts of Creepy Jay watching her through the window made her frantic. But what could she do? *If I told mom, I'll have to admit pleasuring myself. If I tell Darrell, he wouldn't be bothered about that part, but he would go ape-shit on his dad and as much as I'm certain he could take care of himself—the questions of how far it would go was dangerous. Should I just keep quiet?* The thoughts of even knowing CJ was in a room just the other side of the wall between them made her feel sick to her stomach. The idea of seeing him now—scared the crap out of her. Things were not ever going to be the same, again. Not that they were ever good.

Would CJ tell her mom when he was alone with her? *Oh, by the way Ms. Bonham, I was walking by and heard something in your apartment and peeked in to make sure everything was okay. I saw your daughter naked on your couch with her fingers where they shouldn't be.*

The thought made her queasy. She felt like a trapped rodent in the corner of the room who spied the cat on one side ready to pounce and a woman with a broom ready to flatten her into the floor on the other.

***

"Hi, Mom! How was your trip?" Mitzi spit out quickly.

Joyce sensed something was off just by her daughter's tone and demeanor. "Productive! And—Ethan is a very nice man. A real southern gentleman."

"That's great. I'm glad everything went well."

"You seem a bit off the mark tonight. Are you okay? Everything go okay here on your first time being on your own?" Joyce asked and then studied her daughter's response.

"Went great, Mom. Had Violet over and she spent the night—so I didn't have to be alone."

"I was hoping you would have a friend over. I completely forgot to mention it when I talked to you Friday. I'm glad you've found some friends so quickly." Joyce smiled. "Any run-ins with our neighbor?"

"No, not really. He said he hadn't noticed you around one of the times we crossed paths, but I said you were busy with work. I didn't let him know you weren't here."

"Good thinking, Mitzi. You do actually listen to the things I tell you!" Joyce walked toward her bedroom with her overnight bag and Mitzi followed watching to see if her mom noticed anything out of place.

"I have a test tomorrow in English, so I probably ought to get studying."

"I was hoping you were hungry like I am. Wanna head over for a quick bite at the Caper, before they close?"

"I guess I could eat. Sure!" Mitzi answered.

"Let me put a few things up from my bag so they don't wrinkle and then we'll head out."

"Okay, just holler when you're ready." Mitzi turned and headed for her bedroom, scanning the apartment one more time along the way for any signs of anything. She walked by the couch and suddenly noticed her pair of panties, that had been kicked partially underneath by the leg. She looked back toward her mom's room and then quickly bent over and grabbed them.

Joyce poked her head out of her door. "Hey, Mitzi—would you

grab me a Coke from the fridge, please?" She saw her daughter stuff something into her pocket.

Mitzi turned back toward the kitchen. "Sure, Mom. From the can or in a glass with ice?" She nervously smiled at her mom as she passed her on the way.

"Can, since we're heading out." Joyce looked at Mitzi as she went into the kitchen.

Mitzi felt a cold chill like a child getting caught with their hand inside the cookie jar after being told not to get one.

Joyce headed back into her bedroom with a parent's look of concern across her face, but said nothing.

At the Caper, the two ate their meals and talked about the weekend.

"I went to the beach on Saturday with Vio and her boyfriend. We went to about the same spot you and I were at."

"Is this boyfriend the one who drove, or your girlfriend?"

"Kyle drove, but he's a safe driver. It's okay, Mom, remember—I'm not a child anymore, I'm almost nineteen."

"A very protected nineteen, Mitzi. You haven't really been out in the world alone, much."

Mitzi poked some salad in her mouth to keep herself from smarting off to her mom. It was a defensive measure that she had perfected due to her tendency to answer her mom back with sarcasm. She could pull it off sometimes as her brand of humor, but at other times—it just unleashed tension between them.

"How's your salad? Taste a little like leafy sarcasm?" Joyce smiled.

Mitzi returned the smile and looked over at the door when the sound of the bell rang. *Oh, my gawd! Vio, Kyle and Darrell just walked in! What the hell was going to happen now?*

Darrell saw Mitzi at once and gave her a wink which she nervously ignored and looked away quickly. She coughed into her arm choking on her salad.

"Are you okay, sweetie? Your color changed across your face. Can you breathe?" Joyce started to get up and pat her on the back.

"I'm okay, Mom—something just went down the wrong tube."

"Hey, Mitz—are you okay?" Darrell asked with a concerned tone.

Violet rushed over to Mitzi's side. "Hey, girl…" She touched Mitzi's shoulder and leaned down. "…you that choked up to see your best friends? She laughed.

Wiping her mouth with a napkin, she cleared her throat. "Hey, guys. No, Vio, I just swallowed a piece of salad that tried to go down the wrong way. What are you guys up to?"

"Grabbing a quick bite. I need to regain my strength from all that—swimming this weekend." Darrell answered with a wink from behind Joyce's back. "Is this your mom?" He quickly followed up.

Joyce turned her head to get a look at who was talking. "So, you must be Kyle?" She asked.

"No, ma'am, I'm Darrell, Kyle's good friend," he answered as he threw his arm around Kyle. "This is Vio, Kyle's girlfriend."

Mitzi's face began turning beet red.

Joyce looked over at Mitzi and then continued, "So what does this make you, Darrell?" She calmly asked.

"Um…" There was a brief awkward silence. "…I'm guessing Mitzi hasn't talked much about me?"

Joyce looked at Mitzi and then toward Darrell who was now moving around into her view. "No, actually I haven't heard a word about you, Darrell. I'm guessing there's a story that comes with you?" Joyce cocked her head with an eyebrow raised. "One that I am very interested in hearing." She turned back to Mitzi and gave her an irritated look with her forehead wrinkling up. "Pull up some chairs and feel free to share a meal with us."

"Mom, we're about done eating, we don't need to do this right now." Mitzi said quietly, almost under her breath.

"But I want to meet your friends and get to know them, sweetie." She gave her daughter a sarcastic smile as if she enjoyed returning her daughters normal ridicule before she was able to dole it out. "Really, kids, grab a seat."

Kyle pulled out a chair for Vio and then sat next to her, leaving an open seat by Mitzi.

"Is it okay if I sit here, Mitz?" Darrell asked sheepishly.

"It's a free country. I reckon you can sit wherever you like. My mom made that clear." She gave her mother a scornful look. *Oh, this is gonna be fun—not!*

"So, tell me, Darrell—have you lived here long?" Joyce asked.

Mitzi rolled her eyes and poked another bite of salad into her mouth. She avoided looking at Darrell, wondering, but too afraid to see what his disposition was. *The interrogation has now begun. This is exactly why my mother knows nothing about you, Darrell. And when she finds out that you're Creepy Jay's son—well, that is when the inquisition will get worse. Much worse.* She mocked the conversation to herself.

"I've lived here all of my life, ma'am." Darrell answered.

"All of your life, hmm. So, are you a senior also?" Joyce asked.

Mitzi shook her head. *Here it comes, I can almost feel the heat coming off the bright light of the interrogation lamp directed at him, afraid of how he may answer.* Mitzi thought.

"Well, Mitzi certainly knows how to pick a handsome young man." Joyce smiled as she watched Darrell's face begin to redden. "It looks like you two share a matching skin tone and your hair color is even kind of close. Yours has more strawberry…" She looked into Mitzi's eyes. "… and yours lighter blonde, not so much red." She looked over at Darrell. "You make a cute couple, which is what I am supposing you two are? The mom is always the last one to know these things." She looked at the two of them and smiled. "I know, my Mom was always the last to find out such things on me!"

It appeared to Mitzi, that her Mom had decided to cut the line and let the fish on the hook escape for the moment. It wasn't like her. Wasn't she going to ask his last name or anything? Not that she was complaining—just dumbfounded.

The rest of the meal was calm and friendly. Joyce laughed and joked with Mitzi's friends and even Mitzi appeared to let down her guard as she glanced over and slightly up at Darrell. They shared a smile of relief together.

While Mitzi's mom's attention was on Vio and Kyle, she nonchalantly reached into her pocket under the table and pulled out her panties she had tucked in earlier. She nudged Darrell's leg and then leaned over to whisper to him.

Darrell leaned down putting his ear into shot of Mitzi's whisper.

"Here's a little memento for you. Just put it in your pocket and look later when you're alone. Been thinking of you," she whispered at a very low volume, then pulled back and smiled.

As Mitzi and her mom left the restaurant, leaving her friends behind, she almost dreaded the short walk home. *What would be the topic, hmm, I know exactly, and I don't want to have that discussion.* It took almost a quarter of a block down the storefront sidewalk for her mom to break into the talk she'd foreseen.

"Your boyfriend seems very polite and nice. I of course, wish I would have found out about it from you." She glanced over at Mitzi. "I guess you know now for yourself what I was talking about when I said it was a small town. Not many secrets held long in this little burg."

"I didn't want you to freak out, Mom. He's a special guy and I wanted time to see where it would lead, before I had to face your barrage of questions."

"Am I really that bad? I think I showed great strength in holding back and instead was just being civil." Joyce defended.

"Mom! You are wanting to be an attorney—of course you're THAT bad! You were, however, un-commonly gracious with the inquisition tonight. And I thank you for not making Darrell too uncomfortable or shining your bright light too deeply into his eyes. And of course, curtailing his placement in front of the firing squad!" Mitzi tried to refrain from letting her smile show. "I'm not sure he even really felt like one of your versions of a defendant in court. You didn't use big legal words or accusatory baited questions at all. I'm surprised, and I'm kind of proud of you." She looked over at her mom and lightly bumped her in the arm. "Is this you recognizing that I'm closer to being a full-fledged adult than I am a helpless child?" Mitzi asked.

Joyce leaned toward her daughter and placed her arm around her shoulder, drawing her tighter to herself as they meandered home. "This is me noticing that you've been a pretty responsible young lady now for quite some time. It's me giving you some breathing room as you get older, while I fight my urges to overprotect you. It's not easy as a parent—and sometime in your far, far off distant future—you will find that challenge out for yourself! A long, long time away from this moment."

"Okay, Mom. You've made your point. I love you!"

"And I love you, sweet Mitzi B. With all of my heart."

27

Jay noticed Joyce and Mitzi leaving earlier once she'd gotten home. He went out on the deck soon after to enjoy the evening moon over the bay. He needed the calming effect after wondering just how little strawberry-blondie would react once mommy got home. He was thinking about just putting all this BS out in the open for all to see. *I'm tired of Darrell thinking that I was his dad. I'm also tired of playing the fishing buddy game with Gabriel and listening to his so-called words of encouragement and fatherly advice of how to interact with my son; the man just doesn't know the truth.*

Jay spoke out loud, "There were three people in this world that had reached or came close to reaching my 'spiritual' side, and Gabriel, sir, you are not one of them. Ms. Cela, Ben, and Gina are the only ever to come close." He held his tie to Ms. Cela in his hands right at this moment, and he looked down at her handwriting off to the side of Isaiah's verses. Jay read aloud, "I have swept away your offenses like a cloud, your sins like the morning mist. Return to me for I have redeemed you. Verse 44:22."

Ms. Cela's handwriting next to it was—"The lord will wipe away every sin you ever did imagine, like it never got done. Believe and repent."

Jay dropped the book into his lap and he looked out at the beautiful puffy clouds moving through the moonlight over the bay. He thought to himself. *Ms. Cela would love this view tonight. I wished she was sitting next to me, talkin' her talk, and making me feel like there truly was hope. Ben and Gina tried, but I'd let myself get too dark in my thoughts about Gina. It dirtied my goodness when I was around them. Ms. Cela, though, she was still angelic.*

His thoughts were broken by the sounds of footsteps coming up his neighbor's staircase. A split second of nerves hit him. That was unusual. He generally felt no sense of alarm. The women neighbors were up to the top before he could manage to move. He tried to keep from looking at them, as if he would be invisible, but Joyce hollered out to him. He first acted as if he didn't hear them, and she hollered again.

"Good evening, Jay. The moon certainly is beautiful tonight." Joyce spoke.

Jay slowly turned and nodded, "Yes ma'am, it is. It's a nice calm night so far. I smell a storm brewing though."

"You can actually smell a storm coming?" Joyce asked as she inserted her key into the door.

"Yes, ma'am. My nose can smell things other people don't seem able to pick up." He smiled awkwardly and eyed Joyce's little strawberry tart. Daring her to say something about their earlier moment of sharing."

Mitzi felt a cold chill and pushed past her mom through the open door. "Come on, Mom, let's get inside."

"I'll have to listen to this story another time, Jay. It's late and tomorrow is a brand-new Monday."

"Yes, it is. I get some new wheels tomorrow. Got my license again, finally. I've missed being able to drive—I made my living driving over-the-road for many years."

"Congratulations! You be careful out there. G'night." Joyce stepped through the doorway as Mitzi pulled on her arm.

"Don't talk to him so much, Mom. He scares me." Mitzi spoke in a hushed voice.

"What happened to you? You gave me a hard time for wanting

to talk in hushed tones for fear he'd hear us?" Mitzi's mom asked.

"He just creeps me out lately. I feel like he's spying on us all the time."

"Mitzi B, maybe he's just lonely. I don't ever see anybody going over to visit him." Joyce responded.

"If you did see somebody go in..." Mitzi paused for a few seconds. "...they'd probably come out in pieces, neatly wrapped in butcher's paper and plastic bags."

"Mitzi B! That's enough of that creepy talk!"

"Creepy is correct, Mom." Mitzi mocked a shockwave of fear pouring through her body before taking her hand and making pretend stabs into her heart and neck as she slowly staggered toward her room. The room that had more than likely very little dead air-space between hers and—Creepy Jay's.

Jay relaxed back into his lounge chair. *It appeared little strawberry, wasn't up to letting mommy in on their little secret just yet.* He was still rolling the idea of sharing his thoughts of who Darrell's real father was with him. He was ready to be a full-time empty nest with no responsibilities to anyone, but himself.

28

Sheriff Burks despised Mondays. He dragged his uniformed ass up to the door slowly and gave it a tug open. "Morning, Mary Lou," was the only response he could muster as his starched pant legs swished together with every step he took.

"Morning, Sheriff." Mary Lou responded. It was the ritual, almost a game between the two. Who could say the least number of words on a Monday morning?

Sheriff Burks grunted. *I'll be damned if she didn't win again. It ain't fair she's got a damned two-word name.* That was the only thought that echoed in his head. He had other thoughts that were hounding him ever since he'd found out the ex was living in town again, and with the damn daughter he barely knew. He knew he was going to have to go see them soon before it was just a damned uncomfortable bump-in at the Piggly-Wiggly store or bank or what-not.

He sat down at his desk, still huffing under his breath, bitching about his misfortunes. He just couldn't believe his ex was not only living here, but working for that snake of a lawyer Ethan fucking Kendrick. What was the point of him risking his and his men's lives arresting druggies and cons, if that prick was just gonna get 'em released before the cell door slams shut. Bullshit!

Burks drew in a deep breath and exhaled rather noisily through his nose. He was now hoping that no more of his past was going to begin re-appearing also. The ex was enough. Dealing with Darrell and Jay had been nightmarish. This past shit needed to stay buried where it was left. He sure as hell didn't need his wife to know any of this crap that was going on. She'd have his ass for sure.

He suddenly wished he still had some 'trustworthy' deputies he could count on. Like the good ole days. These new young punks didn't understand about covering for each other. Oh, if the swampy bogs could talk. The stories they would tell. Thank gawd for gators and other creepy shit out there that help a guy bury a past.

Burks picked up his phone and when Mary Lou answered, he gave her four simple short words. "Connect me with Kendrick." He instantly dropped the receiver back down and dug out a toothpick from his top drawer while he waited for Mary Lou to get back with him. He knew he'd beat her this time on the word game. No way she could beat four when she buzzed him back.

His phone rang and he picked it up without saying a word. It was Mary Lou and he knew it.

"Kendrick, Line two," was all she said.

Damn bitch beat me again! After cussing his secretary in his head, he picked up the receiver and pressed line two. "Ethan, you SOB I hear you have a new employee. Hope you have better luck with her than I did." He chuckled.

"Sheriff Burks, what can I do you for today?" He responded.

"Well, now, I just thought I'd drop a congratulations to you once I heard the thrilling news. I've been too busy trying to hunt down criminal types and drug lords to drop by lately to catch up." Roy smugly smiled to himself. "I hear you hired Joyce and I thought you might need some words of warning or encouragement from someone in the know about her. She can look like a swan…" He kicked one boot up on his desk. "…but she can be a python, sure as shit." He picked at his teeth with the toothpick again. "You know, personality traits that you would be clueless about." He chuckled again with no immediate response from Ethan. "Traits that take time to learn, if she lets you live long enough anyhow." He chuckled. "Anyways, I meant for Mary Lou to call Joyce, not to bother your busy schedule. All that defending the hardened cons and crooks that my boys apparently waste the taxpayer's dollars apprehending here in Franklin County." Another grunt and chuckle could be heard from Roy. "Could you patch her through to me? We haven't had the pleasure of gettin' together yet and she's been here a whole month or so I hear."

"Well, Roy, I do hear Joyce's daughter is as pretty as she is? I suppose that pretty much seals the deal that she's obviously not from your loins as everyone's been told. But I'll have her call you just as soon as we hang up. I think the lady deserves more than a thirty second warning that a piece of her old luggage is trying to track her down." This time Ethan let out a guffaw. "I may even offer her a stiff drink of some seventeen-year-old scotch I've been saving for a special occasion. You just hang by your phone for a little while and if the lady wants to return this call, I reckon your end will ring. By the way, you need to come out to the house again one of these days and talk 'old times' again. Have a blessed day, Sheriff."

"One quick question for you to let mull in that brain of yours, Ethan…" Roy sat up from his reclined position in an old wooden chair. "…Does she remember you? Does she remember what you did—because I think if her memory was jogged a bit—she just may have a different feeling about who she was working for—don't you think?"

CLICK.

29

Joyce decided not to rush into a call-back with her ex. He hadn't wasted any of his time trying to call me or our daughter back to apologize for being such a dick. He can just wonder why I'm not rushing to kiss his ass like I used to. "The nerve of that crass piece of..." She took another sip of the scotch over ice. "...piece of work." She shivered a bit from the stiff drink and then smiled at Ethan. "Sorry, I about let my evil side show."

"I can't imagine you having one of those. I also can't imagine what you ever saw in Roy Burks." Ethan said.

"What can I say? I was young and foolish. All my girlfriends were getting married and pregnant—or maybe it was actually pregnant and then married..." She sipped from the glass a little slower this time. "...and I guess I thought maybe if I didn't take the only one in line, I'd be left out?" Joyce shook her head. "I still got left out, only with a new baby on the way. He didn't stick around for long, and I'm fortunate that he didn't. So is Mitzi. It's just harder trying to explain that to a little girl that didn't have a daddy for the father-daughter dances or birthdays and Christmas." She looked down at her drink and then up toward Ethan. She caught him either admiring her legs or deep in thought. She wasn't sure. She knew which one she was hoping for. "I'm sorry I'm boring you with this messy past."

"Not at all, Joyce. I just didn't want to patch you through to him, without the option and advantage of having a shot of scotch, first!" Ethan playfully laughed. "Would you be up for dinner tonight? You could bring your daughter if you would like?" He looked at her with comforting eyes. "Or we could use it as a working dinner if that is better? I'm all yours either way if it fits into your schedule for this evening?"

"Actually, I just found out that my daughter has a new beau, so I'm fairly certain she would rather be with him." She smiled with a bit of nervous uncertainty. "Maybe a working dinner? Where would we go where we could do that? I hear the Big Apple on the Bay is nearing completion, but not quite there, yet."

"My house at six? I can either pick you up or give you directions, your choice."

"I don't want you to bother picking me up, especially if you're putting something together. I'll just drive out."

"It's a bit out of the way. I would be okay with you following me there after work, if you're comfortable?"

"Well, I guess I could do that. Mitzi made it all weekend without me. Again, she will probably be thrilled. Maybe at lunch, I'll run home and leave a note and bring something to change into?"

"Something comfortable and casual!" Ethan said with a victorious smile. "My day's looking brighter already, Joyce!"

"Mine too, Ethan."

30

Life is usually slow motion down on the forgotten Gulf Coast. That's what Joyce had always heard. She no longer believed in that fairy tale. Life was speeding right along for not only her—but her Mitzi B, also.

She knew she had always preached to take things slow. The signs in her head told her to do just that—but her heart was screaming to throw caution to the wind while she was young enough to enjoy it and keep up.

Later in the afternoon, when Joyce came back to the office, she found a note with Ethan's address written down on a map, with an area on the coast circled. The town was Carrabelle. On the note was a quick explanation that a meeting had come up and he wouldn't be able to lead the way. It should take her about forty minutes since she didn't know the way and if she liked, she could bring an overnight bag to head back into the office in the light of day instead of the dark of night. He wrote he was sorry, but didn't want to back out of the dinner invite.

He would be there ready to serve by six-thirty and she could leave the office early. He also noted where the spare key was if he ran a tad late or she got there early. 'Make yourself at home as if it were yours. Drinks are in the bar fridge.'

"Well, this is an interesting surprise." Joyce said quietly under her breath.

Joyce walked out to Addison's desk. "I hate to bother you Addi…" Joyce appeared disheveled. "I'm supposed to have a working dinner tonight out at Ethan's home in..." She looked at the note. "...Carrabelle?"

Addison smiled, "Yes, a beautiful home, right on the beach! It's lovely. I've been there a couple of times. You are going to love it. In fact, you won't want to leave!"

"So..." Joyce was afraid to go on. "...everything will be...."

"Oh my, honey. No worries at all! He's a gentleman, I assure you. You're safer out there then crossing the road here in town. I promise. Enjoy your dinner, he's quite the cook!"

"Okay, Addi. You've put my mind at ease..." She smiled and then gave a quick look of fright. "...you won't say anything will you?"

Addi pinched her fingers together and ran them across her lips as if zipping them up tightly. "Not a word, Joyce. Go enjoy! I bet you'll eat out on the deck that overlooks the beach!"

Joyce grinned and headed back into her office. She closed the door and sat down at her desk. She closed her eyes for just a second to gather her thoughts. She said aloud, "Pardon my French." Then she quickly went back inside her head. "What did I do in this world to deserve to be treated so grand?" Now, she almost wished she had asked her daughter to go. *Spend the night? Was this just dinner? Or dinner, drinks, and sex?* Her mind began playing out the entire scenario. She pictured Ethan. He was good looking. He was probably late forties or very early fifties. Salt and pepper hair with even lighter close-cut beard. She imagined his physique to be on the muscular side. He certainly didn't appear to have an ounce of fat on him. His clothing was always current and sport-casual. He looked as if he was an outdoorsy man who probably enjoyed boating and fishing and hiking. Swimming or maybe even surfing?

What the hell she thought to herself. *I'll admit it. He's a dream. Just what did I do to deserve all of this? Where's the cameras someone will point to and say, You're on Candid Camera!"*

31

Mitzi opened the door to her apartment and threw her bags on the couch. She stopped briefly and looked at the couch, then turning to look at the window. *I sure gave CJ one hell of a show with a front row view.* Her stomach rumbled and she suddenly felt as if she may vomit. She rushed out to the kitchen to get a drink of water, and that is when she noticed the note pinned on the refrigerator with a magnet.

Sorry, honey, another unexpected trip for work. I should be home by dinner tomorrow night. There is a casserole in the fridge you can reheat.
I love you,
Mom
P.S. I'm in Carrabelle, Fl about forty minutes east.

Mitzi wadded up the note after reading it. Part of her was happy to have another free night—the other part of her was pissed that she was now playing second fiddle to her mom's work, and part of her was concerned about this Ethan guy, who was her mom's boss. *Was he really working her? Or was he playing her for something else?* She wanted to meet Ethan, that was for certain. *When Mom got home, they were going to have a talk about this new—situation. In the meantime, though, the hell with the chicken casserole!*

Mitzi picked up the phone and rang up Vio.
"Hello?"

"Vio! Guess what?" Mitzi questioned.

"Your mom is gone again overnight? Ha, ha."

"Yes, she is!"

"Get outta here! You're shittin' me."

"I most certainly am not. Call Kyle and have him call Darrell. Let's meet at the pier in an hour to make plans." Mitzi said.

"You got it, girl. See you at the end of the pier."

***

After hanging out together at the pier and eating at the Caper, the foursome headed back to Mitzi's. The sky was dark as they pulled into the drive; Vio swore she saw Chubbs silhouette running off behind the apartment building.

"Hey, look at the guy running off!" said Vio. "It looks like Chubbs."

"No way, that guy's too small and way too fast!" echoed Kyle.

"Did anyone mention to him that we were meeting up back here?" Asked Mitzi.

"No, I haven't seen much of him. I think he's mad or his feelings are hurt. You know, he's got no girl, so he feels left out." Darrell chimed in.

"We have to help that boy!" Vio said. "I can think of one or two girls, especially if he'd try out for the football team."

"It's our senior year and summer practice is over, Vio. Ain't no coach gonna take an untrained, never-played a game a day in his life rookie!" Kyle chuckled.

"I just wonder what he was doing here? Why was he coming to see me?" Mitzi asked as she crawled out of the backseat.

"Grab the beers Darrell! I need an ice-cold brewski—it feels like someone draped a moist wool blanket on top of me!" Said Kyle.

Mitzi began stomping up the stairs toward the door.

"Don't you want us to be quiet, Mitzi?" Asked Vio.

Mitzi glanced over at Darrell and then looked at Vio. "Nope, fuck him, this is my house. I don't care what he tells my mom, she's out probably doing the same thing, but with her boss." She looked back at Darrell to check his reaction. "Besides, we're eighteen and free-will, of-age adults now. We can drink beer, stay out, and make love all we want!"

"Yee haw, gawd bless the U.S. of A and the Florida state liquor laws!" Hollered Kyle. "Hey, Mitz—whose white van is that on your crazy neighbor's side of the drive?"

"It's CJ's. His boss got it for his job. He tried to tell me this morning on my way off to school. As if I gave a shit." Mitzi responded.

"He's got a job? I thought he just hung out here or fished all day at the pier." Answered Kyle.

"Let's just skip the CJ talk. I don't wanna hear it. Let's crack some beers and play some cards or something." Said Darrell.

"Strip poker?" Inquired Vio.

They all laughed, but no one instantly hollered out no.

"Sorry, Kyle, but there's only one guy I wanna see naked. And it doesn't take him losing at cards to get there!" Mitzi laughed.

"I dunno, Mitz—I wouldn't mind taking a peek at Vio in her birthday suit!" Darrell laughed as he eyed Mitzi, who reached over and slugged him in the chest. "Just joking, sweetie. Your hot little package works just fine for me!"

"Your package is perfect too, baby." Mitzi quickly answered back.

***

Jay heard the rebel-rousing kids tromp up the stairs. He put his usual book down on the table and sauntered to his door. *It had been quiet all evening and now the rowdies were home. Just where the fuck was little strawberry's mom at? Things were changing around here and change never brings anything good.* Jay's mood was harsh and his thoughts were not pleasant. He opened his front door and stepped out. It took no time at all to spy the small wooden tile on the deck just steps from where he stood. He bent down and picked it up, not having to look too closely to see what was scribed on the front in black, just like the other two.

KILL.

Jay squeezed his fist holding the tile as if he could shatter it into pieces with his grip. *This game was gonna by gawd stop. I won't have some little shit playing games with me anymore*! He thought as his blood boiled, turned and went inside, walked over to a kitchen drawer and opened it. There he stared at the other two tiles and then picked them up. He looked blankly for a minute while his mind raced. His heartbeat thumped loudly inside his body. He could feel the rage growing in the veins on the sides of his temples. Perspiration dripped down his forehead and into his eyes, causing them to sting from the salt. He began pacing back and forth. Words of fury were screaming inside his brain. He wasn't sure if he was echoing them from his lips or not. His calmness that the Good Book he'd been reading had given him was now a very distant past in the matter of mere seconds. Jay turned toward the door and threw it open, not bothering to close it as he quickly rounded the corner to his neighbor's door.

BAM, BAM, BAM. Jay pounded loudly. "Open the fucking door! I know you're in there Darrell, you little bastard. BAM, BA….

The door flung open and there stood Darrell, with Kyle behind him. The two girls cowered in the corner by the kitchen, each holding a sharp carving knife.

"What the hell do you want, you crazy asshole?" Darrell yelled.

Kyle squared his shoulders as if to send the signal that game-time was about to begin.

Jay drew his closed fist back and then with the craziest gleam in his eyes, he brought his fist toward Darrell in slow-motion as he simultaneously turned his wrist upward and very slowly opened his clasped fingers out to reveal the wooden tiles. "Why the fuck are you leaving these at my doorstep? Do you really wanna go back to the beginning?" Jay stood wild-eyed, waiting for Darrell to respond. Jay moved his palm in such a way that the tiles danced a slow hypnotic waltz in front of Darrell.

"Step your crazy ass back, before I finish what I failed months ago. What Billy failed years ago." Darrell stood firm and Jay looked down toward his crotch as if to watch a wet spot grow bigger, which didn't happen.

"I see you've finally got a handle on your little problem." Jay guffawed as he continued to glare at Darrell.

Kyle stepped forward in a challenging manor toward Jay. "You better run back home, old fuck. If you don't—we're gonna see if angel's wings will help you as we throw you the hell off this deck." Kyle stepped even closer to Darrell and began to edge around him.

Darrell put his hand out to stop Kyle. "I got this, brother." Darrell looked back at his Poppa. "I don't know where or who has given you those reminders of your evil fucking ways—it wasn't anyone here and even if it were—you should take heed. Nobody wants you around here. Nobody gives a shit if you live or die. My Mom doesn't, this town doesn't and I certainly don't." Darrell broadened his shoulders and stood taller as he poked his finger in his poppa's shoulder to accentuate each word he stated. "Go the Fuck away. Runaway, like the cowardly piece of shit both you and I know you are. Last warning, old man. You don't scare me anymore. I'd just as soon kill you right now, right here."

Jay watched Darrell's body language. He knew the boy had changed. He'd grown up and put away childish things. He'd grown muscle and balls. He realized one thing as he stood there confronting Darrell and his friend. He knew he'd lose tonight. It wasn't the time nor place, tonight.

"This isn't over, Darrell. Not by a long shot. You and your friends better watch your step. Like a wolf who's hungry, I'll be watching." He looked over at Mitzi, who was shaking as she clutched the knife. He gave her a quick wink. "Yea, I'll be watching you, strawberry." Jay backed away and grinned a devil's grin as he tossed the tiles onto Mitzi's floor. As Jay turned to walk back to his door, he began singing Blondies hit, 'One Way or Another.' "One way or another…I'm gonna gitcha, gitcha, gitcha. One way or another…." The last thing they heard a minute later, was Jay's door being slammed. It felt as if the entire building shook.

"I'm sorry Darrell, but that is one loosely wired and faulty circuit. A real piece of twisted, fucked up, waste of air." Kyle said.

"I'm sorry guys. I'm sorry you had to see this." Darrell replied.

Mitzi dropped the knife on the counter and ran over to Darrell, grabbing him and nestling tightly. She was shaking like a leaf. "I'm sorry, baby. I'm so, so sorry."

Vio stood staring blankly until Kyle made his way over and carefully took the butcher knife from her quivering hands.

"He's gonna kill us. He's gonna wait until we don't see it coming—and he's gonna kill us." Vio repeated the statement over and over as Kyle held her tightly.

Ten minutes later, they all heard a motor start, followed by screeching tires headed away, down the street.

Darrell peered out through the blinds. "Van's gone."

32

Chubbs had slowed his run down to a tired walk. His out of shape body poured sweat from every fold in his belly. He was tired and sticky. *Maybe this was a stupid idea. Those guys should take care of their own problems. Kyle is a bullshit friend to even suggest this would help anything. Friends—bullshit!* He thought to himself. "They're all having sex like Greek God's and I'm out here snooping around playing stupid friggin' games in the dark." Chubbs mumbled loudly as he continued walking. "I almost got caught by that wild-eyed, sick bastard who killed his own son. I just want to be home. Mom is gonna kick my ass if she catches me. Why the hell do we have to live out on the edge of town? Bullshit, bullshit, bullshit. My life sucks. Kyle and Darrell are both poster boys for girls." Chubbs looked down at his sweat-drenched T-shirt that bulged from his fat rolls and continued talking out loud to himself. "I look like the Pillsbury friggin' Doughboy. Don't even get invites anymore to hang out. Bullshit!"

The headlights slowly creeped up from behind. Chubbs, without turning around, motioned them on with his left hand. The vehicle remained at a snail's pace.

The vehicle tapped its horn with a short honk.

Chubbs turned around and again and motioned the vehicle to go ahead and zip around him as he turned back forward and kept walking. He did speed up his pace as he looked around at the deserted road. *What was this asshole's problem? Some old geezer that can't drive?*

The vehicle suddenly swerved, coming very close to hitting Chubbs and he let the driver know he was pissed by yelling out, "Asshole!" He also flipped him the bird as bold as he could. Afterall, he was just over six-feet tall and weighed about two-sixty. *Who was gonna fuck with me?* He thought.

The white van swerved back over into the correct lane just in front of Chubbs and then slammed the brakes hard, squealing the tires as the brake lights lit up Chubbs' bewildered face.

"What the hell, mister. Are you fuckin' crazy?" Chubbs stated a little less vigorously, not knowing just who was opening the door? The red tail lights kept Chubbs from being able to spy just who was walking towards him. He tried to ready himself to either fight or talk his way out of the jam. "What's the deal, mister? There aren't any other cars out here—you couldn't just go around?" Chubbs asked more on the sheepish side.

He saw the silhouette raise something up high, but he never knew what it was when it came down hard on his neck and shoulder, first grazing the left side of his head. He was on the ground subdued in no time. His left side of his body wouldn't work right. He tried to scoot away, but his right leg would only push him in a slow circle. He felt moisture pouring from his neck and head, but the pain was more of a ringing in his ear and a slight dull ache.

The silhouette stood over him for a second, before an instant pain came in the form of a dull crushing blow to his chest, making it hard for him to suck in air. He just wheezed as his circle became slower until he lost consciousness.

Jay surveyed the area before quickly getting back in the van and backing up beside Chubbs. Hiding the body better if someone should drive by. It took everything Jay had to get Chubbs' fat-assed body into the van. Sweat poured from his forehead and upper body.

He hopped into the van as quick as he could. He looked back through the rear-view mirror at the road and saw what looked to be a puddle of blood where Chubbs had been throttled by the steel tire-tool. He hadn't really thought anything through or made any plan. He'd acted on impulse. Something Jay knew better from his past. At least there was plastic over the floor in the van. Thankful for new vans, so he could use it to wrap the body up. He hoped the storm brewing out over the bay would come into shore and help wash his mess from the road before morning light. He couldn't believe how he'd let his anger take over and get the best of him. Jay wondered what that fat bastard of a kid had been doing up on the deck. He now knew, and it wouldn't be happening again. *Play the jar game with me punk—and you lose!*

Jay remembered there were always reports of sharks being seen up by Carrabelle, a little town east and north of Apalachicola. He'd also seen alligators up in those waters close to shore. It wasn't too far a drive, either. Jay turned his van around and headed towards the coastal waterway bridge to Carrabelle. He kept the van at or below the speed limit and watched closely for any Florida state police cars.

He saw one cop car as he slowly cruised through Eastpoint, but no sign of suspicions. He continued until he was just past Lanark Village.

It was a sparsely populated area with many places to pull over. Picking the right one out on a dark night wasn't easy. It was farther than he wanted to be, but he found the perfect deserted turnoff just about a mile past Lanark Village.

Jay carefully pulled onto the dirt and gravel road leading between the trees toward the ocean. He doused the headlights, leaving only the moon and lightning flashes in the distance to light the way. As the path came to an end, he pulled to a stop and got out to scout the area. He listened for any sounds of people or activity close by. There seemed to be nary a soul tonight.

After quickly opening the side-door of the van, Jay struggled to pull the over two-hundred-pound plastic wrapped body from the vehicle floor. He dragged the dead-weight through the sand toward the shoreline, taking every ounce of energy and muscle he owned. Jay had to take breaks every ten or fifteen feet to re-collect his breath and strength. As he got close to the surf, he looked around and noticed there were still no lights or people to be seen anywhere. He began rolling the body toward the wet sand and as the water rushed up around his ankles, he began unrolling the teen from the plastic.

It had taken nearly an hour to get this far, his victim was surely dead by now. He got the last of the plastic from around the body and it laid on the sand several feet from the water as the wave receded. He began to pinwheel the dead weight out toward the surf, when he heard a gurgle from the carcass' mouth. He stopped and rolled the boy's face towards him and muffled words began coming from his mouth.

"You ain't dead yet?" Jay asked with no humanity in his voice.

"Heee…lp. Can..n't breathe…" Chubbs gasped and spent every bit of the last breath and energy, begging for his life in the broken bits of speech he was able to spit out along with blood.

As calm as a hunter cleaning his fresh kill, Jay pulled his knife from his pocket and unfolded the five-inch blade. He stabbed it into Chubbs' throat and then turned the blade sideways and pulled it across from one ear to the other. Jay then slit the stomach open allowing organs to spill out into the water.

The butcher casually washed the blade of his knife as cold as if he'd just finished cleaning a fish or gutting a deer. As he rested on his knee, the waves continued washing over his legs as he folded the blade back and returned it to his pocket. With each wave, his balance teetered as the large floating cadaver rolled onto him and then back away as the water receded.

He got up and began dragging Chubbs' gutted body out as far as he could. Jay didn't want to go too deep because of all the blood in the water. He felt confident that either the bull sharks or the alligators would quickly smell the blood and come in to feast on the fat easy prey chumming the water. Between the two, the body should be unrecognizable by morning.

One last tug and then Jay walked around and gave Chubbs a push off. He moved inland away from the bobbing body and then dipped down underwater to clean himself off. Quickly making his way up to the tree line, Jay found a downed limb and drug it back to the beach, where he swept the trail and his footprints from the sands etched memory.

He looked up at the lightning in the distance and the darkening clouds blowing nearer. *The storm is gonna beat me home. I'll be driving back in a pouring rain. Perfect.*

Jay moved the van to another pull-off on the opposite side of the road and parked, making sure there was no blood or evidence where the body had been. He then ran across the road and with that same branch, swept up footprints and tire tracks in what was left of the light of the moon.

Dark, hard rain was rolling in quickly and he needed to get back to Apalachicola and get tucked in. Jay's brake lights faded into the darkness as he headed west down the coastal highway towards home. He felt confident his mess had been taken care of. He'd now need to come up with a plausible alibi and story. Those thoughts spun around his mind the entire drive back. All hour and thirty-five minutes of the drive, most of it in heavy rains.

This hadn't been his first crime of murder that he'd committed. It was however, the first one in many years. This one was different in the fact the body was so obese. His past experiences had been much more petite. The thought reminded him of the things he needed to check on. Things that may still exist. Mementos. Treasures kept from sins of his past—hidden in his farmhouse walls in the shop, along with other well concealed things. These were sins, he recollected, even God would refuse to forgive. Memories so dark, he'd pushed them way deep inside. He didn't believe even Ms. Cela or her Good Book could give him the answers of true redemption. His judgment game had run much deeper than he'd let on to anyone, especially Ben and Gina.

Oh, Gina. She was a beauty. A sweet, hot-ass and very petite beauty. A pleasurable hmmm, type of groan, was the sound that tucked the evening in for him as he pulled into the drive with his lights out. Two a.m. No lights on at the neighbor's house. Perfect.

33

Mitzi stirred for just a second, imagining she heard someone on the deck. She quietly crept out of her bedroom in the dark. It was hard to see with no moonlight shining through the pulled blinds.

She carefully stepped over Vio and Kyle, who were sound asleep. She reached the window and twisted the blind giving her the ability to see the driveway and the bay. The white van was there. *I wonder when the crazy bastard came home. I wonder what tomorrow will bring. Will CJ have cooled down?* Mitzi felt a quick chill run from the top of her head down to her toes all at once. The rain continued to fall heavy from the sky as the lightning occasionally lit the walls around her, adding to her sense of fright.

Mitzi looked at the door one more time to make sure it was locked, and then tip-toed back into her bedroom where Darrell lay quietly sucking in heavy breaths and exhaling loud sighs. She suddenly felt sick for him. Knowing how horrible it must have been growing up with a monster like Jay, doling out cruel punishments and harsh words of criticism and loathing.

Mitzi just didn't understand it. Darrell somehow retained such a sweet character even being raised by someone full of so much hate. He was charming, handsome, and full of compassion. She hated to see what he'd faced earlier this evening. The unfounded accusations and threats. Her nose began to run as the tears filled her eyes. All she could do was look at the man she'd fallen in love with so quickly. She wiped her tears and sniffed as she remembered being a smart-ass the day they'd met, when he dropped the note from his pocket and she bent down to pick it up. She smiled and quietly laughed at picturing the look of shock on his face when she said he was such a fine ass. She giggled again out loud and Darrell stirred.

How could anybody want to hurt a guy like him? The hate in Jay's eyes was almost like a rabid animal that didn't understand why it wanted to lash out and hurt the one in front of it. He was proof that there was evil in this world. Cold, heartless evil.

Mitzi softly crawled back into bed and snuggled into Darrell, like spoons. When she'd read the note her mom left, she instantly looked forward to more incredible sex with him. She hungered for it.

The mood had changed with what happened and now she was swallowed up with sadness for Darrell. Tonight, had been a teeter-totter of emotions. Happiness, laughter, friendship, love, lust, fear, and now sadness. All she could think of right now was nurturing her guy. Protecting him as best she could. Letting him know she loved him deeply and would be there for him. No matter what kind of monster he'd come from. She felt in her heart, that Darrell didn't have an ounce of Jay's nature in him. Jay was devil spawn. Darrell was a complete opposite of that. She looked forward to their future, having a home together and making babies. She knew it was going to happen, she felt it in her soul. They were meant to be together.

34

Cat worried and missed her boy. She'd missed most of the beginning of his life once he was about five or six; drowning her days in alcohol to escape Jay's torment. Now recovered, she was enjoying the closeness they had renewed for the three and a half years that Jay was gone. The two became a family again, along with the Watkins, who were almost like her parents.

Now she was back to being alone. Her baby, who had grown into a man in what seemed almost overnight was seldom home. They rarely shared a meal, he wasn't coming home on any kind of a regular basis, and when he was there—he wasn't mentally there. He was lost in his own head, or in his part of the room behind the quilt.

Cravings for the bottle worked their way back into her thoughts occasionally. But she was too strong to go there. Cat knew the pull of whiskey would be too strong to let her escape its grip if she succumbed. Another dangerous temptation that kept knocking on her door was Jay. She wondered if he had been brought back into her life for some specific reason. Did God do things like that? If so, what reason could it be? To help him in his time of desperate need? Cat knew Jay hurt inside. She always knew he had past pains he kept at bay, held just below the surface of sight. There were times in her loneliness, that her body ached for the closeness and touch of a man. She hadn't been with one for a long, long time. Jay was the only man—except for the traumatic incident with Roy Burks.

Many times, those lustful thoughts led to unpleasant memories she held back, much like Darrell had squashed deep down. Jay was the king of bad memories. Jay had his ways of unpleasantness with her too. She had felt the same at times with him as she did with Roy. Jay could be such a cruel man.

Was Darrell happy, she pondered? Did Darrell hold her traits or would his father's demons overtake him at some point in his life? She'd never seen those struggles of hate and anger show in him, and if anyone had the right to be angry or harbor hate—it would be Darrell. She missed seeing him in church on Sundays. The subject never came up in the short times he was around these days, but Cat knew it was an important subject and made a silent promise to herself to talk to him about keeping his salvation alive. She reached up instinctively and clasped the cross and locket that seemed to help calm her worries. As Cat stared at it, she was surprised the gold finish hadn't been rubbed off completely from all of her life's worries that had drawn her to clutch it lately.

Time was moving in slow motion but the days somehow raced forward without hesitation. A funny thought. How could such a thing be?

***

Jay lay in bed mulling over what the evening had brought. He replayed the nights events for reasons other than the charge it gave him. He was worried he may have left something behind that may point a finger at him. He was certain he'd covered his tracks, but it had been a long time since playing a game like this one. He knew lack of practice brought mistakes. Mistakes that could make a big difference. *The look on the fat boy's face was priceless as I walked toward him.* Jay thought to himself. *Scared little bitch wasn't so calm and cool like when he was planting wooden tiles on my deck. He'd learned his lesson just a little too late. You play with matches, you get burned.*

Jay pictured the thrashing bull sharks feeding and fighting amongst each other over the meaty body. Or maybe a grandpappy alligator dragging him down to the bottom. He knew one thing for certain, his little friends would always wonder if he'd had something to do with his disappearance. That ballsy pretty boy that stood behind Darrell would surely be next. He didn't like the look in that boy's eyes. *He was trouble. Him and his fucking hot rod muscle car. Spoiled piece of crap, but I'll show him. Judgment has been done, nothing left but deciding the punishment and implementing it.* His veins began to bulge in his temples and his head throbbed. *Composure. I need to practice composure. No signs of fear or guilt. Practice the look of concern with just the right mix of complacency.* Jay practiced his response in his head if he were to be questioned.

"Yes, I've seen the boy around. Those kids were noisy when Joyce wasn't home. I think she travelled with her new job. Of course, the one you say is missing hadn't been coming around with the others much lately. I don't know if they had a disagreement or—you know, the chubby one wasn't paired up with a girl like the other two boys seemed to be. Shame he's missing, I hope you find him real soon." Yeah, Jay thought to himself. Compassion, open some questions of an argument or reason why the others didn't want him around, and just enough complacency to let the officer know that they were kids and he really didn't have much interest in them.

Jay wondered if it would be Sheriff Roy Burks that would come visit. *That chicken-shit bastard. I dare Roy-boy to do a damn thing to me. I got dirt on that pecker-head. Roy wouldn't want to open that can of worms from his past with me.*

Jay would take the van tomorrow and make sure it was clean. Spic and span throughout. He would also disconnect the odometer for the work trip he was taking tomorrow, just in case. He needed to go to Tallahassee to pick up some specialty lighting fixtures and supplies for the restaurant.

Perfect timing, he could see if there was any activity going on in Lanark Village. Afterall, the criminal always returns to the scene of the crime.

Jay laughed out loud.

35

Kyle drove Vio, Mitzi, and Darrell to school and they headed to their usual south lawn table to wait for Chubbs.

The four talked about feeling bad leaving him out of their foursome.

"I'm gonna find him a girl!" Vio said. "He's a good guy and deserves a girlfriend."

They waited for Chubbs until the bell, but never saw him.

"I think he's pissed at us." Darrell said. "I'll talk to him in class if I don't catch up to him in the hall. I have him in fourth hour English. Mr. Wise actually lets us sit at the same table, go figure?"

Mitzi leaned in and kissed Darrell when they parted ways inside the building. "See you at lunch?"

Darrell smiled, "Well, I kinda' have plans with Angela for lunch, today." He grinned an evil grin and Mitzi slugged him in the arm.

"Darrell, you better watch yourself." She turned away and then touched her butt. "Remember this? I'll let you touch it later—but, you gotta be only mine!" She winked and swung her bottom back and forth dramatically as she walked away. She cupped her hand and then turned it over her shoulder, waving goodbye to him.

***

Darrell had gone the first two hours without seeing Chubbs. It was unusual. They were the friends that always met in the morning and shared laughs. *He must really be pissed or sick?* He didn't really worry about it until he was called to the office, having never seen him and wondering why the office would call him down.

***

The apartment was empty and no one around. The storm passed through sometime in the night. The rains were heavy at times but were now settled.

Jay crawled on the gravel under the van and located the odometer cable. He disconnected it and then crawled back out from underneath. He lifted the hood as if he were checking the oil and doing maintenance. He'd planned everything out to the T.

He walked around and then opened the side door. Everything looked good and clean with no signs of anything out of place. He would still give it a cleaning when he got to Tallahassee. Inside and out. Also, underneath.

Jay hopped in and started it up, backed out, and headed off down the street.

***

Chubbs' mother was frantic. She'd gone to bed before Chubbs got home. That wasn't all that unusual, but upon opening his door and his room not appearing he'd been home—that had never happened before. She knew his best friend lived with the Watkins, so she hurriedly looked up their number.

"Hello, Reverend Watkins?"

"Yes, speaking."

"This is Anne Deeks, Chubbs' mother…" Anne's voice was shaky. "I was wondering if Darrell had left for school, yet? My boy didn't appear to come home last night, and he's never done this before. I'm hoping he was maybe there with Darrell, because of the rainstorm last night?"

"Let me go check Ms. Deeks, I haven't seen him or his momma this morning, but I'll go knock on their door. You just hang on for a second." Gabriel took the few steps from the phone and knocked on Cat and Darrell's door.

"Be right there." Cat answered.

The door opened and Cat appeared. "Morning Reverend."

"I have Ms. Deeks on the line. She was wondering if her boy Chubbs stayed here last night with Darrell?"

Cat's mouth fell open a bit. "Darrell didn't come home last night. He's done this several times in the past week or so. Is something wrong?" A look of worry passed across her face.

"We don't know nothin' yet, don't put the cart before the horse." He turned and made the few steps back to the phone and picked up the receiver. "Ms. Deeks? You there?"

"Yes, Reverend, I'm still here, any word?"

"No, ma'am, it appears Darrell didn't come home either. His mother says it's not been the first time in the last week or so. How about Chubbs? He been missing in action overnight before last?"

"No, sir, this is a first." Her voice began to quiver. "What should I do? Oh, Lord, I hope they're both okay. That was a terrible sudden storm last night. Oh, Lord...."

"Now, Ms. Deeks, don't go worryin' yet. Call the school and see if he checked in today." Gabriel looked over at Cat and whispered, "When I get off here with Ms. Deeks, you do the same, Cat."

Cat nodded, now carrying the worry of two mothers. She instinctively reached for her locket and nervously rolled the cross and locket in her fingers. She bowed her head and closed her eyes. *Dear Lord, please be with Darrell and his friend. Please let us have them home safe and sound.* She opened her eyes after saying a quick prayer and tears began to spill over onto her cheeks.

"Alright, Ms. Deeks, you be sure and give me a call back when you find out anything. I'll do the same." Gabriel hung up and then handed the receiver to Cat, so she could call the school.

One mother received the news she'd prayed for—while the other did not. There were calls made to the sheriff's office and officers dispersed to both boy's homes. An officer arrived at the school and just before lunch Darrell was called to the office.

Mitzi would wonder where he was and why he didn't meet her on the south lawn at lunchtime.

***

Jay slowed down when he neared the spot he'd first stumbled onto Chubbs. As he drove past, he noticed no blood stains in the street or signs of a scuffle at all. *Good. So far, everything is working out fine.* He sped up and headed out of town toward Lanark Village on the way to Tallahassee as planned. Forty minutes later, he was driving slowly by the spot his evening escapade ended. Again, everything looked quiet and undisturbed. No signs of any foul play or activity. He wondered about the body, was it taken care of by one of nature's predators? Did it wash out to sea, never to be seen—or had things gone the other way? He hoped it hadn't washed in and become beached where a fisherman or tourist would find it, or smell it in a day after the hot sun baked it. He pictured the sight in his mind and someone pushing on it and little sea crabs rushing out from the insides. The thought made Jay experience a quick shiver under his skin.

Jay accelerated and steered the van on down Highway 98 toward Highway 319 to Tallahassee, his trip was a roundtrip drive of about four hours. He figured after picking up his materials, he would be home by five or five-thirty. He needed to stop up around Sopchoppy and re-connect the odometer. That way it would have made up for his trip last night as if it never happened.

He loved when a plan came together. And this plan was doing

exactly that.

***

Darrell told the officer that he or his friends hadn't seen Chubbs much since before last weekend. He told the deputy he thought Chubbs felt like a fifth-wheel in their group now he and Mitzi and Kyle and Vio were dating. "You don't think anything has happened to him, do you? I mean, maybe he just needed some time or maybe he found a new friend? Something!" Darrell shook his head. Guilt began to overwhelm him. "I'm his best friend—Hell, as far as I know, us four are his only friends." He dropped his head toward the floor.

"Son, let's not get too worked up yet. It's still early. Technically he hasn't been gone long enough to be deemed a missing person." The deputy said.

Those two words sank into Darrell's brain and made this whole thing real. *Missing person. More than likely, my best friend was now a missing person. What the hell could have happened? Where could he be?* He needed Mitz and Kyle and Vio. He needed comfort. Darrell needed to know his best friend who'd stuck with him through all the cruel shit he himself had been put through, was alright. Safe. Darrell needed Mitzi's comforting body nestled into his. The only person he could think of who may be sick or horrible enough to have anything to do with this—was Jay. But Chubbs hadn't suffered any run-ins with Jay, as far as he knew.

"You're not planning on leaving town anytime soon are you, son?" The deputy asked.

"No, sir. Am I a suspect or something? I mean, he is probably okay, isn't he? This kind of thing happens, doesn't it? A guy just wanting to be alone to get over things?" Darrell rambled as he searched for the answer that would fix everything.

"We'll get to the bottom of the situation, son. I'm just obligated to ask you if you plan on being in town for a while?"

"Yes, sir, I am. I live here. Been here all of my life." Darrell answered.

"Oh, I know who the hell you are, son." The deputy responded.

Mitzi walked into the office as she too was called down. She heard what the deputy said to Darrell and stood in shock.

"Just what the fuck do you mean by that?" Darrell loudly questioned.

"Yea, Deputy, what the fuck?" Mitzi echoed.

"Settle down, son, you too, Miss. Take some breaths and ease down." The deputy stated.

"I don't appreciate your last statement. Totally uncalled for. If you want to be a prick—I can step down to that level—dick." Darrell was red-faced, his veins beginning to bulge from his temples, his jaw wrenching.

"I've heard you Caders are all hotheads spoiling for trouble." The deputy puffed up.

Darrell didn't know it, but the sheriff ordered the deputy to try and bait Darrell to test his temper, hopefully provoking him into confrontation. It wasn't proper procedure, but it was Sheriff Roy Burks town, his way of doing things.

"Don't let him bring you to his level, Darrell. We know you've done nothing wrong. You've got the three of us as your alibi." She looked at the deputy. "All night long. No worries, Darrell." Mitzi said in a louder than normal conversation tone.

Darrell smirked at the deputy and walked over to Mitzi, taking her into his arms.

Principal Bingham spoke up after witnessing the deputy's demeanor.

"That's enough of that type of talk Deputy. I'll not have that in my school. You can tell the sheriff any more questioning of my students will have to happen at the station. This is not your interrogation room."

Tammy Hatley, the principal's secretary, clapped her hands in adoration. "Yes, sir, Charley! Thank you, for sticking up for our students! Do you want me to call security to usher this 'officer' off the property?"

"That won't be necessary, Tammy. I think Deputy..." Principal Bingham leaned over to see the officer's nametag. "...Deputy Bill Glenn won't mind seeing himself off the property—will you Bill?"

The deputy turned and began to walk toward the office door. He stopped and turned, beginning to respond, but the Principal cut him off.

"You be sure and tell Sheriff Burks, you have been asked not to return and if this is the standard form of questioning my students—I'll need to see Mr. Burks in my office, before any more of my students are harassed by his men." Charley took the steps to get closer to Deputy Glenn. "You might want to remind Roy he is an elected county officer, and this is election year. These derogatory and intimidation tactics are inappropriate for our students—period!" Mr. Bingham stepped back and held out his arm toward the door.

When the deputy left the room and the office door closed—everyone in the office clapped their hands loudly. "Bravo, Mr. Bingham!" Was repeated by those same adults and kids.

Darrell fought showing a smile, to no avail. Mitzi squeezed him tight.

Mr. Bingham patted Darrell on the shoulder. "You've been nothing but a fine student, Darrell. There is no excuse for these kind of gestapo tactics this deputy displayed here. I'm sorry on behalf of the people who have elected this misguided sheriff, term after term."

Mitzi knew Principal Bingham held no clue he was talking about her estranged father. She didn't really know her dad but knew if he told the deputy to treat a student like that, it was all kinds of wrong.

36

"So, what in the hell happened to Chubbs?" Darrell questioned the other three. "This is weird."

Mitzi spoke up, "I was thinking, creepy."

"Yeah, like as in Creepy Jay." Vio said. "Sorry, Darrell."

"Guys, you don't always have to say sorry after every comment. I know what he is. He is creepy. But he's so much more than just that. He's volatile and dangerous. I don't think of him as my dad or even family."

"Hey, Mitzi, what time is your mom coming home tonight?" Kyle asked.

"I'm not sure. Who knows now-a-days? Her new boss calls, and she jumps through his hoops." Mitzi answered with a hint of disgust.

"Hey, girl, at least she's out there showing that gorgeous body she has! I'm only eighteen and I'm jealous of her ass!" Vio's eyes rolled as she smiled, trying to lighten the mood.

"So, is—you know—CJ over next door?" Kyle asked.

"I have no idea. I don't know what to do. I know I should tell my mom, but…" Mitzi sounded scared about something. She thought to herself about the peeping tom thing with Jay.

"You okay, Mitz? I think you just changed color on us." Vio leaned in and put her cheek against Mitzi's forehead to check her temperature.

"I'm fine! I'm just weirded out about Chubbs, and Jay, and of course, last night. It's all just—just really getting to me." Mitz managed to squeak a fake smile to Vio. "That was awesome how Mr. Bingham stood up for you today, Darrell!" Mitzi said, to direct a change away from the attention she was getting.

"I would never have pictured that happening," Kyle added. "Not from that old goat!"

The group was just sitting around talking to take their minds off their friend that was missing. The truth was, each held a gut feeling something terrible must have happened, but talking about it would make it feel more real.

Footsteps sounded from the outside stairway. They sounded like women's heels.

"My mom must be home." Mitzi got up from the couch to meet her at the door.

"Wow! A room full!" Joyce glanced around quickly to each kid that was here. "Why the gloom and doom look?" Joyce asked as she stepped into the living room, observing the sober faces. "I know it's Monday, but come on guys!"

Mitzi caught her mom's attention with her serious look. "Chubbs is missing. His mom said he never came home last night."

"Oh, I'm sorry. Surely, he will show up soon. Big seniors his size, don't usually just disappear. He may be at another friends place?"

"Mom, we are his friends. Probably about his only friends and we haven't seen him since Friday at school."

"Falling out between you all?" Asked Joyce.

"More like he didn't feel like he fit in since we've kind of—paired off." Vio answered. "I was looking for a girl to introduce him to, but...."

"I see, so now you all are feeling guilty?" Joyce smiled. "Maybe, just maybe, he knows your guilt and he's punishing you?" Joyce answered.

"Oh, mom, I can't see Chubbs doing that to us. I think it's something far more sinister. In fact, we all do. We're just avoiding talking about it."

"Has Jay left you alone?" Mitzi's mom asked.

All three looked at each other briefly before Mitzi spoke up. "Pretty much. It seems someone is messing with him and he thought it was us. Which of course, it wasn't."

Kyle's eyes quickly looked to the floor. Joyce caught the uncomfortable moment with Kyle.

Joyce eyed each of them separately, looking for the one other than her daughter who might possibly cave with some truth. "Pretty much? That begs to have further conversation, Mitzi. Who is gonna speak up first?"

"It was no big deal, Ms. Bonham." Vio spoke up. "I just thought there was going to be a fight. Kyle would have chucked him over the deck, but Mitzi said no. You'd have been proud of her."

"Maybe we should have the police come over and have a talk with Jay?" Joyce stated.

"Mom! It's taken care of. No need to stir a settled hornet's nest."

"Well, I'd like some more explanation other than what you've offered. I need the facts!" Joyce said.

"Can we do this later?" Mitzi asked. "I'll fill you in after everyone goes home, Mom."

The blank stares of the others looking at Joyce, forced her to awkwardly concede. "Fine, Mitzi B, but you better not hold back!"

Mitzi wasn't sure what she'd just gotten herself into, but it was better than having her cross examine everyone all together—just in case the scene on the couch with her was forced into the explanation. No matter, it was obvious Mitzi wore a new nervousness in her expression, instead of relief.

Joyce headed on into her bedroom with bag in tow.

Darrell leaned over and in towards Mitzi's ear. "You okay? The color in your face is all over the place."

"Wanna go outside and talk for a moment—alone?" Mitzi

asked.

"Sure." Darrell leaned back and away for a moment and then looked towards her mom's bedroom. "Hey, guys, could you stay inside a moment? Mitzi and I need to chat really quick."

"Sure." Kyle answered and Vio nodded in agreement.

The two got up and walked outside on the deck, both looking over to see if CJ was outside on a chair. Noticing he wasn't, they walked over and sat down.

"Can you keep your temper under control and make a promise and keep it?" Mitzi gave Darrell a very stern look. A look that told Darrell she was very serious.

"Wow! You have an 'I'm not f'ing kidding look' across your face and in your eyes. This must be monumental stuff." Darrell's eyes looked to the deck floor momentarily before he lifted them back to face Mitz. "If it's this serious—I guess I will have to."

"I'm not joking, Darrell. This is going to make your blood boil, but you need to know, and I need you to promise to do nothing about it. Nothing!" Mitzi's intense stare into his eyes told him if he wanted to know what the problem was, he would have to agree and mean it.

"Yes, Mitz. I promise to do nothing." Darrell braced himself for what was to come.

"Well…" Mitzi began with hesitation. "…I don't have long to talk more than likely, so I'm just going to have to drop the hammer and get it out." Her body quivered briefly as she began to continue. "The other night after the beach and you guys had gone home…" Mitzi looked away and toward the bay. "…and before my mom got home…" She paused again.

"Yes? Just spit it out, Mitz." Darrell reached out and touched her arm.

"I was lying on the couch soaking in the cool bay breeze, reminiscing of our beach time…" She turned back and smiled at Darrell who cocked his head like a small puppy would in wonder of a strange sound it just heard. "...and I was very, very happy with that moment we shared. I uh, I began to touch myself and it led to taking my clothes off...."

Darrell's imagination was moving ahead wildly as his body was showing signs of its own as he waited in anticipation of where this story was headed.

Mitzi could tell Darrell was becoming aroused. She knew it would change shortly. "Anyway, I of course was enjoying the moment and forgetting the window was open, and I may have become a little vocal as I continued..." She reached over and pulled Darrell in closer so she could restrain him. She knew where his instincts would lead him when she got to the end of her story. She nervously continued. "...I heard something that drew my attention quickly from myself and what I was doing and looked toward where the sound came from..." She held his wrists tighter. "...the open window. And—and as I focused on the moment..." She looked away briefly and then back to Darrell's eyes. "...that's when I saw him peeping in at me."

Darrell's arms and entire body tensed in that moment. His hands squeezed the wooden railing of the deck as his head went toward the sky and then slowly back down, turning toward Mitz. "That son-of-a-bitch was watching you?" There was silence for about three seconds. "That motherfucker was watching you through the window while you were thinking about you and me?" Darrell backed away from the railing and then turned slightly to pull away from Mitz and change his direction to CJ's front door around the corner. Darrell sucked in a deep and loudly drawn breath.

"Darrell! You promised! Don't do it. It's not worth it..." Mitzi grabbed his arm with both hands and squeezed as her nails unintentionally dug into the skin of his wrist. "...it won't do anything but harm! I just wanted you to know in case I need to tell this to my mom or the police. Jay didn't do anything—but watch. I made noises and he must have heard them. He didn't do anything to me."

Darrell froze in his tracks and his head dropped as he stood there. It was as if Mitzi were looking at a robotic mannequin that suddenly lost its power and ceased. His head slowly turned back to Mitzi. "It's not fair. You make me promise something that is now impossible for me to do. And you know what I want to do."

"I know, Darrell. I didn't tell you to cause conflict. I told you so you would know before anyone else did in case I have to talk." Mitzi chose not to tell Darrell what Jay slipped up and said that caused her to look toward the window. She knew it would be a lit fuse on the situation she could not put out. Jay's words would drive Darrell to break his promise in an instant and she didn't want that. He was already a marked man with her dad—Sheriff Burks. The entire Cader family was.

Darrell and Mitzi just stood in silence, looking at one another and then looking away, only to look again to each other.

The door opened and Joyce spoke out immediately as she stepped onto the deck. "Hey you two, you left your friends not knowing what to do. What's going on? Did you guys come out here to get your stories aligned?"

"Mom! Stop talking like an attorney!" She'd turned and gave her "the look" moms were very familiar with when they'd upset their daughters.

"Ouch! Daggers!" Joyce tried to smile, but she still wore a look of concern. Something wasn't normal or right in the air tonight and she was a mother. She owned the acquired and necessary radar to read between the silent lines. "I have an idea, Mitzi B." Joyce cleared her throat and dropped the level of interrogation in her voice. "Why don't you ask your other two friends to call it a night—and then you, Darrell, and myself will figure out what's going on in a civil and quiet discussion. Okay?"

Mitzi stood still for a moment looking at Darrell and then back to her mom. She knew this situation was beyond the point of just dissipating on its own. She knew they just needed to face it.

There was no sarcastic humor or punchline which could recreate the moments already spinning out of her control. It was time to drop the evidence on the table and beg for mercy from the court.

37

Jay was still awake and held a glass to the wall and to his ear. He tried to listen to the conversation through the wall. He heard crying and what sounded like words of assurance from Joyce and Darrell.

"Gawd damn it! The little red-headed treasure trover is fessing up? Shit is coming to a boil quickly. I'm gonna have to think up some sort of defense and defer tactic." Jay wore a look of worry across his face as he began pacing back and forth and then again to the wall with the glass in his hand.

He thought to himself. *I'll have to throw the fact out there that I'm not Darrell's poppa and that I've known for a long time. That should throw a turd in their soup they'll be cooking up. Afterall, why would I care anything about any of those little troublemakers if I weren't any kin to them?* Jay began speaking his thoughts aloud. "I keep to myself. Of course, I watched a free teaser show. I heard a scream and came running prepared to help, but instead was enticed by a sex show. I'm a man!" He began getting more agitated and spoke more loudly as he continued. "What man wouldn't watch a nasty little young thing gratifying herself on the couch? You'd have to be queer not to. I'm a lot of things—but I'm a man who likes pussy and not a damned thing a man is equipped with. I'm normal!"

Jay's rationale was dissipating quickly as signs of his psychosis took over. If he would have been in his little dirt-floored shelter in the Bronx, he would have been stirring up a hell of a dust storm inside as he paced in circles.

At a brief instant, something in Jay's apartment caught his eye. He stopped immediately. He stared at his chair in the corner. The chair he spent many hours mulling over Ms. Cela's Good Book. There it was, nestled on the table-top beside the chair. It usually called out to him to come over and pick it up and read—but tonight the voice inside his head was telling him to do something totally different. He stopped mid-step. His head and body quivered from the top of his head to the bottoms of his feet. He felt a cold shiver and then his insides heated up like a boiler ready to blow steam.

Ms. Cela's Book sat there silent, but voices echoed inside his ears. The tips of each ear felt the heat from his chest. Jay's gut felt like retching as if a demon were poking him from the inside trying to find an exit. Jay's attention was drawn away from himself and back to the Book sitting on the table. He felt as if the pages were daring him not to come seek the knowledge they held. Taunting him to a point he stared quizzically at it. As if he were answering someone talking to him, his mouth began to open slowly. "Me? You think you can rule me?" The smile began to envelop his mouth and suddenly took a course change. The turned-up edges straightened abruptly.

"I'll not answer to you anymore. I'll not be Jesus' slave either. I and only I rule and judge! You've tried to take my power away from me!" Jay's eyes were black and dark. He stared at Ms. Cela's Bible in rebuke. "I'll not be divided anymore as if I'm a piece of meat torn in two! I'd rather be shark bait like the little fat bastard who dared to provoke my anger!"

After a few seconds of deafening silence, Jay stalked over to his chair and leaned to grab up the Bible he'd been conversing with. He opened it up and grabbed a handful of pages ripping them from the binding. Jay held them up in front of his face and spit on them. He tossed the Book into the corner and it landed with a loud thud on the floor.

Jay's eyes focused on the wadded pages he held in his hands

and he seemed to quietly study the words written upon them. After several moments, a cold wave of grief washed over him. His eyes narrowed slightly and then he dropped to a humbled and empty stare toward the ground.

Jay turned and fell back, finding himself landing in his reading chair into a submissive position, his wrists turned outward as the pages fell to the ground around his feet. "Lord, why do you let these demon's toy with me? I'm lost. I'm dead to this world." He gazed down to his hands which lay open having no feeling. Jay tried but he couldn't close his fingers. It was as if they no longer submitted to his control. A tear poked out from each corner of each eye. Jay tried to mentally forbid them to expose themselves or spill over the edge of each lid, but he failed his attempt. Each tear left a wet trail behind itself as it journeyed down his cheeks and into the newly close-shaved stubble that was left shadowing his face. He looked like a newly broken man, again.

38

Chubbs' body had indeed been a meal for the creatures of the ocean. The sharks must have smelled the blood in the water and taken advantage of the lifeless carcass. The dark silhouettes cruised in taking turns biting chunks off and swimming away only to return for more. His body bobbed up and down with each attack through the early morning hours. What wasn't devoured slipped down below the water's surface and into the currents which live beneath; carrying him farther away from the place he'd called home. Apalachicola.

Several days passed as the conversations and questions grew in the little town on the forgotten coast. Chubbs' friends would wrestle with guilt more each day, blaming themselves for ignoring him as new love and hormones took control over their own bodies and minds.

The sheriff put out an all-points bulletin asking for anyone who knew anything or had seen him to call or come forward. There was talk from the small shops to the marina and gas stations. People wondering if Apalachicola entertained a new predator in its midst. Doors were locked at night that used to remain open. Children were no longer allowed outside to play under the streetlamps in the fading summer twilight.

Chubbs' mother spent every evening on her porch swing praying for God to allow her son to come up the sidewalk and home.

Darrell's anger with his poppa grew deeper and deeper.

Cat saw the despair in her boy's eyes. Not knowing what to say or how to approach him, she fell into a depression that threatened her to reach for the bottle again. Gabriel and Gloria prayed for Cat and the townspeople several times through the day and night.

The news of an Apalachicola High School senior's vanishing seemed to spread like wildfire throughout Florida and the surrounding states.

Sheriff Burks worked his way through a list he'd created of people who recently crossed paths with Chubbs. It was a quiet, unspoken list of possible suspects which would soon make his way to Jay's name. The sheriff intentionally kept Jay's name from the front of the list for a specific reason. He looked forward to and yet also dreaded that conversation. Roy owned a past and buried within that past is where he wanted it to remain. Jay could shed unwanted light on his own skeletons of the past, and he knew it. It would be a career ender if the stories ever came to light. He knew Jay also realized this fact and would have no problem spilling the beans to save his own ass. An ass that was more than likely guilty if there was a crime involving Chubbs' disappearance. There lay the dilemma.

Roy's quiet little town was on the verge of becoming "a royal fucking quagmire." It was a statement spoken rather loudly one late afternoon while he paced the floor of his office. He stayed late that night along with an old friend he'd kept close at hand in the right bottom desk drawer. Old Grand-Dad, rye mash bourbon. One hundred proof Kentucky straight bourbon whiskey and a loyal friend of his from way back in the day. The rush of cinnamon overpowered the sweet-caramel and vanilla undertones and upon the second shot, Roy could begin to taste the burnt oak which always went well with his Oliva Connecticut Reserve cigar. Lately, he was going through both vices on a regular basis, but it relieved the tension enough to let him get the shuteye needed to see the next day through."What a damned mess." Roy belly-ached again as he sank lower into the seat of his worn leather desk chair while propping his short fat legs across his desktop. His mind drifted back to those days of yonder. The women, the other "friend" and the one time shit spoiled the whole damned setup. A piss poor decision made by the one and only..." Roy let out a long drawn-out sigh before continuing. He lifted his gut so he could access his belt to let it out a notch or two for comfort. "...Ethan fuckin' William Kendrick. You sorry, son-of-a-bitch." The man that just had to taste the sweet honey from a nest of killer bees. "Yes siree, you spoiled the stew pot for us all—you, no-good rich bastard." Roy would never forgive him. Because of Ethan—and his taste for other men's women.... *And now somehow, one of 'em was workin' for him. A bee that was once upon a time mine, even though I didn't want her baby makin' ass.*

39

Nineteen days passed and there was nary a sign of Chubbs or any answers of what may have happened.

Kyle was feeling the guilt inside. He had an idea of who was responsible for Chubbs missing. He also felt guilt from what could be his part in the matter. He quietly stretched out on a towel at his favorite spot at the beach on St. George Island. His sunglasses not only blocked the sun from stinging his eyes—but they also shielded the guilt which screamed from them today. *Vio could surely spot something up with me lately if she tried. Damn my idea of suggesting Chubbs plant little taunts around CJ's door. I need to figure out a way to see what that sick asshole did to him. I need to get revenge for Chubbs.* Kyle sniffed and glanced over toward Violet, who was lying next to him. He thought for a moment he'd spoken his confession out loud and turned to check for her reaction. *I must have only thought it. It's gonna be the thing that puts me in the damn looney bin though. I bet CJ caught him and buried him somewhere in the swamp land. It's my fault. I should have done my own dirty work. I'll get him, though. That's for damn sure. He'll pay.*

***

Mitzi woke up for the second day feeling like crap. This vanishing of Chubbs was working on her. She'd also noticed she wasn't alone. Everyone was acting different. Even her mom lost some of her zest for work. The entire town was reeling in awkward pain.

Mitzi got up and went into the bathroom. She looked into the mirror and rubbed her red and tired eyes. As she leaned over to grab her toothbrush, she checked herself out. Mitzi kind of took a double take as she looked at the reflection of her boobs. They looked bigger. She placed her hands on them and massaged herself lightly and then pushed them together. They felt tender to her touch. They were bigger. She smiled at herself in the mirror, enjoying the sight of her body and how it had changed into a beautiful carbon copy of her mother's.

Suddenly a cramp in her stomach hit and she got the toilet seat lifted just in time to retch her guts out as she dropped to her knees.

"What the hell?" Mitzi wondered and then leaned back over for round two.

***

"Sorry, Darrell. I'm not feeling too good. This whole Chubbs thing has me sick to my stomach." Mitzi's eyes were beginning to form tears. "I just can't seem to function. I'm worried, I'm petrified of what may have happened to him and if the same will happen to one of us?"

"Mitz! Chubbs is gonna show up somewhere and soon. He couldn't have just disappeared." Darrell tried to console her, but even he had a feeling they may never find Chubbs. "No way you can make it to school, even after lunch? I want to see you. I need to see you."

"I'll see—but at this point, even my mom said to stay home." Mitz sighed. "She doesn't even look at me the same way after our talk and me fessing up to what your dad saw me doing. It's like she's ashamed of me."

"I bet she's not so innocent herself, Mitz. Don't worry about it.

She's just overwhelmed by all this craziness like you and I and everyone else in this town. Apalachicola went from a treasure from heaven to a curse from hell overnight. It's shaken everyone, not just you and our friends." Darrell paused. "Can I at least come over after school? I promise to leave Jay alone."

"My mom hasn't banned you yet!" Mitzi replied.

40

Jay answered his phone on the third ring.

"Hey, Jay! We need you to go over to Ebro and pick up some custom paintings from the artist. They're for the restaurant. Gina picked them out the other day but didn't have room to fit them in the car."

"Sure can, Ben. You need me to leave today?"

"I hate to give you such short notice, Jay."

"Ben! Glad to do it. I've been feeling useless here lately. Only so much pier fishing a man can do!"

"That leads me to another topic Jay. I've been looking at a little sport fishing boat that's over in Pascagoula! Pictures look sweet and the price sounds very reasonable. It's a Carolina Classic 35. Know anything about them?"

Jay's jaw dropped. "I haven't really researched boats for many years. I wouldn't have any ideas of value?" He answered.

"We may need to head over that way next week and look her over, maybe give her a test ride..." Ben hesitated, "...She got pretty banged up when her mooring broke free during Hurricane Fredrick. She was practically new. She needs some aesthetic repairs, but that is all, supposedly."

"That sounds great! Count me in." Jay's face grew the biggest grin as his past dreams came to mind. "I'll be over shortly to pick up the list of paintings and the address."

"Actually—Gina may ride with you. She wants to look over a couple more of the pieces since you'll be taking over the van. Is that okay with you?"

"Hey, you two are the bosses! I don't mind though." Jay's days had been a back and forth between depression and the fear he was losing control of his surroundings. This news about a fishing boat in his possible future was the news he needed to hear. His demeanor changed instantly. The thought of being around Gina for the day just sweetened the deal. The whip cream on top of the sundae! He no sooner hung up the phone with Ben when his telephone rang again. Jay thought maybe Ben forgot something to tell him, but it was Cat that said hello.

"What can I help you with, Cat?" Jay asked in an uneasy tone as if he were expecting a chore he wouldn't enjoy.

"I'm worried about our son, Jay." Cat spoke quietly and Jay could hear the uneasiness in her tone. "He hardly comes home anymore or it's so late I never see him. I know he's grown, but he's still in high school. And now with his friend disappearing…" Cat's voice quivered. "…I'm worried to death. What can we do?"

Jay fought the urge to laugh out loud and he was sure Cat could sense his lack of concern without the laugh. "Now, Cat—you're right, he is almost a grown man. A man with raging hormones and finally the balls to have a female companion. I'm surprised you see him at all. Lord knows if I didn't live next door to his new squeeze—I'd never see him either. Of course, we aren't on the same terms—relationship wise, as you two are." Jay cleared his throat. "You do realize I think I know who his real father is—don't you?"

"I've told you over and over he's yours, and I don't know what else to say. I really don't want to go over this again."

"I know you say it, I'm just not sure I'm buying it anymore. I mean, he has finally stepped up and shown some intestinal fortitude like Billy—but I just don't see my biology in him, if you know what I mean?"

"I didn't call to argue, Jay. I called out of concern—mainly for

Darrell, but also for you."

"Not your job to be worried 'bout me anymore, sunshine. You're free to be a single lady again as far as I'm concerned. Ain't nothin' there but the paperwork anyways." Jay let the line go silent for a moment as he listened for a response. When none came, he proceeded, "I thought at first we could maybe pick up where we left off—I mean, I thought things would be different, but yet the same." Jay was silent again as he hesitated how to steer the conversation.

Cat began to answer, "I was hopin'...."

Jay interrupted her. "I have to be able to trust—even if it's news I won't like, I have to believe..."

"Gawd damn it, Jay!" Cat interrupted. "I told you Darrell is yours. What more can I say? A woman just knows, and a woman would have to cheat, which I wasn't—you were the one out bedding down any girl who would drop her panties.

"Awe, there it is, Cat. Layin' all the blame at my feet. Maybe—just maybe, you were too drunk to know who was down there between your legs. Ever wonder 'bout that? I bet Roy remembers!"

CLICK.

The phone connection between them went dead with only the sound of a dial tone.

"That cheatin' whore isn't gonna ruin my good news!" Jay practically yelled the statement. The veins began to bulge out from his temples. He knew he was right. He had no doubt who Darrell's real daddy was. Not only did Darrell bare a great resemblance to Roy—he owned the same pussy disposition as Roy did. "Ain't no damned way that bastard is mine. I ain't havin' no part of it."

Jay finished getting ready to go to Ben and Gina's house to pick up either the paperwork or Gina. He still hoped it would be Gina. He also hoped she would be dressed to please. "It's a shame and a waste of her attributes to be where she is—but that's where she is." He said with a hint of anger mixed with sadness. If he were Ben—

he wouldn't let any man take her out of town alone. Especially a man like himself.

41

Gina climbed into the van as Jay caught a glimpse of her breasts almost jiggling out of the top of her blouse. He smiled to himself quickly.

"Long time no see, Jay! Almost like old times." Gina looked over and smiled. She glanced down a moment and quickly realized she maybe should have worn something more conservative. She'd always flaunted what she had though. Why change now?

"Yep, like old times." Jay rebutted along with a smile.

The awkward silence quickly set in.

Gina's eyes showed the awkwardness she felt too, almost instantly. She decided quickly she wasn't going to have it last long though. By the time they were crossing the John Gorrie Memorial Bridge, she had Jay laughing and smiling. "Almost reminds me of our trip in the Caddy, headed out of Manhattan!" Gina chuckled.

"That, is one place I do not miss!" Jay appeared to be in thought for just a moment. "It's been at least four months since then. A lot has changed." He shook his head. "…I do miss Ms. Cela, though."

Gina agreed instantly. "What a sweet, sweet soul. I still think of her and of course, Meesh, my friend that overdosed." Gina's eyes saddened briefly.

"I don't miss the harsh cold, damp air. I also don't miss begging and dumpster-diving for food." Jay replied.

"It's hard to remember you that way." Gina answered as she looked over at him, noticing his physical changes. "You've gone and become a handsome man!" She smiled and winked.

"Well, that is very kind of you, although I don't see it. I don't know of any Floridian women that would agree either—there aren't any lined up at my doorstep." Jay chuckled.

"Well, that's a damned shame, because the ladies obviously don't know what they're missing."

He glanced over and winked at her. "Obviously!" He replied as his gaze fell again to her jiggling cleavage. He felt the tightness in his jeans and needed to make an adjustment for comfort. He tried to nonchalantly solve the problem, but he saw her look out of the corner of her eyes and then smile. She knew exactly what she was doing to him. His mind went into overdrive imagining the different ways he would attempt to satisfy her wants if the chance ever arose.

"Ms. Cela. I wonder how she is doing?" Gina changed the subject by attempting a drastic turn, a move just short of throwing a verbal glass of cold water onto his crotch.

"She must be a hundred." Jay replied in a tone sounding somewhat disappointing.

Gina decided to be brave. "I'm just gonna throw this out there, Jay. You and I are friends enough to be honest, aren't we? I mean, we've been through quite a barrage of different circumstances normal people don't usually bridge together, right?"

Jay hesitated with dread where this turn may be headed. They only had about twenty-five minutes left until they reached Ebro, but there would be the forty-minute ride back to face each other's company. "Yes ma'am, I supposed we have, but I'm not sure this sounds like a comfortable driving conversation."

"I like being straight forward, I'm just that kind of a woman."

Jay nodded in agreement. "I see it in you." He smiled at what he'd just said.

"I know that I don't dress like every other lady in the world. I of course had a job that wasn't your typical Pollyanna job either." Gina paused.

"Yes ma'am, again, I would agree. I'm still wondering just where you might be going, though."

"I know I catch you looking me over a lot. It happened several times on the way here from New York."

"Now, are you trying to embarrass me? Cause— I'm not sure you're capable of that. I'm a pretty harsh man." Jay glanced to his right to face her, and then smiled, his eyes staring directly into hers and then rolling down to her cleavage, blatantly.

"Jay—I swear I've felt my tits and ass burning from your gaze many times since we've met, and I'm used to it, believe me. I've lived with lustful stares with my clothes on and off. It's all part of the job in my past." Gina wondered if she should have just stayed quiet, but she had a question that had bothered her since the night they met. She was determined to have it answered today, while they were alone and without Ben to get in the way.

"You're a very attractive woman. In fact, you have one of the most fetching bodies I've ever seen—and the sexual prowess to pull it all off." Jay stared straight ahead down the highway. He suddenly looked over and before he stopped to think about it, he spoke abruptly. "Gina, I gotta speak honestly to you, since you said you liked that…" Jay paused momentarily as if rethinking his response before continuing. He looked intently into her eyes. "…I'd fuck you the minute you invited me. That's a fact and I'd admit that you'd probably be my final coupe de grăce." He held his eyes firm, locked into hers. "I know that's forward, and Ben would fire me in a minute for thinking it, much less speaking it to you. But damnit all to hell, you're a work of perfection and I'd be remiss not to just lay it out there." Jay then turned to face the road ahead again.

Gina was momentarily speechless, but she never so much as blushed. She'd gotten part of her question answered, but there was still more she struggled with from their past. "Okay—that's bold, but fair enough. I mean, I did ask, so thank you for your honesty."

Gina stumbled over her words for a second or two before continuing. "I'm going to be the forward one now, it's my turn, okay?"

A crooked smile fell across Jay's mouth. Gina watched it form in the corners and then tidal wave across his entire face. She didn't give him time to respond.

"I'm just wondering why, when I entered Ben's apartment and you stuck the gun in my back..." She hesitated as if she really wasn't certain she wanted the answer, but decided to slowly continue. "...why didn't you take me into one of the bedrooms and rape me? I mean, Ben was hogtied to a chair?" Gina stopped briefly. "I just would have expected a guy who wanted to hurt another guy, would have seen the opportunity and taken advantage. Especially, if he was as enamored with my body as much as you say you are?"

"Never crossed my mind at the time. I had other business to tend to and you were a surprise. I could pull over onto one of these dirt and gravel roads and do it now if you'd be so inclined?" He kept looking forward straight ahead.

"I dreamed you did. It was cruel and horrible." She watched his reaction and mentally hung on for his response.

"It could be I suppose, but it could be filled with passion and pretty dang incredible too." Still his eyes remained glued to the windshield ahead as he continued to drive.

Gina noticed his gripped hands on the wheel were flushed red with his knuckles becoming whitened. "I imagine it could. You are very attractive now that you're cleaned up—and I do still have that need and desire to be the focus of other men's attentions. You know, old habits are hard to break." Gina knew what she was doing was wrong and maybe even dangerous. She'd become filled with boredom only working on the restaurant. Ben's attentions were engrossed with the future, while the present went unnoticed. Her mental attentions were now focused on a sudden whim of sexual desire. She felt stimulated but vulnerable as she sat alone with Jay in the van. She almost craved to have Jay be forceful in his advancements. She was clueless why, but suddenly she blurted it out before her lips could seal it in. "Pull over, Jay." She stated in a gravelly demanding voice that was spiked with carnal hunger. She suddenly felt animalistic and out of control. Gina now realized she spoke the words before she could stop them and take them back.

Jay spied a road up ahead and put his blinker on. His pants were tight and bulged. His heart was pounding like it hadn't since...."

Jay worried with one question. Would he be able to stop with just the sex? His mind raced back to the keepsake trinkets of others he'd kept and hid in the walls of his shop. The work it had taken though was always worth the effort. He looked over at Gina, who now looked slightly frightened, which titillated him even more. He continued down the gravel road and deeper into the woods until it finally ended at a river. There was no place to go but to turn around and leave the same way they entered. There was no one there but them and the van to be seen. His heart was banging inside his chest as he looked over at Gina. She was perspiring profusely, and he focused on the little sweat droplets that rolled from her face down her neck and were now forming a trail between her breasts. He looked up into her eyes and said one word, not giving a hint if it was a game or not.

"Run!"

42

Both doors to the van were left wide open. If someone were to stumble down this dead-end road, the scene would cause an uneasiness at best.

Jay slowly walked through the brush in the direction Gina ran.

Did she wonder if this was a game? He wasn't sure himself. He wanted this, but he also just found out from Ben that a fishing boat was in his probable future. *That was something I'd dreamed about from the day I ran away from my dad. I'd worked hard and saved for it.* Then that one day as a young boy, he'd come home and found Ms. Pasterknack raped, tortured and dead along with his dreams of buying that boat—as dead as she was. *But now, I had a second chance, and this crazy bitch was toying with me—or setting me up for failure with her husband.*

As he scanned the woods and listened for footsteps, he couldn't turn off the thoughts of his past and how this would affect his future, one way or the other. It was a different game of chance than the Mason jar and now with her out in these woods—it was out of his control. *The outcome would shake out much like a tile would, either a life-long dream answered by Ben or one of ravaging Gina, the most desirable woman I've ever craved. I might get both, if Gina keeps her naughty little mouth shut!* The only thing he knew for certain was that she was out there all alone, and his hormones were raging. *She had crossed over the line today, and she was gonna get what was coming to her. She'd called the game—dealt the card— and called my bluff. It was time for her to pay the piper—then I'll see what my outcome will be.*

"Gina!" he yelled out. "Come out, come out wherever you are…." Jay felt his heart thumping and the heat hanging in the air made him sweat bullets. He hollered out once more, "We can call this whole thing off—last chance to keep your goodies wrapped up to yourself." He smiled wickedly, knowing that was an outright lie. "Last chance baby-doll!"

There was no answer.

Jay stopped walking in the twigs and leaves to listen. He could hear rustling in the branches to his right. He quietly moved slowly and followed the swooshing of tree limbs and the crackling of footsteps on the dry ground. He stopped again to listen. It sounded as if the movement had changed and was now heading back towards him. Jay leaned against a tree trunk, hidden, and he waited.

***

Cat slowly came out of her room. She hoped Gabriel and Gloria were upstairs or out doing chores. She didn't want to face them. Her eyes were red and slightly swollen and her mind was a mess. A broken-hearted Cat was thankful the Watkins were not drinkers because if they were, she would surely be hunting down a bottle of anything containing alcohol. How could Jay have talked to her like that? And that gawd damned accusation again. As she stepped through the front door and onto the porch, the swing to the left called her name. As a girl, her front porch swing had always been a favorite spot to sit, especially in tough times. She found it soothing to swing her problems away. It worked as a child.

Cat pushed back with her feet, closed her eyes, and began to let her mind drift back to those years before Darrell was born. They were good years for the most part. She'd had her suspicions of what her husband was doing the evenings he would have to park after driving all day. She'd of course heard about the truck lot girls who would bounce from rig to rig, selling sex for drugs. There was always something on the television about it. Either girls getting caught and arrested, or disappearing without ever being heard from again.

Cat had seen her husband's mood begin to change when he would come in the house after being gone all week. He was colder, easier to agitate and spending more time in the shop. Sometimes for hours without coming inside the house when he'd get home. Even his pride and joy, little Billy, would get on his nerves more and more. Of course, Billy worshiped the ground his poppa walked on. He talked all week about where his poppa could be and what surprise he would bring home to him this time?

She also remembered the day the young police officer knocked on her door. Officer Burks. He'd come to ask some questions about Jay. Nothing condemning or anything like that. He just wanted to know Jay's truck plate number and the color of the cab. He said it was just for his records. Truck rigs had been stolen lately and he was wanting to get ahead of any problems before they possibly happened. He was young and handsome. He made her feel pretty and desirable again. It wasn't anything special that was said, it was just the way his eyes looked at her. As he walked out to his car and climbed in, he did turn and smile big to her, but she figured she'd never see him again.

Cat had been wrong though; she saw him a week later when Billy was in school and she'd come into town to shop for groceries. It had been a long walk from the farm into town and now she had two armloads of groceries to walk home with. It seemed innocent enough to accept the officer's offer to drive her back home. It was a horribly hot early afternoon.

Cat pushed again with her feet to continue the motion of the swing. She found herself pushing harder as her mind continued forward in her memory of that day.

Officer Burks carried her bags in, and she offered him a cold glass of lemonade. She remembered what he'd said to her after taking a sip from the glass. He smiled as he stared at her and said, "This lemonade starts off sour but ends with a nice, sweet taste. I bet that's just how you are in the bedroom—ain't it?" Cat remembered she was so caught off guard that she didn't know how to respond.

"Is the boy in school today?" Officer Burks asked.

"I just don't think you should be asking questions like that, Officer. I appreciate the ride, but I think it's best if you leave now, before Billy or Jay get home."

Burks looked at her differently than before. His eyes became cold and determined. "It's only fair ma'am—I gave you a ride, it's your turn to reciprocate. It's just the neighborly thing to do." With that, Officer Burks began to advance forward towards her. He held his finger up to his lips, directing her to stay quiet. "Where's your bedroom, Miss Catrina?"

Cat led him down the hallway, sheepishly. She had no idea of what to do, but she was certain he had plans—plans that would change her forever.

The porch swing stopped abruptly, and Cat's eyes opened wide as she rushed to put her hand over her mouth. She hadn't cheated on her husband. She'd been forced. It was a memory she'd kept locked away for nineteen years, pretending it never happened. She never told Jay and as he became colder and meaner, she knew she could never let him know. She had to protect Darrell as best she could, even though she knew deep down Darrell was from Officer Burks' seed, not her husband's.

Cat reached for her locket. The comfort that she always wore around her neck since she'd found it again. She knew she'd only done what she had to and that no one would ever believe a word she would say. When Burks became sheriff several years later, she knew her silence was all that kept it from happening again.

Cat rubbed the outside of the locket as the cross dangled below. She looked down at it, seeing the gold plating was about rubbed off where her thumb and forefinger clasped it. It was now a tarnished dull silver color in those spots she held tightly. A sign of the many worries she'd dealt with. Cat always knew that Darrell was indeed the outcome of that hot summer afternoon. *I kept that damned day a secret to myself, never telling a soul. It was a blessing and a curse all wrapped up in one bundle. Now, that bundle was grown up and all I had left from the years with Jay and Billy. And that bundle is slipping away from my grasp and it hurts all over again.*

She'd recently thought a lot about Jay. *Maybe, just maybe me and Jay could repair our past? When I saw him in the cemetery at Billy's gravesite, he looked like the old Jay. The happy Jay. The man I fell in love with that sunny day on the boardwalk.* But that man was still dead in his soul. She began to see it quickly after he got out of jail. She'd wondered if Roy had taunted him by telling him about that long-ago day, but when he walked out with Darrell and the rest of the entourage—she realized by their facial expressions, Roy more than likely had said nothing. She looked at Roy and could sense a fear of Jay and possibly even Darrell. Roy looked angry, along with a mixture of lament thrown in. *I didn't know where that look came from. He sure as hell wouldn't even look my way. Did he even ever put it together about who's boy Darrell really was? Am I the only one that knows the truth? What would Darrell think of me if he ever found out?*

Life looked up on one side for her, and slowly fell apart on the other. Jay still housed the demon inside of him. She could feel it and the feeling planted a seed of dread inside her heart.

Today, with the phone call she'd made to Jay—that seed had sprouted and was deep-rooted already. *The garden between us held no beautiful flowers anymore, only thistles and briars, things which caused only ugliness and pain.*

43

Gina slowly made her way back toward the van. Her mind was racing inside. There was struggle within. Her unspoken loneliness now lit with the old familiar matches of lust, but she also wrestled with the new-found love and desire for a faith in God. She was second now to the new business with Ben but desired Jay in a salacious way. It was an internal battle between physical wants and mental guilt. She knew this was wrong. She was confused.

Gina stopped suddenly as if a premonition warned her. She listened and slowly turned to look behind—Jay's hand slowly laid across her opposite shoulder, palm down as fingers tightened their grip, squeezing into the muscle.

"Well, hey there pretty lady…" Jay leaned in—real close. His breath heated the lobe of her ear as he continued his sentence in a hushed tone. "…I've been lookin' all over for—you. Seems I have a new itch that only you can scratch." He pulled his mouth away slowly and Gina's neck prickled up with goosebumps. His hand pushed her in the direction of the van that was now in sight.

Gina stumbled as her legs became jello. She almost fell to her knee, but a sudden burst of energy seemed to rush through her body. She pulled her shoulder away from Jay's grip and stood straighter while she moved forward toward the van under her own power. She looked back at Jay who was one step behind. Gina winked at him. "Race you to the van." She took off.

Jay stumbled and lost a step as Gina gained a small lead. As they came closer to the van, Jay caught his balance and was close to cutting her off.

Gina never looked back to see how close he was. She knew it wasn't far behind. When she got to the van she quickly turned and went for the driver's door. Before she could put her fingers under the car door-handle, she let out a quick scream when she saw something from the corner of her eye. Out of breath, she turned in time to see Jay slide around the front of the bumper. His feet slid across the gravel in an Elvis-style maneuver and stopped short of running into her.

Jay was breathing heavy as he struggled to get his words out. "You…" He drew in a big breath and rested one arm on the van and the other around Gina's waist. "…you sure are making this whole scenario today interesting." He drew in another full breath.

"My body is saying yes—but my brain is saying, stop and think this through." Gina responded as she too drew in large breaths.

"Why, I think we're beyond the figuring out if it's gonna happen…" Jay looked at the perspiration stains on her blouse and then let his eyes move towards her sparkling cleavage and smiled. "…this was your idea and your deal. There ain't no backin' out of it after you got me all worked up inside." Jay let his hand drop down to her waist as he eyed her over. His hand slid lower and around her shorts until his fingers were touching her backside. "Hmm hmm…" He lifted his head until their eyes were locked. "I have been dreaming 'bout this little rendezvous for quite some time. I'll make it better than your dream was." Jay winked and began moving her around the front of the van and toward the sliding door on the other side.

Jay's hand clicked the handle and the wide door slid toward the back of the van, revealing a roomy area with packing blankets for the artwork. "Hop up in there, sweety and make us a comfortable spot to get to know each other."

Gina's eyes began to dart from Jay to the inside of the van. "So, there is no talking you out of this now that I've gotten second thoughts?" She leaned in and lifted her knee onto the van floor.

Jay watched intently and got more aroused as she began to climb in the van. Her shorts were tight which showed her panty line, leaving hardly anything to his imagination. Jay drew in a deep breath and let it out very slowly as he continued staring. "I just don't think that would be fair to either of us. We had our moment that brought us here…" He reached up and slid his hand between her legs as she started to crawl on both knees toward the folded blankets. "…it seems we ought to continue that moment to completion—now that we're here and all. We've already wasted the travel time. It'd be a shame to do it for nothing when we both all hot and sweaty."

"But…" Gina began to stall. "…we could always just climb in and continue on to the art store and pretend this never happened. I won't say anything."

"I know you won't, now spread them blankets out and start getting those shorts off. We ain't got all day. We got places to be and I'm far too worked up to go without losin' some of this tension that's all built up."

Gina reached farther toward the other side and grabbed a couple of packing blankets. She was making resolve with the fact she was going to be having sex with Jay.

Jay just stood in the opening by the door and watched as his cravings became more carnal by the second.

44

Darrell's name came over the speaker system, asking him to report to his counselor's office. He looked up at the speaker hanging on the wall above the chalkboard. He then looked to his teacher, Mrs. Clayton. She nodded acknowledging the announcement and mouthed, "It's alright, you can go," as she tilted her head toward the door.

Darrell wondered what was going on, but put his book in his backpack and glanced to the back of the room at Mitzi. It was the only class they shared and when his eyes met hers, she held the same look of confusion. He turned away and moved toward the door. He glanced at Mitzi one last time before he disappeared into the hallway.

Ms. Ashland's office was two doors down from Principal Bingham's, which the door was closed on both. He hesitated a moment and then reached out and lightly knocked on Ms. Ashland's door then nervously stuck his hands in his pocket.

A couple of seconds later the door swung open and he was greeted with the counselor's smiling face.

"Hello, Darrell. Come on in and sit down." She stepped to the side and pointed to a chair which sat in front of her large desk. Instead of walking around to her desk chair, she reached for a chair against the wall and slid it closer to Darrell's before sitting down.

"It's okay Darrell, you aren't in any trouble. I was just having a conversation with Principal Bingham, and he wanted me to touch base with you. He filled me in on a conversation you had with a deputy out in the office a while back." She gave Darrell an assuring smile.

"Yes ma'am, Principal Bingham really stood up for me to the deputy. It was real nice of him. Has anyone here heard any news on Chubbs?"

"I'm afraid not yet, but my concern is how you are doing? You've come a long way, Darrell. I remember the boy who showed up here your freshman year—you have changed drastically both physically and emotionally. You're barely recognizable! I just want to make sure you are dealing with all this okay. I usually call a parent, but you're eighteen now and I thought I would just have a chat with you." Ms. Ashland smiled again before continuing. "I remember when you kept to yourself pretty much!

"I see you now and it looks as if you've matured considerably and made many friends. It's your senior year and there have never been any problems we've needed to have concern over."

"It's nice that you're showing concern for me, ma'am, but I don't understand the reasoning now. Are you worried I may do something?" Darrell questioned.

"No, nothing like that at all. It just seems almost overnight you've grown from a young man who struggled socially last year and this year you came back a different young man. I just want to make sure since we are early in the year that you are truly doing okay. I don't want to be presumptuous, Darrell, but we know your father is back in town and we just want to check to make sure your after-school life is on track as well."

Darrell hesitated and seemed to search his words carefully. There was some uncomfortable silence between them.

"I'm not trying to pry, Darrell, I'm just concerned and trying to make sure you are okay. The school has been very proud of your accomplishments. You're on track for some scholarships if you keep your grades the same for the year." Ms. Ashland reached out and touched Darrell's shoulder briefly. "Principal Bingham has told me that you are in the top three percent with your grades. That's impressive!"

"My situation with my dad is—complicated." Darrell looked up and into Ms. Ashland's eyes directly. "I'm sure you know all of the headlines, as I'm sure the entire town knows. But there are things that aren't in the headlines. You're right, he is in town, but I stay away from him as best I can. He may have thought he could waltz back into my mom and my lives—but he was wrong." Darrell looked down to his feet and then back up with more directness. "There won't be any problems concerning myself and him and the school—if that's what your concerned about. We aren't close and I would rather just keep it that way. My mom was hoping things would work out between us all, I think." Darrell shook his head as he continued. "But I don't see it ever happening. He's a fraud and she's too smart to fall for him again. I know I am. He killed my brother, and she and I will never forgive him for that. But he is no problem for me or the school."

"I'm sorry, Darrell. I didn't mean to re-open any wounds. I was just concerned about you and how you are personally doing. I'm here, as is Principal Bingham or any of your teachers, if you need anything." Ms. Ashland reached over again and gave Darrell's shoulder a light squeeze of assurance.

"Am I free to go back to class?" Darrell asked.

"Yes, and if you ever need to talk about anything..." Ms. Ashland paused.

"Yes ma'am, I appreciate you offering." As Darrell started to round the corner on his way back to class, he turned and glanced toward the offices. He saw Principal Bingham's door open and Ms. Ashland walked in before the door closed behind her. "What the hell was that all about?" Darrell said under his breath.

45

Ben was talking with the construction site manager and asking about meeting the deadline. "I'm having the artwork picked up today. I'm hoping you can start the final clean-up and hang the pieces by Wednesday. Are we still on target for a soft opening next Thursday?"

"Yes sir, I don't foresee anything that will hold us up, Mr. Dane. My men are installing the main window that views the bay today. That is going to be quite some view!" Bob the supervisor said.

"You and your men have done an incredible job. The place looks spectacular." Ben replied.

"Your wife has done a great job designing the interior." Bob confided. "We'll be finishing up the kitchen appliance installs today and into tomorrow. It's down to the punch list items now!" Bob rolled up the print and patted Ben on the arm. "Mr. Dane, it's been a pleasure working with you."

"Bob, it's Ben, just Ben. We've been working together long enough now to be on a first name basis. I'll check back in the morning. I have some last-minute errands." Ben was excited. Earlier he set reservations for three at Salt Water Jacks on Beach Front Road in Panama Beach. He'd been told it was top notch. "Hey Bob, have you ever eaten at Salt Water Jacks in Panama City?"

"Mr. Dane, I mean, Ben—I ate there one time with my wife, way back in the day. You know when new love is in the air! It cost me a week's pay, but it was the best seafood I'd had ever—and the dessert it led to later was worth every dollar! If you know what I mean!" Bob's face turned red after he realized how he was talking to his client. "Yes sir, Ben. I've eaten there. Why?"

Ben chuckled. "Glad to hear! I have reservations for myself, Gina, and our partner, Jay. Kind of an early celebration of the upcoming grand opening!"

"They should love it, Ben." Bob said.

"Well, I'm out of here, Bob. I have some last minute things before I surprise them in Ebro at the artist's shop! We'll talk tomorrow!"

Ben wanted to have everything set up special. He'd reserved the very best table in the house which overlooked the beach, and sunsets were always gorgeous on Panama City Beach, or so he'd again been told. Gina worked so hard putting things together in the restaurant. Her design sense pulled everything together. Ben never realized just how talented in blending colors, fixtures, styles, and artwork she was. Life was great and he wanted to share his gratitude. He also knew Jay was struggling with his new life and the fact he wasn't clicking with his family like he'd hoped. This surprise should catch Gina and Jay off guard and show them his appreciation for all they've done. Ben knew he'd been focused on the restaurant and kept them both on the back shelf. When he became driven with something, it was his way of keeping motivated until the task was complete.

46

Gina slowly unsnapped her jean shorts and slid the zipper down. She looked up and saw Jay lost in the moment of watching her. *Should I kick him in the balls and try to run? Or should I let him have his way and tell myself it was rape?* She didn't want to appear frightened. She didn't want to give him any pleasure. She'd been in spots like this before. The line was blurred this time. She asked for the situation. Her insides were battling. Part of this whole scenario excited her libido and the other part filled her with fear and guilt. She'd seen the danger in Jay's eyes. She sensed he was not new to forcing himself on someone. *Was it force? My heart is racing but my body is craving.*

"Well, little Miss Gina? Time is a wasting! It's time to let the kitty out to play." Jay's face tensed and his eyes darkened in that moment. He began to unbuckle his belt as he crawled inside the van.

Gina slid her shorts down to her ankles and laid back as Jay made his way in front of her. She hoped it wasn't going to be like her dream. She wanted to fight her compelling desire to pleasure him. She wanted to be able to label it rape in her mind. She closed her eyes as Jay pulled her underwear down.

***

As the van pulled off the gravel road and back onto the highway toward Ebro, road noise was all that could be heard. Gina looked out through the window to the right, watching tree after tree become a blur while Jay looked straight ahead with focused intent on the road.

In Gina's mind, she wrestled with the act. She acknowledged to herself she felt dirty and adulterous. She tried to console her actions by Ben's admittance he'd slept with a dancer the night he met Jay, even though she told him he hadn't truly cheated. She knew this was different. They were married and there was no painting this any different than it was. Adultery. She also tried to reason a way of imagining Jay could have mentally forced what happened between them. Afterall, her dream almost foretold it. She had felt stalked by him from the first few miles in the Caddy as they left New York City. *Could it be possible? Could Jay be some form of a devil?* She tried to slowly turn her head toward him to see what expression he was wearing, but she couldn't persuade her neck muscles to respond. She was glued to the side window view. *Would Ben be able to tell? Did I now wear a bright red scarlet letter "W" for whore? What would Jay do? Would he hold this over me and use it, so he could fuck me whenever he wanted? The silence feels booming.*

Gina looked down at her leg. It was beginning to twitch. She could feel a moistness on her inner thigh, and it made her nauseous knowing someone other than her husband had been inside of her. *I'm responsible for letting it happen.* She and Ben had refrained from sex from the time they got back together until they were married. *And now, I've thrown all that trust away. Would God dare forgive me? Could I ever forgive myself? How can I look into Ben's eyes ever again without seeing Jay's eyes intently staring down into mine while he was inside me? A memory I'll never be able to un-see.*

Gina turned and stared straight through the front windshield, her mind a jumbled mess. She hoped Jay's brain was frying like eggs on a hot skillet. *Mine certainly are.*

Suddenly without warning she boldly blurted out, "I hope you're fucking happy." She paused. "Actually, let me rephrase that. I hope you fucking die. In fact, why don't you just aim this van towards a tree and gun it?" She turned to see his response. "Or are you too big of a pussy?" Her head shook back and forth along with an all-knowing smirk.

Jay's foot forced the accelerator pedal to the floor, throwing them back into their seats. The engine roared as the van built up immediate speed. He raised his voice in a yell to overcome the engine's noise. "You really want me to do this?" Jay smiled a wicked grin. "Because I sure as shit will. You don't dare a man who lives on the edge of his own fucking worthless world. I got nothing to live for, Gina."

Gina saw the speedometer read eighty miles per hour. She never batted an eye or showed any fear as she boldly shoved her middle finger into his face and yelled, "Do it motherfucker! You killed my world today you gawd damned demon!"

Jay made a sharp swerve toward the opposite edge of the road to a line of moss-covered oaks. The van went into passing gear as he mashed the gas pedal harder on the floorboard but then suddenly jammed on the brakes, hard. The van skidded down the empty highway parallel to the tree line, screeching to a stop, leaving some forty or fifty feet of black tire marks behind them. He then looked to his right to see Gina still glaring at him with no expression. Her eyes empty and hollow.

"I killed your world? Honey, you begged for this. You've been flaunting your tits to me from night one. You're the stripper who likes to tease men for tips!" He stared back just as cold and hard as her. "You got what you wanted. Jay reached into his pocket and pulled out a fist of paper money and threw it at her. You got what you deserve, and there's the tip! Now, live with the wrath of it, baby-doll." Jay moved his foot from the brake to the gas pedal and pushed down until he reached the speed limit. "I killed your world…" Jay repeated in a mocking tone, shaking his head. "You're lucky I quit with just the sex. My urge was to…" Jay stopped his sentence cold and looked back to the road ahead.

As they pulled into Ebro, the silence was abruptly broken by Jay. "We're almost to your artist's place. Are we good now?" he paused. Can you pull this shit off as if nothing happened or should I just turn around and leave you back in the woods where you got your thrill?"

Gina sat still and quiet, no emotion showing in her expression and then she turned to face him. "What did you mean you quit with just the sex? What am I supposed to take from that? Are you a woman beater too? Maybe a killer?" Gina looked over and into his eyes. She searched deep into his darkness, trying to coax the answer. "You've killed before, haven't you? I mean, other than your son." Gina's head tilted as she suddenly felt a glimpse inside his madness. "You've killed women before, just for the thrill?" Gina never hesitated her focus from his eyes. Gina's eyes searched even deeper within his in almost a challenging stare. "You're one sick fuck and you shouldn't be allowed to live. But you know that, don't you, you bastard."

Jay sat at the intersection waiting for the light to change. He thought he saw the red become green from the corner of his eye, but he wasn't about to look away from Gina's challenge, so the van remained stationary at the light. "I've done a lot of things in my life that people wouldn't understand or approve of." He smirked and his eyes seemed to set deeper within their sockets as his brow furrowed. "I'll not be judged by you or any other. I was judged all my young life and I'm above that now. I'm the judge."

There was a tap of the horn behind him. Jay turned back to the intersection with no acknowledgment to the driver behind him and mashed his foot down on the gas pedal. "I'm the fuckin' judge. No one else can judge me." Jay's veins bulged from his temple as blood pulsated in surges, which could be seen by Gina. His knuckles blistery white as his hands tightly gripped the steering wheel. Gina was suddenly rattled by what had just taken place. Her hand clenched the van's door handle as thoughts conspired internally. *Should I open the door and jump?* Gina's eyes darted back and forth, scanning their surroundings, searching for a bystander that could protect her if she braved the sudden action.

Jay missed his turn and instantly twisted his head toward Gina. "Gawd..." His lips pursed as he bit at his lower lip. "...damn it! You got me so riled I missed it."

Gina could tell he was losing it quick. She hadn't seen this side of him—ever! Her eyes continued to search the streets and sidewalks as her gaze darted between Jay and the outside of the van. She looked at the speedometer briefly. *Thirty miles an hour. That wasn't fast enough to kill me, but I may not be able to get up and run. Why the hell did I put myself into....*

Jay glanced over and saw Gina obviously planning an escape. He reached over and smacked her on the shoulder. "Don't even try it, Gina. I got nothing to lose." He grabbed a handful of her blouse in his fingers. "You try to bail and I'll stop this van and drag you back in by your fuckin' neck..." His eyes penetrated hers. "...then I'll drive back to the river and bury your ass..." Jay's mouth then turned from a stern straight line into a turned-up leer. "...Of course, after we 'make love' again." He finished the statement with a cackle and a gleam in his eye.

Gina's grip loosened and her hand fell away from the handle. Her head dropped in defeat. *I've made a horrible, irreversible mistake and I will have to live with it in total secrecy and silence for the rest of my life. However long or short that will be. I mustn't ever drag Ben into this.* Her head remained lowered into submission, without a tear being shed as she softly spoke, "I'll not cause any trouble for you. Please just promise me Ben will pay no price for any of this." She tilted her head subtly to meet his gaze. "Please don't ever speak of what we did."

"Well now, Gina..." After seeing he'd won the battle, he returned his focus to the road ahead. "...I can see you're bein' real sincere..." Jay cleared his throat a bit. "I think I could manage to make that little promise, seeing as it works for both of us..." He turned back again briefly to see if her attitude was still to his liking. "...I may of course..." Jay cleared his scratchy throat one more time. "...need some form of reminder occasionally—of why I'm keeping Ben out of this...."

There it was. His ace in the hole, so to speak. That son of a bitch is going to be calling whenever he wants seconds—or thirds, or....

Gina turned back to her side window, she'd played her game and lost. *My new life was finally a gift after all the hell I've survived. Now—it's a curse, a forever masquerade of happiness and a plaything on the side for a living, breathing psychopath.*

Gina looked to her left at the stranger who barged into her life uninvited only to be shown mercy by Ben and her. She couldn't even muster up any more contempt or regret. She was spent. Their eyes briefly met for a moment and she answered in only one word.

"Okay."

47

The last of the artwork was packed into the van. Gina was inside talking to her artist friend and Jay sat in the driver's seat, impatiently waiting. That's when a large white Cadillac convertible pulled into the drive next to him. He looked over to see Ben's smiling face. *What the hell....*

Ben's face beamed as he swung the big white door open and stepped out.

Jay watched as Ben made his way over toward the van window. Ben obviously held no clue of what happened today on the deserted gravel road. He was far too jolly in appearance.

Ben reached the van's driver side door and put his hands on the window frame. "Hey there, Jay! I bet you didn't expect to see me over here!"

Jay sat, trying to overcome the feeling of being unprepared and stunned. "No sir, Ben, this is the last way I would have expected today to turn out."

Ben reached inside to pat Jay on the shoulder. "I have a surprise for the two of you!"

Jay glanced toward the door of the art shop to see if Gina was headed out yet. He looked back to Ben. "Surprise, huh? You do seem to be full of those." He answered in a drawn-out sentence. It's funny how the incident earlier with Gina caused Jay no fear or discomfort at all, but the simple showing up in surprise fashion from Ben was causing extreme paranoia. Jay kept glancing to the door and began to open the van door to step out. He was certain he should walk over and somehow give Gina warning and a wink. He should give a nod that trouble would go down if she didn't play her cards right.

Ben helped open Jay's van door. "You look kind of flush, Jay. The heat and sun working on you today?"

Jay quickly retorted. "My system still seems to be on a New York comfort level! The humidity is still being rough on my body."

"We'll talk dinner plans when Gina comes out. Is she about ready?" Asked Ben.

Let me run inside real quick and make sure she hasn't picked any more pictures out! You can wait here; I'll fetch her and be right back." Jay winked.

"Don't tell her I'm here, yet! Let it be a shocker!" Ben smiled.

"Indeed, it will be!" Jay responded with a forced chuckle. He rounded the van and walked up to the door and knocked before turning the handle and pushing the door open. Jay turned and gave a smile to Ben as he disappeared inside. "Gina?" Jay spoke as he walked back toward the gallery. "You still in here picking paintings out?" Jay made his way through the opening in the hallway into the gallery where he saw the artist and Gina talking. "Gina, I'm not supposed to tell you, but Ben is outside and says he has a surprise."

Gina looked up and said something to the woman and then hugged her. "I'll be in touch Judy. I absolutely love your work!"

"I'm thrilled that they will be hanging in your new place! Thank you!" Judy answered.

Gina walked toward Jay and gave him a look of concern. She leaned in and whispered as she looked back at Judy and waved. "What the hell? What did you tell him?"

"Nothing. Just play it cool and there won't be any problems. Just pretend I didn't tell you anything." He pushed her in front of himself as they headed out through the door toward the parking area.

Gina turned back to Jay and gave him another stern eye before facing forward and suddenly pretending to spot Ben. "Ben? What in the world are you doing here? Did you come to pick out some more artwork yourself? Or to make sure I wasn't spending too much money purchasing extras?" She smiled as she contained her uneasiness making her way to her husband.

"I came to surprise you for all of your hard work! Jay's also. I know I've been ignoring you both and I've come to make amends! Salt Water Jacks overlooking the beach! Five-star cuisine and a celebration of what's about to be a big step for us all!" Ben was smiling ear to ear.

"I'm hardly dressed for anything over a quarter-star, Ben. I'll just excuse myself with the van and you and Gina can celebrate together. I'm not feeling all that well, anyway." Jay reached over and patted Ben's shoulder.

"Nope, Jay. I won't accept that." Ben grabbed his hand. "We can stop and get you two a quick outfit change on the way."

"I couldn't, Ben. But thank you for the nice intentions. It means a lot." Said Jay.

"Honey, it's been a long day. Maybe we should postpone and do it closer to home? Another time when we know the plans." Gina chimed in as she looked at Ben and then glanced to Jay.

"Seriously? I've gone to some effort here to show my appreciation to you two. I know I've ignored you." Ben's shoulders began to droop.

Gina looked at Jay. She did not look forward mulling through an evening at a nice restaurant with her husband and the man she'd just cheated with today—she was however, now filled with more than enough guilt not to ruin his joy and plans. "Jay, I'm up for a nice dinner, if you are? Let's give Ben the company he deserves tonight. If you want to beg out early after we eat, Ben and I can finish up. Home is only forty-five minutes away, after all."

Jay hesitated and squirmed in place a bit until he finally agreed.

"Perfect! You two deserve this so much!" Ben poured more gratitude over them.

They stopped and found suitable clothing and then Jay followed in the van to Salt Water Jacks on the strip.

Jay watched from behind as the two conversed in the Caddy ahead of him. He tried to keep his imagination at bay. *After all, everything looked friendly. It doesn't appear Gina is spilling any details of what happened. It would be a shame if I had to do something off-the-cuff to solve a problem. The quick action with Chubbs was unplanned. It'd been a while since I'd needed to clean up a mess like this from letting my anger control me. I'd rather not have to repeat such an evening unless it was totally necessary.*

Jay watched the interactions between Ben and Gina very closely during dinner. When he felt assured all was good, he began his exit strategy on leaving and getting on the road home.

Ben held up a glass of non-alcoholic champagne as the waiter passed a glass to Gina and Jay.

"Feels like a not-so-distant past at some of the restaurant experiences we three shared together in New York! And—on our way here to Florida, also!" Ben moved his glass toward the middle of the table and nodded for Gina and Jay to do the same. "Very soon, we will be able to do this together at the Big Apple on the Bay! Here is to good friends, a great future, and a promising shared fortune. Cheers, partners!"

CLINK.

The juice sparkled as each held the glass to their mouths and drank in unison. Jay's and Gina's eyes bounced back and forth between each other and Ben.

Jay got up from the table and finalized his plan to get on the road by shaking Ben's hand and thanking him. He then turned to Gina and smiled. "It's been a perfect day working with you, Gina. I hope we can do it again, real soon."

Ben got up and thanked him for taking care of his wife, and then mentioned traveling together to check out the fishing boat he'd mentioned earlier. "Maybe after the weekend?"

"Yes sir! Yes sir, indeed!" Jay answered as he looked over at Gina and smiled. "That would be just fine. Finer than cat fur!" He winked.

48

The drive home in the van was tranquil. No conversation to grind through or eyes masked with tension, ready to spar. Instead, Jay was alone, his mind muddling through the hour he and Gina spent at the dead-end gravel road near the river. Those hungering moments he could feel her fear and dread. Then, of course, the friction they'd shared between their bodies. His hair prickled over his scalp. The recollection boosted his heartbeat and pushed him into arousal. Gina somehow gave him the obsession to quickly perform again. That wasn't like him. He usually needed to either roll to his side and fall asleep, or in his past, start the implementation of clearing the area of evidence.

I think Gina enjoyed our time together today—once she shook out the collywobbles. Jay made a mental note of how desolate the spot was. *Not a soul around. Add to the fact there were woods with soft soil and a river where one could wash themselves nearby. It would make a quick close dump site if I were ever to need one.*

Jay shelved his previous thirst for hunting, kidnapping, sexually assaulting young women, and then hiding the evidence. *It had been at least four years since my last conquest. How many had there been before? I would have to go through my keepsakes to be accurate.* Jay hadn't tried to search the hidden cavity in the south wall of his old shop next to Cat's and his old farm house, since he'd returned to Apalachicola. His other souvenirs were apparently undisturbed also.

Gina today, stirred the beast which previously lay hibernating down deep within his psyche. Jay believed before today he'd possibly conquered the once hungered desire. He most certainly had gone through scenarios inside his head when he stumbled upon women he was attracted to. Women like Gina, or Joyce. For that matter even younger girls like Mitzi and her friend Vio, but he'd left it within his mind. He let the inner beast toy with those fascinations, but he'd kept the cage door closed on his boogeyman. He'd almost released it unintentionally when Mitzi put on her little show.

Today was a different avenue I hadn't been down before. Gina herself brought up the conversation of sex and rape. I knew she'd played with me visually, flaunting her hot, tight body. I never did understand why Ben would let such things be worn by his wife. He surely was aware of her parading her body around. She literally showed me her breasts every chance she got. I ain't fuckin' stupid. He thought. *She knew what she was doing from the get-go. Gina wanted to be raped by me. It was a mental violation she'd intentionally toyed with herself. She was used to being the one in control, using her body to get what she wanted. With me, she dared to be submissive. To be the dominated and violated one. Gina got scared when she imagined how far I just might go. If she only realized how close she'd come to taking her last breath from this world. Sharing that final moment with only me. My judgement, conviction, and sentence.*

Jay's mouth began to turn upward in the corners, forming a troubling smirk. *I had to fight every damned one of those urges not to strangle you. Not to let my fingers reach out to your throat and tighten as I watched the fear die away—behind your eyelids— my eyes fixated on yours. My manhood still inside you. I would have been the last thing you felt and the final image you ever absorbed as you faded into the darkness. The light of life dimming to the flicker of a moth, left to become hollow eyes with no more gleam contained within. Just like Lila Pasternack, God rest her precious soul.*

Jay's body stiffened as he sat steering the van wheel. He quickly returned to his thoughts after realizing he was still indeed driving. His eyes weighed heavy in the darkness at this late hour. He was intoxicated with his daydream of Gina and his past.

In keeping a grip on myself, I gave up the rushing tidal wave of energy that would have come from stealing a memory to take with me. A last memory of you, Gina, along with a keepsake to relive it whenever I felt the urge to. Would the devil inside of me let go and slumber again? Or would he instead be constantly pushing to escape, now that he was awakened?

"Oh, Gina. You have no idea what you've provoked inside of me." Jay said aloud, no longer able to contain his internal voices to speaking only inside his head. He looked up to the moon which attempted to hide behind the dark sky, and white, thick clouds. "Yes, the moon is my monster, and the clouds are my thin veil to attempt caging him inside—deep within. But what can a floating cloud confine?" A look of perplexed concern passed across Jay's face as a sudden memory of a different time popped into his head.

Words came to him as clear as a pane of glass and in Ms. Cela's voice, inside of his head.

"But I tell you that anyone who looks at a woman lustfully has already committed adultery with her in his heart. If your right eye causes you to stumble, gouge it out and throw it away. It is better for you to lose one part of your body than for your whole body to be thrown into hell…."

Jay was momentarily speechless. He had no idea how he could remember the verse from Matthew, so clearly. "Ms. Cela!" Jay screamed aloud. "It's too late for your God's words! I've gone past just lookin' and moved right to the dirty deed! It couldn't be any worse a sin if I'd choked the life outta' her dirty sinnin' body."

49

Joyce and Mitzi sat on their couch watching the breaking news. The headline put immediate anguish and tears in Mitzi's eyes. Her mother sat trying to console her as the news story continued.

"Tonight, authorities have found the remains of what they believe to be the body of a young male in his late teens. The remains have been sent off to the Florida State Crime Lab, where they hope to get confirmation of who the remains belong to and just what the cause of death could be. The partial body was oddly found washed up on the beach in front of the Florida State University Coastal and Marine Laboratory, established and constructed in 1949. The university facility sits on twenty-five acres taking up the harbor side of Alligator Harbor. That peninsula is about forty-five miles south of Tallahassee.
"The Florida State authorities are searching records of missing persons from around the area. Again, no identity has been named, as of yet.
"Moving on to local weather, Jamie Wampler will let us know what the weekend weather is shaping up to be...."

"I just know it's Chubbs, Mom." Mitzi reached up to wipe the tears back. "I need to see Darrell, Kyle and Vio." Mitzi tried to get up from the couch but fell back into her mom's side. She reached around Joyce's neck and tucked her head deep into her shoulder and continued to bawl as her stomach did flip-flops.

Joyce attempted to calm her down, "Now, Mitzi B, honey, we don't know that for certain…."

"Mom! It only makes sense; we haven't heard a thing from him and now this?" Mitzi's sniffles continued as she tried again to pull herself away from her mother.

The phone rang from the wall phone between the kitchen and living room. "I'll get it Mitzi."

"If it's Darrell or Vio, I want to talk!" Mitzi cried.

"I know, sweetie. I know." Joyce answered her daughter as she pushed herself up from the couch and reached for the receiver. "Hello? Yes, yes she and I were just watching." Joyce turned to her daughter. "Yes, Darrell you can bring your friends over." Joyce paused as she listened. "Of course, Darrell. You all are welcome to stay if it's okay with your parents. Mitzi needs each of your comfort, too. I'll tell her…" Joyce held the phone away. "…they are all heading over, Darrell, Vio and Kyle." Joyce held out her hand and motioned Mitzi to lean toward her so she could give comfort. "We'll see you soon."

CLICK.

50

Jay flipped the radio on once he'd pulled away from the hotel restaurant, hearing a shocking story. He hit the brakes hard as he approached the Apalachicola city limit sign. A couple of the pieces of artwork slid to the front of the van and slammed into the back of his seat pillar.

The station mentioned the remains of a teenage boy have been recovered from a beach near Alligator Harbor, just as he'd turned it on.

Jay's attention perked immediately. "What more could this damned day bring?" He banged his fist on the dashboard. "Son-of-a-bitch!" He knew this day would more than likely come. He just kept telling himself that there would be no way to tie anything to him. *I know I didn't leave any evidence. That fat boy's body sure drifted a long way away. There couldn't possibly be anything identifiable left.* Still, there was always a feeling there may be one thing he'd overlooked. This wasn't his first rodeo and he'd gone through this mental questioning and anguish before, but always in the past, nothing became of it.

***

Mrs. Deeks sat bawling on her couch in front of the television. Chubbs was all she had and now and she just knew he was gone forever. *Why would my baby have been in the water? Why would my boy be out there all alone?* Those were questions she would be asking forever, unless the police could find answers.

***

Mitzi B heard footsteps coming up the outside stairs. She held the door wide open and was in Darrell's arms before he hit the top step. Vio and Kyle were right beside her with their arms around her.

Joyce peeked out from the bedroom door with sadness and concern. This kind of thing never happened in Apalachicola and most assuredly wasn't the kind of affair that usually affected her daughter. This was a first. *Thank you, Jesus, it wasn't my daughter in the news. Thank you for her good friends to be here for her. Please let Mrs. Deeks get an answer that will give her comfort.*

"Come on inside, the breeze is cool out here tonight. I'll make some coffee or hot chocolate." Joyce offered.

Four tear-filled high-schoolers ambled inside making their way to the couch as Joyce headed into the kitchen.

Ten minutes later, Mitzi heard a sound she thought was a car outside. She got up and peeked out through the window and saw the sheriff's car out in the drive. "Mom! Dad is headed up the steps?"

Joyce flew out of the kitchen and to the window. "I wonder what the hell…" She stopped herself. It was a little late, but it was a noble attempt. "I wonder why he is here this late. Or at all?"

Sheriff Burks walked past their window, not paying any attention as he passed.

Joyce looked at Mitzi. "He's going to Creepy Jay's door?" Joyce said in an odd form of question.

"Damn straight he is Mom! Maybe he is going there to arrest him!" Mitzi replied before she realized what it would imply to Darrell.

The room fell silent as they all strained to hear what was going to happen.

"I don't think he's home." Kyle remarked. "The van wasn't out front when I pulled up."

"That's right." Agreed Vio. "Kyle's car and yours, Ms. Bonham, were the only ones."

Joyce side-stepped to the front door and opened it, standing just outside to see if she could hear anything. Four kids piled in closely to eavesdrop also.

They must have appeared to look quite funny as Sheriff Burks rounded the corner to find them precariously standing half in and half out of their doorway. At least it's how Joyce felt as Roy rounded the corner and then cracked the smile she hadn't seen in years.

"Well, well, what do we have here? We trying to see how many bodies one can fit in a doorway at…" He looked down at his wristwatch. "…ten fifty-two p.m. on a Wednesday evening? Or could it be y'all just trying to be the first one out to see the handsome sheriff of this fine town?"

"Hello, Roy." Joyce stuttered as she'd been caught off-guard.

"Don't you mean, Sheriff Roy?" He chuckled.

"Well, hello there, Miss Mitzi. Ain't it a little late to be havin' friends over on a school night?" Roy said sarcastically.

Mitzi looked straight at him and guffawed. "Just like you to 'play' the great concerned father. Where ya been the last nineteen years—Daddy dearest?" She turned and walked back into the living room before he could answer.

"Why don't you two go back in and comfort her." Joyce smiled at Kyle and Vio. "Thank you for being here for her." As soon as the door shut, she turned back to her ex-husband. "You son-of-a-bitch. You've been nothing to that girl of yours and you have the balls to puff up and treat her like shit in front of her friends?" Joyce shook her head. "I guess it's nice to see you at least finally grew a set. It's just too bad you still don't know how to use 'em."

She turned to head back inside.

Roy stared at her backside as she began to reach for the doorknob. "Yes siree. I do remember what a sweet ass you have. It always was such a fine tight thing. Seems it didn't take long after marrying you I had to carry a marker around with me…" He pulled up his officer's belt which carried his weapon and ammo along with his radio. "…yeah, didn't take long before I needed to mark that ass to find it, 'cause you quickly turned all ass, every damned bit of you."

He began walking and as she turned towards him, he tipped his round brimmed hat, smiling. "Evening, ma'am." And walked back down the stairs without another word.

"You're still a worthless little squirt of nothing. I'm surprised you had enough in your tiny testicles to even be a donor dad. Mitzi is the best thing you ever did in your pathetic little life and you don't even acknowledge her birthday." Joyce spoke it loud enough for Roy to hear. "How many other kids in these parts you reckon you've deserted after impregnating their mommas?" She shouted and then slammed the door.

Sheriff Burks barely made it to the bottom step before a white van turned into the drive.

"What the hell do we have here?" Jay said aloud as soon as he spotted the sheriff's squad car. "This night is getting more and more troublesome by the minute." Jay rolled his window down. "You know Sheriff, a man could actually park his own vehicle in his own damned drive if you'd move the unwelcome wagon outta my way."

Roy meandered up to the window. "Just the man I came to see—Billy Jay Cader. Been listening to the news on this van's radio? It is actually news to you, ain't it?"

"Just what are you implying? Just 'cause you hide behind a badge, don't mean you get outta havin' your ass kicked for making unfounded accusations!" Jay pulled the handle and threw the door open, slamming it into the sheriff's belly. "Oops, forgot about how touchy this new van door can be. You'll excuse me, won't you? Or are you here to falsely arrest me again?"

Burks smiled. "Now, Billy Jay, there's no reason to get ugly. I'm just here lookin' to clear you from having anything to do with Chubbs Deeks disappearance. I suppose you heard they've more than likely found his body over on Alligator Harbor?"

Jay smiled as he stared hard at Roy. "I did hear there was possibly a teenage boy's remains found out east. Didn't hear they identified anyone yet." Jay climbed out of the van and stood rolling up the window. "You gotta wonder what makes these crazy hormonal boys do foolish things like swim alone in the gawd danged ocean in the evening. Everybody knows that's when the sharks come out to feed. Pitiful training by some daddy who shoulda' known better. I'd bet there's a girlfriend involved somehow. Maybe broke his heart by dumpin' him."

"Billy Jay, you are some special piece of shit, ain't you?" Burks replied.

"There you go with the pleasantries and professional talk—and on an election year!" Jay answered sarcastically.

"We can spar all night long..." Roy cleared his throat. "...or we can go upstairs and get these details I need outta the way. It's up to you, boy." Roy smiled as he moved his hands to his side, near his weapon in a display of authority.

"Now, don't go getting' antsy to pull your piece and shoot me. That'd be a lot of paperwork and explainin' to do." Jay started walking toward the wooden stairs. "I suppose if you're really serious 'bout talkin', you best be following me, it's been a long day and my energy has gone to shit." Jay looked back as he got halfway up the stairwell and gave Roy a big knowing smile. "You and Ethan still throwin' those special parties out at Ethan's little beach shack?" Jay cackled. "All the town's most important men—bangin' drunk school girls and swappin' doped up wives?" Jay turned back to see five people peeking out through Joyce's window.

Sheriff Roy stopped with his hand rested on the rail. He sucked up two deep slow breaths before he continued up to the top. His brow suddenly sweaty from the second climb up the stairs or the conversation. Roy crested the last stair, this time as he passed the window, he stared at each face peering back at him.

Jay's door no sooner closed before Roy got in Jay's face. "I got so many ways to make you disappear Billy Jay, don't you ever damn forget it." Roy didn't sway or hesitate in his aggression.

"Sit down, Roy. You look flush. You havin' a stroke or somethin'? I got no intention of sayin' anything." Jay stared back, matching the sternness of Roy. "I don't need your shit up in my face makin' accusations. You don't know a damn thing you're talkin' 'bout. I, however, do know about the parties. Remember? Don't threaten me. You've put me behind bars for the last damned time. Got it?" Jay stared intently into Roy's eyes. "I've been to the glass house, Roy. I do know a big round ass like yours…" Jay's eyes began to twinkle. "…would be passed around more than a collection plate at a Billy Graham revival. Might be a little different for you on the receiving end. Your dates won't get you all doped up either. They'll want you to remember your experience—specially bein' a locked up dirty sheriff!"

Roy stood there; his belly sagged over his belt buckle as he still sucked deep breaths from climbing the steps. "I can't do anything about the expectations of the State Police. Consider it a warning that they are involved in this investigation. I don't know for sure you had anything to do with that dumbass kid's disappearance, but I can't—I won't cover anything up for your worthless ass either." Roy pointed his finger directly at Jay. "You stumbled onto something you never should have. You should suffer yourself some memory loss of those parties, before somebody helps you out with it—permanently." Roy turned toward the door. "That's not an idle threat, Billy Jay, consider it a semi-friendly warning." He gave Jay a cold smile as he opened the door. "And by the way, your felon ass shouldn't be able to vote, so I'll take any fucking tone I want regarding my civility with you. Remember that." He winked as he left, leaving the door wide open behind him.

"I ain't no gawd damned felon, Roy! I was acquitted!" Jay was livid. *The gall of that son-of-a-bitch to talk that way to me. I could gut him and cook his grits. In fact, I think I'll start off with a little entré tonight!* Jay stewed a minute longer and then went into the bathroom to relieve himself.

As Jay stood looking down at the toilet, his bladder emptied; he imagined the feeling of throwing Roy over the balcony. He smirked. *I'll do one better. I'll let somebody else take care of that. And I know just who can be pushed into doing it.*

He gave himself a couple of shakes and looked down to tuck himself back in before zipping up. That's when a quick flashback came into his memory. He glanced at what his hand was holding and smiled an evil grin as the scent of sex wafted up into his nostrils. He remembered where it'd been merely hours ago and started to get an erection. Then, the thought of Sheriff Roy overwhelmed his thoughts. How he barged into his evening making threats right here inside his own home. He tucked the now flaccid extremity back into his pants and zipped up. *I'll fix that pompous bastard. I'll fix him good.*

51

Jay knocked loudly on the door. He looked over just in time to see some eyes peek out from behind the window, partially hidden by curtains.

"I need to talk to you Darrell." Jay spoke loudly. "It's something of immediate interest to you."

Joyce cracked open her front door slowly and leaned out. "Jay, this is not the night for this, it's late and the kids are already struggling with some news that is more than likely bad."

"Yes ma'am, I just heard. But I have some important news to give Darrell. It's news that can't wait any longer." Jay insisted as he started to put his hand on the door.

Kyle and Darrell rounded each side of Joyce and pushed on through the door past her. "The lady said it wasn't a good time, psycho!" Kyle yelled as he came face to face with Jay.

"Now—hot-rod, I got no argument with you. But I do need to have a word with my…" Jay stopped. "…with Darrell." Jay replied as he turned his gaze to Darrell, who was standing beside Joyce in the doorway.

"I got nothing to say to you, Jay. Nothing." Darrell said.

The door was wide open now and Jay could see the two girls in the background with wide eyes and open mouths. A look of shock and fear across their silent faces.

"Do you wanna know who your real daddy is, Darrell?" Jay questioned in a sarcastic tone. "I think it'll be quite the shocker. It surely blew my mind, even though I wasn't surprised your momma cheated on me."

"What the hell are you talking about? My momma never cheated on you. You're a gawd damned liar." Darrell answered.

"Oh, I realize it's a kicker to hear, but wait 'til you hear who the culprit is! It's a bombshell!" Jay's eyes were wide open. The whites were exposed all the way around each eyeball. His veins were bulging from his head, neck, and arms. "The son-of-a-bitch was just here—in fact, if you hurry, you can wave bye-bye to your real daddy! He's backing out of the drive right now!"

***

Sheriff Burks was backing down the driveway when he turned back and looked out his windshield. He glanced up to the top of the stairs where Joyce's door was wide open. There was a crowd standing out front. He leaned closer to his windshield, squinting into the dark to see what was going on. "Oh well, shit! What the hell are you up to now Billy Jay?" It appeared as if he was possibly causing a disturbance! Burks hit the brakes and slammed the gearshift back into drive and began to pull forward where he'd just come from. "You son-of-a-bitch, Billy Jay."

"Hey, look, Darrell! Daddy is coming back! He must a forgot to give you a good-night kiss!" Jay chuckled a wicked laugh.

Kyle gave Jay a swift shove and he stumbled backward into the railing, almost tumbling over before sliding to the ground. "Go the hell home, psycho!"

Darrell just stood staring blankly.

Mitzi ran up to Darrell and clutched his arm. "Oh my gawd, Darrell!" And then she stopped in her tracks. Her hands fell away from him as if something commanded her to release him and back away; words ceased from leaving her mouth and her expression changed from shock to self-disgust. She glanced down at her hands as if they were contaminated with bile. Mitzi began to shake her head back and forth. "You...you...oh my gawd...you're my..." Mitzi stuttered in disbelief. "...that...makes...makes you...my...brother?" Her knees began shaking, looking wobbly as jello. She fell forward clutching her stomach at first, and then grasping at whatever she could to keep from hitting the ground. It happened to be Darrell's torso that was closest. Mitzi reached, grabbing handfuls of his shirt and pants as she slid to the ground.

Darrell stood in shock, attempting to sort out what Jay and then Mitzi just blurted out. "You're my sister? Oh, gawd! No! I slept with...I...we...this can't be!" Darrell stepped backward as Mitzi clutched the floor and was on her knees, head planted in the carpet.

Sheriff Burks hit the top step out of breath, his hand on the butt of his revolver. "What's going on here?"

The entire area, inside and outside, were filled with shock and silence other than the gasps that left Joyce's and Vio's mouths. Jay was starting to pull himself up to his knees, Kyle was standing his ground ready to take Jay on, and Mitzi was collapsed on her knees inside in front of Darrell. Vio just stood speechless, now trying to construct in her head what was happening. Joyce covered her mouth with both hands turning from one side to the other and back like a motorized robot, not knowing what else to do. It was mayhem that exploded from nowhere.

"Stay on the ground, Billy Jay. Don't move a damned muscle!" Sheriff Burks commanded. "Joyce, what the hell is wrong with Mitzi? Go tend to her!" Burks then looked Kyle up and down. "Stand down, son! Back the hell away. Get inside and sit yourself down on something!" Sheriff Burks surveyed the area quickly, looking for any other possible threats. "You, Darrell! Go sit down."

Darrell snapped to for a moment and turned his stare to the sheriff. "You're my Dad? What the hell? Explain that."

Sheriff Burks looked back at him; it was as if the world stopped spinning and no one moved or was even present except for himself and Darrell. "What in hell are you talking about, son?"

There was a brief break in conversation, and all was still for a millisecond. It was right before all hell broke loose. A calm before the storm.

Mitzi lifted her head up off the carpet just in time to loudly wretch as vomit shot from her mouth, exploding all over the carpet. She coughed and spit before round two. Her body shook and she spewed again and began wiping her mouth with her shirt as she made quiet spitting sounds.

"Mitzi!" Joyce pushed her way over and dropped to the floor as she reached to pull her daughter's hair from the mess. "Are you okay, baby? What's wrong?"

Mitzi coughed a time or two again before slowly lifting her head to look at her mom. Tears were dripping from her eyes as she struggled to speak, and then suddenly she just it blurted out, "I'm pregnant, Mom. I'm pregnant." She rolled away from her mom into a ball on the floor and loudly cried out. "He's my brother, Momma. The daddy is my brother."

Joyce didn't know what to say. The world was moving in slow-motion and it seemed no one was in control of anything.

Darrell looked down at Mitzi. He looked at Joyce and then his eyes moved around the room, spying Vio and then Kyle, then a glimpse of Jay outside on the floor of the deck. He somehow looked past the sheriff and focused on Jay, who was leaning against the railing in a seated clump. Jay wore a dumb-founded smile across his face, as if he'd seen a cat screwin' a dog. That is when everything clicked in Darrell's head. The anger began to steam. The fury inside began to come to an instant boil. *The love of my life—is my sister? She's pregnant with my baby? What the hell relation does that make us? Why would God let the world cave in on me and crush us like this?* Darrell's muscles tightened as the implications of what was said began to sink in. His stomach began to hurt. The walls began to close in on him. He took deep breaths, sucking in as much air as he could. His eyes suddenly came into focus and standing in front of him was Sheriff Burks.

Dad? No damned way. That's just not true. It's not possible. Darrell looked at Mitzi now on the couch bawling. He thought again of the words that came out of her mouth and shocked him. *"I'm pregnant."* What should normally be a happy moment between two people who love each other, was now a dagger shoved into each of their hearts. Suddenly the situation was sick. An abomination of their relationship. It brought disgust and vileness to the most beautiful memories they were making. They would now be the circus act of town, the freak show. Chatter would be heard from every person behind them. *That asshole of a father never told Mitzi? My mom never told me? Jay?*

Darrell instantly saw red. Everything was shades of fire. He looked around the room trying to get the color in his head to change, but it wouldn't. His temples pounded against his skull, crushing his thoughts into shards of painful grief. His ears were burning as if hot pokers were being shoved inside them. In an instant he became a dangerous bomb ready to blow. He felt like a pressure cooker on the stove, the pressure valve shaking wildly and hissing on the lid, about to malfunction. Darrell's pressure limit was about to give way. He caught Sheriff Burks look over at Jay and then back at him and guffaw. The valve blew off the top of the cooker. Darrell's demeanor instantly popped from being shocked and displaced to violent and angry. There was no time for anyone to respond to his actions.

Darrell was on top of the sheriff before Roy ever knew what hit him. Roy's hand still on the butt of his gun, but Darrell never noticed. It didn't matter; Darrell moved so quickly; the sheriff never foresaw the need to draw it from its holster.

Sheriff Burks was on his back trying to block the rapid barrage of punches that were connecting with his face and throat. Roy attempted blocking with one hand as he suddenly dropped the other to his side and reached for his revolver. His hand held the grip briefly before a different hand appeared and pushed Roy's away, pulling the weapon from the holster.

Kyle now held the sheriff's weapon and stood over them.

Jay yelled from outside, "That's right, hot-rod, keep the fight fair!" The first thing Jay noticed was no dark spot ever appeared on Darrell's crotch. He smiled and sat back against the railing as he watched each fist connect with Roy's face over and over; the blood splattered more with each blow until Roy's face was barely recognizable.

Joyce was screaming as she tried to grab Darrell's hands between punches. Vio was crying and holding Mitzi tightly, blocking her view of what was happening.

"Enough—enough! Stop, Darrell! You're killing him!" Joyce yelled when she realized she couldn't physically grab his hands to make him stop.

Darrell's adrenaline died down and he fell off to the side of Roy, who laid motionless, letting out an occasional groan and spitting blood from his mouth and nose.

Joyce ran to the phone and dialed 911. After making the call, she was able to take the time to try and console her daughter; her daughter whose life just exploded into something that would be impossible to understand. She clutched her stomach with one hand. It appeared to be sending sharp pains while she struggled to pull her daughter up and onto the couch.

"Ms. Bonham. I'll clean the mess up if you tell me where the cleaning supplies are." Vio quietly stated.

"That's okay, honey. We probably shouldn't touch anything until the police get here." Joyce answered.

Roy's moans became louder as he started to move around. "What...wha...is everybody...okay?" He tried to lift his head. "...is there any...fuel...fuel leaking?"

Jay got up and walked in, leaning down by Roy. "It wasn't a car wreck, Roy. You just got your clock cleaned, that's all." Jay smirked. "These kids these days..." He chuckled. "...it's tough bein' the dad of a hot-tempered boy, ain't it? Just the cost I guess."

"You better shut your mouth old-timer. You're just about to feel some pain yourself." Kyle stepped over beside Jay, almost stepping on his fingers which were spread out on the floor. Kyle pulled the revolver up and pointed it at Jay's forehead.

Vio turned around and faced both Kyle and Jay.

"Kyle no! Put it down! Don't do it! Can't all of you see what you've done to Mitzi and Joyce? And in their own home!" Her voice cracked.

Kyle glared at Jay and began to lower the gun. "You don't know how lucky you are, CJ."

"CJ?" Jay spoke aloud in a questioning tone.

Kyle stood over Jay with a smile. "Creepy Jay. You know, your nickname, it's what everybody calls your creepy ass."

Vio went into the kitchen after seeing Kyle settle down. She quickly soaked a dish towel with cold water and then entered the living room and leaned down the opposite side of Jay, beside Sheriff Burks. "Sir, this is gonna sting, but you might want to hold this to your face; it's swelling up pretty badly."

The sound of sirens gave notice the police and ambulance were close to arriving.

Jay looked down at Sheriff Burks. "How we gonna play this? You gonna lock your boy up?"

Roy looked at Jay, barely making out his face through his swollen eyelids. "Fuck you... and..." Blood sprayed from his mouth as he spat words out. "... your damn boy." The words were garbled as they mixed with the mouthful of blood. "... I don't know what... the hell you...you're... talkin' about, you...son-of-a...bitch..." His words trailed off as his eyes rolled up under his brows.

"Oh, he's yours, alright, no doubt about it." Replied Jay as he pushed himself up off the floor.

Joyce got up from the couch to prepare for the police. She walked over to Jay and quietly spoke to him.

"Did you know my daughter was the sheriff's daughter also? Did you know Darrell and Mitzi were siblings all along?" Joyce looked at him with disgust.

"No ma'am. That's news to me tonight. I just recently put two and two together about my wife cheatin' with ole Roy Boy. Looks like your family is a little tightly knitted together." Jay smiled a nasty smile and winked.

"You're a sick bastard, you—creepy piece of shit..." Joyce sneered. "...I hope you're happy with ruining my daughter's life."

Jay quickly spouted back, "I ruined it? Hell, I helped bring it all to the light of day..." Jay stared back hard. "I ain't the one bangin' my sister. I helped inform them of their family ties. Hell, Ms. Bonham, I'm more of a hero in this shameful genealogical affair of yours!"

Jay never saw Kyle's fist as it connected with his eye and cheek. He just wilted to the ground with one punch. There he lay, next to his nemesis, the sheriff, as still as he could be. Kyle then removed the sheriff's revolver from his waistband and laid it on the coffee table.

Kyle rubbed his hand as he looked down studying his swelling knuckles. "I've had all the crap out of your mouth a person should take. I've been waiting to close your pie-hole since the day we met, Creepy Jay."

The police and ambulance both arrived within seconds of each other. Two deputies were the first up the stairs and at the open door, hands on their weapons for the ready.

Joyce, Kyle and Vio immediately began talking at once, trying to tell what happened. The room sounded like a crowded ballgame with the rumble and shrill screams mixed together. Mitzi was crying, her head buried in the couch pillows. Darrell sat beside her not knowing if he should touch her in attempting to console her, or not.

Jay rubbed his cheek and cupped his eye as he struggled to sit up. The smile on his face didn't seem to fit the situation as one of the deputies watched from the corner of his eye.

Two paramedics stood at the open door, surveying the situation, waiting for the deputies to give them the all-clear to enter and treat the sheriff and any other injured. One deputy looked to the other saying briefly, "What a friggin' quagmire!"

The two deputies finally got Joyce and Vio settled down enough to separate the males in the room so the medics could come in and work on Sheriff Burks. After a minute or two one of the medics looked up at a deputy. "Injuries appear to be superficial, sir. Looks a whole lot worse than it is. He's gonna be sore for several days, but I don't believe there is any brain damage. We'll transport him to Tallahassee Memorial Hospital for x-rays and a plastic surgeon to check him out more thoroughly."

Jay quietly scoffed at the medic's comment. "Of course, there ain't no brain injury…" He paused. "…the poor SOB don't possess one bigger than a gnat's ass!"

No one paid any attention or laughed at Jay's attempt at humor.

After the medics removed the sheriff from the scene, the two deputies separated all parties and tried to get quick statements about what happened. Darrell and Kyle were loaded in separate squad cars and another was called to take Jay, where they would be taken to the jail for further questioning.

As soon as the last deputy car left, Joyce and Vio continued to attempt consoling Mitzi, who was still bawling horrendously. The living room stunk with a combination of vomit, heavy perspiration, and a strange metallic stench from all the blood. It was an odor that began to overtake their sense of smell.

"Ms. Bonham, I'm gonna attempt to clean up in here for you. Can I open the windows to help with the smell?" Vio asked.

Mitzi looked up and into her mom's eyes. She sniffled several times and tried to speak, fighting all the fears invading her mind. She finally mustered the nerve to push the words out into an apology. "Momma, I...I'm so sorry...for...but...I..." Mitzi's tears flooded her eyes and rolled down her cheeks, carrying mascara lines with them. "...I know...I...shouldn't have...you know..." Mitzi couldn't bring herself to say what she knew she wanted to say. "I...love him...momma. What...(sniff)...do I do?

I...I...can't just...just stop...I don't know..." Her head fell back into the side arm of the couch and her sobbing became almost unbearable to Joyce. Joyce reacted by lying closely to her daughter and squeezed her with calming and loving affection.

Vio looked over at the suffering her best friend was enduring. She couldn't keep the scenario of what happened out of her own thoughts. *Oh my gawd, what would I do if I found out Kyle was related to me? Mitz and Darrell are so much in love. A baby? Mitz and Darrell are having a baby? What is going to happen? And when others at school find out....*

52

The deputies walked each of the three detainees to separate cells. Kyle and Darrell's cells were side by side with a concrete wall separating them. Jay's was across the hallway from them, visible by both.

Darrell began pacing immediately like a caged lion, trapped and uneasy about being locked up in a tiny space.

Kyle banged on his cell bars, then gripped them, trying to shake them loose, to no avail, only causing a quiet rattle from the door hinges.

Jay sat on his cot watching. He'd lived this experience before. "You boys might as well just sit and simmer down. Time's gonna be standin' still for now. At least there ain't nobody here who can rape you—not 'til the glass house, anyway, that's prison slang for the penitentiary, boys." Jay ended his sage advice with a chuckle, before continuing, "Assaulting a sheriff is no small offense, son. And hot-rod—disarming a law officer …" Jay continued, "tisk, tisk." He paused for effect. "…well, that never deals a man a winning hand."

Darrell rushed to the bars, gripping them, and staring into Jay's darkened cell. "Don't ever call me son again. In fact, just shut your worthless nasty pie-hole. You did this to me." Darrell continued to stare at Jay with a spark of wrath in his eyes. "It wasn't enough you playing your damned Mason jar game every Friday before beating me and Billy? Now, you need to ruin Mitzi's life too? You don't deserve to live. You never deserved my momma, and she sure as hell didn't deserve you."

Jay just sat in silence with his back against the cinderblock wall behind him.

"I swear, I'm going to kill you one day. You'll pay…" Darrell smiled an evil grin at Jay. "…for what you've done to Billy, me and Mitz…" Darrell paused. "I'll show no grace either. Just—like—you."

Jay laughed loudly. "Yes siree—son—you may not be from my loins…" Jay answered as he climbed off the cot. "…but you sure as hell have a big part of me inside a you, like it or not."

Kyle reached his arm through the bars towards Darrell's cell. "Brother, I'm with you, anytime, anywhere. This garbage needs taken out, burned and buried."

"This is my problem, Kyle. I'll handle it alone. I appreciate you, but you've gotten too involved already." Darrell answered.

Jay sneered. "Little boys, plannin' their little revenge—man style." Jay sauntered up as close to the bars as he could, pressing his face firmly against them. "You got plans for your momma too? She's the one who caused this little—quandary. Damned woman couldn't keep her legs together when she was drinkin', I reckon. She must have really been stoned to lower her standards to ole Roy." Jay shook his head and laughed. "Gives me the willies just picturing it. How about you, son?" Jay backed away from the bars. "Oops, I forget—that's your daddy I'm talkin' bout. Pardon me, but it is rather humorous for the local lawman to have had the tar beaten outta him by his young'un that nobody knew 'bout. Wonder if your lady will name the little bastard after him—if he's a boy, that is, could be a pants-wetter too." Jay returned to his cot and laid down. He began humming a familiar tune before breaking into singing the words, "Rock-a-bye baby in the tree tops, when the wind blows…."

53

Cat was beside herself from the first phone call she'd gotten in the middle of the night from Darrell. He'd used his phone call to not only ask for help, but also to question her knowledge of the latest news he'd been blindsided with by Jay. "Is it true, Momma? Is the damned sheriff really my poppa? Did you cheat with that bastard?"

Cat was silent. Shaken to the core by the entire phone call. She stuttered through her thoughts and words. "Now, Darrell—it's…um…it's compli…complicated. I…um…I never…did cheat on…Jay.…" Her sniffles and confusion could be heard by Darrell over the phone.

"Momma! What in hell do you mean it's complicated? You either did or didn't sleep with him.…" Darrell paused, not able to believe or understand what he was hearing. "…were you drunk? Is that your excuse, Momma…?"

"I was raped, Darrell! That son-of-a-bitch raped me way back when…" Cat interrupted and blurted out loudly before bursting into tears. "…your poppa was outta town…and…I was headin' home…with…with a heavy armload of…of…groceries.…"

"Momma! You need to get a lawyer and tell 'em about that…I…I…" Darrell began stuttering like he used to. "…I beat…beat…I…beat…his…fa…face…in. I'm…I…in…trouble. Ba…ba…bad…trou…ble."

"Darrell, honey. Breathe. Take your time and breathe. You did what…now?" Cat cautiously asked her son. She could barely understand.

"Momma...I...beat...beat...Sher...Sheriff...B...Burks..." Darrell drew in deep breaths, attempting to halt his stuttering. He concentrated, looking upward as if to plead with God to let him speak. "You...you...gotta...call..." He drew another deep breath. "Call Joyce Bonham...she...she's...Mitz...Mitzi's...mom...and a...and a...lawyer or something...."

"Times up Darrell Lee." The deputy standing beside him declared. "You're gonna have to hang up now, son."

"But...I..." Darrell was saying.

CLICK.

Those were the lasts words Cat heard from her son that night.

Gloria and Reverend Gabriel walked into the kitchen at 2 am. "Who was calling on the phone at this hour, Cat? Is Darrell okay?" Gloria asked.

Cat broke down immediately clutching Gloria as she dropped the phone on the floor and collapsed to her knees.

***

It didn't take long in the small town of Apalachicola for the story to get out in various forms of the truth. Like a bleeding foot in the middle of chum water, the story was attacked and chewed upon by every reporter and local who smelt the blood of a tasty story. It was a bull shark's dinner. It was shameful.

By Friday afternoon, pictures of Sheriff Burks' battered and bandaged face were displayed on every news channel. News crews from all the major networks across Florida along with the surrounding states, swarmed the front of the Franklin County Jail; hungry to be the first to break any tidbit of detail or information that led to the arrest. Billy "Jay" Cader and son Darrell Lee Cader along with an "as-of-yet, unnamed third male" were now the headlines.

News Flash:

Reporters were chased away from the Apalachicola High School campus and parking lot today. After a call from Principal Charley Bingham reported to the State Police students were being accosted as they tried to enter the school grounds and building this Friday morning. Franklin County deputies were brought in to disperse the crowds. More from Tallahassee News 12 after the local weather....

54

Ethan William Kendrick sat in his conference room with Joyce Bonham, her daughter Mitzi, and Catrina Cader.

"Looks like we have our work cut out for us ladies." Ethan looked down at some papers lying on the table in front of him. "We are definitely going to have to do some digging and find anything that can help us out. Catrina—your accusation will most assuredly stir up quite a bit of raucous. Are you sure you're willing to testify? Your private life, family life and sex life will be put out in public and scrutinized in every way possible." Ethan leaned in toward Mrs. Cader as he placed his hand over hers. "The defense will throw anything and everything at you to paint you as less than honest along with accusations of promiscuity."

"I know, Mr. Kendrick, but it did happen and now my son's life is on the line…" Cat sniffled and held a Kleenex up to her nose. "…I have to protect him and let the town know what our sheriff was capable of back then. Lord knows what he does now."

"With my relationship to Joyce and her daughter—I'm contemplating passing this to another attorney; one I of course, could strongly recommend."

Ethan moved his hands back and shuffled his paperwork nervously. "I'll need to do some thinking along with some research. I wouldn't want it to be a problem once we get involved with this case." Ethan Kendrick showed a bit of stress in his face which Joyce didn't understand.

Joyce spoke up. "I'm not sure I understand the word,

'relationship'? I work for you, and Mitzi is my daughter—but that's not qualified as a—personal relationship, is it?"

"Well, Joyce, we have several things going on here, of course. First, is the relationship your daughter and her boyfriend, the defendant, have. The fact she is your daughter along with the fact she and Darrell may very well be related..." Ethan stated as carefully as possible as he rested his elbows on the table, moving his folded hands up to his chin. "...and of course, you being an employee of the firm—my firm—and quite frankly as a defense attorney, I've had a relationship with Sheriff Burks on numerous occasions. Seldom a favorable one, but it could be a conflict in the eyes of the court."

"Ethan—my daughter—and Cat's son, Darrell, need you." Joyce implored. "We'll pay whatever it takes. It will need to be in payments, but...."

"It's not a matter of compensation, Joyce. If I feel like I can take it on without endangering the case, it will be pro bono, of course." Ethan replied.

***

Sheriff Burks was released Friday evening from the hospital. He left through the back door to avoid the press. He knew he needed to talk to an attorney quickly. There were many factors that needed some advice to mitigate the effects to a minimum. He would need to call Ethan. He quietly spoke aloud to himself. "I hate to beg that SOB. for anything. But I sure as hell don't want our past to come back and haunt us." He shook his head back and forth, the movement caused pain to his still swollen face and neck. "He'd better help me, or...."

***

"Roy, damnit, it's not smart calling me. Can you get away without being followed by anyone?" Ethan spoke quietly into the phone receiver.

"Ethan, this could be trouble for you too. I'll sneak away to wherever you wanna meet. Just make it soon." Roy answered abruptly.

"Tomorrow night at 9 pm, at the beach house. Don't be followed." Ethan hung the phone up immediately.

"Why the hell is he making this so damned clandestine? People know we know each other. I'm the gawd damned sheriff and he's an attorney for cryin' out loud."

***

"The fucking squad car? You bring the squad car to my beach house? What are you thinking? And my gawd—your face looks like you've been in the ring with Muhammad Ali. That boy, Darrell did this to you?" Ethan opened the garage door for Roy to pull his car in out of sight. "Are you certain you weren't followed?"

"I'm sure, I'm sure, why are you so damned jumpy? That's not like you." Roy retorted. "And yes, that boy Darrell did this. His dad, Billy Jay Cader, told him I was his damned dad!"

"Do you not understand the gravity of the probable charges you're facing? Rape! And you're the sheriff! Possible father of the victim's son? This isn't just going to disappear! What the hell were you thinking? The doped-up girls out here in the beach house weren't enough for you back then?" Ethan asked sternly.

As the two climbed the steps and entered the house, the garage door closed behind them hiding the squad car. Roy quickly spoke. "Yeah, about that. Jay…."

Ethan interrupted. "If this is more bad news, just wait a minute. I need a tall glass of bourbon to settle this disturbing shit I'm already aware of..." He made a bee-line to his bar and pulled down two glasses and a bourbon decanter. "...our entire damned worlds are crumbling, aren't they?" Ethan opened the freezer and placed ice cubes into two crystal highball glasses. He then picked up the decanter and motioned Roy to the two leather chairs out on the covered deck which overlooked his view of the beach.

The two sat on the overstuffed chairs, each nestled in to figure out what steps should be taken. The sun began to sink lower in the sky which caused the rolling surf's crest to glisten in the fading light. Sounds of the waves washing to the shore echoed repeatedly.

"Look at this view, Roy." Ethan poured a glass and passed it to him and then filled his own. "You're gonna fuck this whole life of mine up that I've spent so long obtaining." Ethan shook his head as he turned and directly held his eyes firm towards Roy's. "You just couldn't keep your dick in your pants? I mean, really! We had access to young, hot girls, and women any fucking weekend we wanted...."

Roy interrupted. "I know. Believe me, I know. It just happened." Roy looked away at the sunset to avoid Ethan's condemning stare. He paused and rolled the cubes of ice around in his glass of light brown bourbon. "I was helping her home with her groceries and..." Roy lifted the glass to his lips, the ice tumbled and clinked as he sipped. "...her husband and kid weren't home and..." He gulped another swallow and made a face from the sting. "...damn, she looked so good. The way her dress just clung to her jiggly ass, her long slender legs sparkling sweat from the heat of the day." Roy seemed to be drifting back into his sweet memory lane of that past. "...I'm a man, Ethan—a man who has needs" He looked back at Ethan's dark eyes. "...it was forbidden fruit. The girls were always so out of it—they never knew what was happening to them. The drugs not only dulled their senses—it took away some of the pleasure I wanted—I needed."

Ethan shook his head as if he knew and understood what Roy

was saying.

"But Catrina Anne Cader—well, once the predicament she was in—took hold in her mind…" Roy's straight lips began to curl upward. "…well, it was damned arousing. The fear in her eyes of what was about to happen. The tension it all caused in her lady-parts. The panic in her breathing. Hell, the pleading and begging for me not to follow through…" Roy's eyes turned again toward the coastline. "It's power like you've never felt. Nothing like the doped-up girls, just rolling around naked in a fog. Catrina felt what was gonna happen to her. She'd resigned herself to it, but I could feel the fear when I was inside her." Roy turned back, holding the nearly empty glass of bourbon up to his mouth for the last swallow. He gulped it down and smiled. "It was all I could do to never grab her again and relive that moment. But I never dreamed she'd tell her husband I was the one that fathered that boy."

Ethan returned a quick smirk. "That may be the one moment in your life you live to regret. You may be asking yourself in the future as you possibly put a bright orange jumpsuit on…" He continued as he stared out at the horizon. "…if gettin' those brief few seconds of …" he paused to hold his glass up to enjoy the smell of fine bourbon before sipping it. "seconds of…the power and pleasure—were really worth it." Ethan quickly swallowed the last quick gulp and let out a long, slow breath. "Those few seconds of power just spilled out and were lost to memory. The outcome now, however, is a different story. A possible lifetime of regret."

They both sat in silence in their chairs, seemingly attempting to absorb the orange and pink sky. The uneasiness in the air seemed to steal its magic.

55

The news crews slowly began to break down their cameras from their tripods and load up their vans in search of the next headline. Life in the small town inched its way back into the quieter, cozier clamshell it was previously kept; protected just a little more from the clamor of the rest of the world.

The crews would return at some point in the future, the town was well-aware of that. They'd lived through this dirty-laundry entanglement before. There would still be entrenched journalists in the shadows, digging and prying for treasures of yet unrevealed morsels they could bring to light. When something big enough or nasty enough broke—the flood of media would return to re-ignite the flames of the town's blight involving the Caders and any other ugly festering mess tied together to them.

***

"Cat, you can't stay cooped up lying in bed until all of this disappears." Gloria pulled her up and into her arms. "You've done this before, child. Don't let this drown you once again. You're strong! You are one of God's most faithful!"

Cat's gloom-filled eyes looked up and into Gloria's. "I failed my boy yet again. He's sittin' in a cold cell, just waiting to be sent up the river and then crucified."

Gloria pulled her in tighter to herself and Cat surrendered into her bosom with sobs.

Cat continued in a muffled voice, "Darrell's suffering because I kept my dark secret from him…" She sniffled. "…from him and my husband…and…and now…."

Gloria began stroking Cat's hair and intermittently rubbing her shoulders as Cat continued to stutter, "…now the both…both of them are caged like…like animals…like rabid dogs…the only family I have left…."

"I know it's not the same, but you have Gabriel and I, sweetie. No matter what happens in this hell-filled world, you're our family and we love you, but don't give up on God and what he can do."

Reverend Gabriel stood just outside of Cat's room and listened to the sadness overtake the woman who'd come from the worst of times yet risen above it all. She and Darrell were on the topside of overcoming such violence and desperation, but now it all came flooding back. Gabriel turned from the door and walked out onto his porch. He lifted his head up to the star-filled heavens. "I know you got your reasons, Lord. It ain't mine to reason why or question, but the sweet woman inside is sufferin' somethin' bad. Lord, please lift her and Darrell up. That young man is warrior strong, but still the boy who needs your guidance. Please use him for your good. Please cast out those demons inside Jay and wake him from ignoring the life you've called him too but instead he chooses to ignore. Wrap this broken family in your comforting arms and heal them with your love and righteousness. Thank you, gracious and Almighty Lord. Amen."

***

The waves slapping against the shoreline were a constant and never-changing reminder of how the world never stops its forward movement. It doesn't matter to nature what human characteristics come and go. The order of God's planet persists on. Storms, droughts, earthquakes, and fires—the waves continue to roll in and out never changing their given purpose.

Humans bid good or evil, come and go with everchanging moods, strengths and weaknesses; sometimes falling by the wayside until they vanish into the dust. But those waves roll in, washing clean what lies underneath; and then gently rolls steadily out, stealing the memory of what was beneath it, only to disappear into the ocean's vastness.

About the Author

Eli Pope lives with his family and two dogs in the heart of the Ozarks. He is currently working on several writing projects including upcoming additions to The Mason Jar Series.

His love of writing is his escape from the everyday grind of working full-time in the real world of paying the bills and providing for his family.

This though, is his passion, along with painting and creating. Pope is a proud member of the *Springfield Writers Guild*.

(Author's Note) Thank you for taking time to read 'The Judgement Game'. I hope you enjoyed it.

Please leave a reader review with amazon.com, goodreads.com, barnesandnoble.com and other online retailers. I would greatly appreciate it.

Eli

COMING SOON by ELI POPE

BOOK 3 - THE MASON JAR SERIES
THE GLASS HOUSE

NOW AVAILABLE

THE MASON JAR SERIES – BOOK 1
THE JUDGEMENT GAMES
By Eli Pope

THE WANING CRESCENT
By Steven G Bassett

Visit *elipope.com* to keep up with upcoming books and projects. Occasionally, Eli makes available to purchase paintings and artistic creations. He lists them on his website.

3 dogsBarking Media LLC strives to bring you quality entertainment. Please let us know if part of our product is not up to your level of satisfaction as a loyal customer.

Contact us at:
3dogsbarkingmediallc@gmail.com

Made in the USA
Columbia, SC
30 June 2024